CONFESSIONS OF A LOST KID
Neighborlee Book 1

By
Michelle L. Levigne

www.YeOldeDragonBooks.com

Previously released as:
GROWING UP NEIGHBORLEE, 2017
Revised

Ye Olde Dragon Books
P.O. Box 30802
Middleburg Hts., OH 44130

www.YeOldeDragonBooks.com

2OldeDragons@gmail.com

Copyright © 2020 by Michelle L. Levigne
ISBN 13: 978-1-952345-00-5

Published in the United States of America
Publication Date: May 1, 2020

Cover Art Copyright by Ye Olde Dragon Books 2020

Welcome to Neighborlee, Ohio.

Where? Somewhere on the North Coast of Ohio, south of Cleveland, right off I-71, north of Medina, in the heart of Cuyahoga County.

What is it? That's a little harder to explain.

Neighborlee is a place you need to experience.

The most important thing you need to understand: Neighborlee is *magic*. Some people say the town is alive. It exists to protect the weird and wonderful (and sometimes a little bit scary) from the cold, practical, material world.

More important, Neighborlee protects the outside world from the weird and wonderful that come to visit … and sometimes come to stay.

First stop: Divine's Emporium, a four-story Victorian house sitting on a hill overlooking the Metroparks. Whatever you really need, you can find at Divine's. Even if you don't know what you're looking for when you walk in the door. The shop is often bigger inside than it is outside. Angela is the proprietor. Please stay on the first floor. You don't want to find out what is hidden and locked safely away upstairs. Like Aslan, Angela is good, but that doesn't mean she's safe. And neither are the secrets and wonders and doorways to other worlds that she protects … and keeps securely locked.

Come in and explore. Meet the people who help Angela guard Neighborlee. Share their adventures of magic and wonder, danger and sacrifice. You never know who or what you'll run into as you walk the streets and listen to the stories of their lives.

Chapter One

My name is Lanie. I'm one of the Lost Kids. Not that we think we were lost, *per se*. Don't get me started on the whole Superman routine of being sent away to protect us. Although it would sure be an ego-boost, wouldn't it?

I'm getting ahead of myself.

What or who are the Lost Kids? Every few years, a child just shows up on the outskirts of town, or within four miles of the borders. Old enough to be self-mobile, but not old enough to communicate, or remember anything once she or he learns to talk.

All these Lost Kids end up at the Neighborlee Children's Home. I've checked. Mrs. Silvestri, the administrator of NCH while I was there, kept good records. The mystery of the lost children was something of her hobby.

While many abandoned or misplaced or lost children who ended up at NCH are identified and claimed, some never are, no matter who looks and what questions are asked. Never reported missing. No DNA markers to link them to someone even years later.

For the most part, Lost Kids grow up and graduate from NCH and make good lives. Most don't leave Neighborlee. When they marry other Lost Kids, things sometimes get interesting.

Most don't leave.

Other than the ones who vanish mysteriously.

Again, I'm getting ahead of myself.

Some Lost Kids develop interesting little talents. Nothing spectacular like being bulletproof or X-ray vision or time travel. What we can do… Well, that's where my friends and I come in.

I was found on Old Mill Road, August 9, a Monday, after a torrential rain. I was curled up in the shelter of one of the humongous blackberry patches that still to this day line both sides of Old Mill Road, heading down into the quarries.

Mr. Lawrence's truck bottomed out in one of those Godzilla-sized ruts. That muddy water splashed my face and I let out a holler. Mr. Lawrence, for all that he was in his eighties, had very good hearing. He slammed on the brakes, jumped out, and proved his eyes were still twenty-twenty when he saw me crawling out from under the brambles, wearing nothing but a thin white T-shirt and diaper. I had probably crawled in under the blackberry brambles to eat, since my hands and mouth were smeared with berry pulp.

The Lost Kids have been around in Neighborlee long enough for a tradition to develop. Since we're never old enough to talk and say who we are, we need names. Our names come from the road or building where they're found, the month, the day of the week, and whoever finds them. If I had been a boy, I might have been called Larry or August, or maybe just Gus. Someone suggested Mona for me, since I was found on a Monday. Mona Miller? Ugh. Mr. Lawrence said I reminded him of his daughter, Elaine, because of my dark curls and getting all messy with the blackberries. I was just about a year old, but I knew enough to get at the berries and feed myself. He wanted to name me for his daughter. So that's how I became Lanie August.

Usually, when Lost Kids get old enough, around high school age, we're allowed to choose our names and legally change them. Most of us just change our last names. For instance, Ford Longfellow chose his name because he was going through a poetry phase in high school. My friend, Kurt was happy with his last name of Hanson and stuck with it.

I went into Willow Cottage — the baby cottage — at NCH. My birthday was listed as August 9, until all the queries and searches and notices posted through official channels brought someone to claim me. But nobody did.

I spent the next four years relatively sheltered in the baby cottage. We had our own courtyard and playground, separate from the rest of the NCH campus. Part of that was to prevent what Mrs. Silvestri called the "shatters." Face it, babies are much easier to adopt out than older children. How kind is it to let the older girls get attached to cuddly, living dolls and then go through the pain of losing them when they're adopted out?

The tall wooden fence separating the baby playground from the main playground had gaps in it that got wider every year. The babies got to know everybody else in the orphanage before we graduated out into the general population. We made friends, we knew who we liked and who we didn't. We learned who the bullies were, and which older boys and girls would defend us before we got dropped into the swim of things.

Not that there were hundreds of kids at NCH, with the babies in solitary. Far from it. The highest population ever recorded topped just over one hundred, about fifteen years before I was a resident. We were a family, not prisoners. We knew we were protected, and even if we didn't have blood relatives, we belonged to someone.

I graduated from the baby cottage on my fifth birthday and transferred to Oak Cottage, my home until I turned eighteen. I was the only one graduating, in preparation for the start of the school year. There were only five of us in the baby cottage and I was the oldest. Mrs. Silvestri explained all the changes in my life, introduced me to my new housemother, Miss Abby, and then took me shopping. I would be going into Kindergarten in less than a month, and my fifth birthday was a big occasion.

Outings with Mrs. S were special occasions. We all loved her, even if she did rule with an iron fist and no one could ever get away with anything. The important thing was that we knew she loved us, fiercely, like a lioness. No one ever made fun of her children or pushed us to the back of the line. No one pried into our lives and put us under a microscope, and then when they decided we weren't useful, relegated us to the trash, the way the Grandstones did.

The Grandstones were Neighborlee's resident robber barons and spoiled rich kids, with the attitude that they were entitled to everything and anyone they wanted. If they had to rewrite history to prove it, they would.

Mrs. S took me to lunch at Miller's Diner, where I had my first ever peanut butter chocolate malt. I knew Stephanie Groves, the waitress who took care of us. She was an NCH graduate who came in once a month to do crafts or bake with the children, or just play games with us. Many of the Lost Kids came back to NCH and repaid the debt of love and care they had been given.

After lunch, we went to Divine's Emporium and I met Miss Angela. Divine's is an old Victorian house, one of the oldest in town, painted olive and gold, with all the fancy gingerbread trimming and gables and skinny windows and a deep porch and a flagstone walk and a wrought iron fence across the front. It sits on the edge of a somewhat steep hill, at the end of a dead-end street, looking down over the Metroparks. The hill isn't too steep that deer can't come up the slope to Angela's garden in back. They don't pillage her garden like they do other gardens in town, and she puts out salt licks and bins of grain and fruit for them. All the animals that come to visit behave themselves in Angela's garden.

That's the outside. The inside…is a wonderland. Lots of rooms that, from the outside, should be small, yet feel huge on the inside, filled with a wonderful hodge-podge of treasures. Lots of secondhand items, with Divine's doing a booming resale business. A glorious mixture of pottery and crystal, rag dolls, candles, used books, wind chimes, old furniture, nostalgia toys, a tiny soda fountain/coffee shop tucked into a corner, jewelry, vintage clothes, apothecary jars full of penny candy, and the Wishing Ball.

The Wishing Ball, that day I first saw it, sat on the marble countertop in the main room of the shop, next to an old-fashioned brass cash register. It was about the size of a bowling ball, something along the lines of those gazing balls that some people put in their gardens, but dark, with metallic rainbow streaks all through it. The colors seemed to move. Not when I was looking straight at them, but as I turned my head, or from the corner of my eyes. The stand was a coiled, dark brass dragon, the long tail wrapped around twice.

From the moment I stepped into the main room with Mrs. Silvestri, the Wishing Ball caught my attention. I walked as close to the counter as I could get before I lost sight of it, sitting up on the counter above me. Mrs. Silvestri didn't stop me when I headed straight over there, but came with me. Well, she was holding my hand, after all. Looking back, I think she wanted me to see it. Taking me to Divine's, taking me to see the Wishing Ball and meet Angela, was something of a test.

Warning: If Divine's Emporium doesn't like someone, they don't hang around Neighborlee very long. People who resist the "go away, we don't like you" sensation long enough to become conscious of it describe it as itching powder under their skin. If they dig their heels in and stay in town, they usually go kind of crazy. Not a fun, genial, wacky old favorite aunt kind of crazy, either. The nasty, megalomaniac, "the world owes me" mindset that deliberately picks fights over stupid, worthless matters. If there was a Wikipedia listing for Neighborlee, and a definition of the Neighborlee defensive effect, here there would be a note saying, "See: Grandstones."

Divine's welcomed me, though. I stood staring at the Wishing Ball, my hand firmly tucked in Mrs. Silvestri's, just amazed. I wanted to get up there, and I was playing with the idea of using my *trick* to get up to the counter for a closer look, when Angela walked into the room.

I had discovered my *trick* quite by accident, just a few months before. I was momentarily unsupervised in the cottage, wanted a cookie, and didn't want to wait for someone to open the cupboard and get it for me. So I climbed up onto the table in the kitchen and walked across it to the counter. A logical progression for a nearly-five-year-old, right? The problem was the four-foot gap between the kitchen table and the counter. I didn't stop to think, I just took a running leap, like I had seen someone do on TV the night before.

My jump took me up to the top of the cupboards. I hung in the air for a good ten seconds before drifting down to the shelf where the cookies sat out in plain view.

I could fly. Kinda-sorta fly. Not zipping through the air like a jet or a certain alien superhero. More like controlled gliding, or going straight up, hovering, and coming straight down. When I got older, that talent made it possible to get incredible photos. Again, I'm getting ahead of myself.

As a nearly-five-year-old, I had no idea that I couldn't or shouldn't kinda-sorta fly. I just figured it was another ability that was part of growing up, like tying my shoes, counting past one hundred, telling time, and reading. By this time, I had figured out that learning a new *trick* before one of the adults showed me how to do it earned unwanted attention. I didn't get in trouble for learning to read and tie my shoes faster than normal, but the fuss and extra attention made me uncomfortable.

Explain to me why it's so unusual to learn how to read by leaning over the shoulder of the person reading to us before bed, and picking out the words on the page and following along? Just pay attention, and it's easy to learn dozens of necessary *tricks* to get along in the world. Of course, being less than five years old, I didn't have that reasoning worked out in my head, I just did what worked.

By the time I walked into Divine's, I had figured out that it was smart to keep new *tricks* hidden until I saw other kids my age doing the same thing. So, I kept quiet and practiced at night, when everybody was asleep, or when I was alone on the playground behind the cottage.

That day in Divine's, though, I cast caution aside, ready to raise myself up for a closer look at the Wishing Ball. I was still attached to Mrs. Silvestri, like a kite on a string.

Angela walked in just as my feet got about three inches off the floor. She smiled at me, winked, and flicked her fingers at the floor. I settled back down. She came around the counter, pulled out a four-step ladder, and put it next to the counter on the end, giving me a more ordinary path up to the Wishing Ball. Right that moment, I knew this pretty blonde lady who smiled at me like we had an enormous secret was going to be a very good friend. Mrs. Silvestri introduced me to Angela while I climbed up. Then she told me it was called the Wishing Ball.

Angela was, is, and likely always will be, one of those ageless women, with a long, oval face and sculpted cheekbones. She has an incredible, thick, long fall of hair in a dozen shades of gold, with hints of strawberry in it, and big eyes that are different shades of blue, depending on her mood. The day I met her, she wore her usual handkerchief print blue dress with draping sleeves and no waist, what some might call a granny dress or hippie dress.

"Do you know what a wish is, Lanie?" Angela asked me, once I was settled on the counter, with my legs hanging off the edge, braced on one arm and gazing into the Wishing Ball.

"It's something you want really bad lots, only it's kind of hard to get." I saw her reflection next to mine in the dark rainbow swirling surface of the ball. "And sometimes it's something you want really bad lots for other people, because they need it a whole lots more than you."

"Really? Like what?" Her smile turned thoughtful, and she glanced at Mrs. Silvestri, who was standing behind me with one hand resting on my back.

"Like…" I turned to look at Mrs. Silvestri. Thinking back, I can't really say what concerned me more. Revealing orphanage secrets? Or revealing that I was very good at standing by the fence and listening to the children talking and playing on the other side of the tall wooden slats? "Ginny Olsen wants her aunt to come back from

Indiana and adopt her."

"How in the world…" Mrs. Silvestri patted my back and let out a sighing chuckle. "Ginny's only worthwhile relative is a missionary in India. She wants the girl, but the other relatives won't let her have custody or take her out of the country. Yet none of them want custody themselves. They'd rather let the government be responsible for her." She stepped around to look me in the eye. "Where did you hear that, Lanie?"

"At the playground."

After staring at me for a moment, Mrs. S laughed. Then she kissed my forehead. Angela smiled and nodded, and for the first time I got that full-chest feeling that was partly relief, partly amazement, and the knowledge that I had pleased her.

Angela showed me how to put my hand on the top curve of the Wishing Ball and make a wish for Ginny. She told me wishes made for the good of other people were always much stronger than wishes for ourselves. Then she told me to make a wish for myself. I wished for another book like *Half Magic*, which I had just finished reading. Angela then gave me a peach-flavored licorice whip from one of the dozens of apothecary jars behind the counter. How did she know I loved peaches? She helped me down the ladder and told me to go look in the book room.

Not until I was curled up in my new bed in Oak Cottage that night, with my new book, *The Time Garden*, by the author of *Half Magic*, did something occur to me. No one had showed me where the book room was on my first visit to Divine's Emporium. I just knew. Or perhaps more accurately, the wonderful magical weirdness that filled the shop guided me to the book room.

As I worked my way through the shelves to Edward Eager's books, I heard Angela and Mrs. S talking on the other side of the shop, and figured they were taking care of adult business. When they caught up with me, Angela told me the book was my birthday present. Then we went on a tour of Divine's. They both said I could come visit whenever I wanted, but I wasn't allowed to walk to that side of town by myself until I was twelve. While I could walk to school by myself, it was different going to Divine's, because I had to cross the main street, five lanes, that cut Neighborlee in half. NCH and the Neighborlee City Schools campus were on one side of the street, and Divine's, the shopping district and municipal section of town and the quarries and Metroparks were on the other side of the street. Angela assured me there would be plenty of older boys and girls who would be willing to be my escorts for visits.

I decided right then and there, I couldn't wait until I grew up. Something told me that being able to come see Angela by myself would be very important. Why did grownups have to put so many dumb rules on us?

Three days later, I met Kurt.

Chapter Two

I knew who Kurt was, but studying the world through a half-inch-wide gap in a solid wood fence made for some slightly warped images. I hadn't really talked to him because the boys usually didn't come near the fence and socialize with the babies. Everything we learned about the boys at NCH, we learned from the girls, or we eavesdropped on the adults. That meant we heard about the nice boys, the ones who defended the younger children from the bullies, the boys the big girls had crushes on, and of course, the bullies. Kurt was supposed to be nice, but only three years older than me, he hadn't built up much of a reputation yet.

I had decided I needed to practice my kinda-sorta flying, to show Angela what I could do next time we met up. I already had it in my head that just going up and down, or gliding, wasn't good enough. Maybe she could help me figure out how to fly like Superman. I found a sheltered spot at the far end of the field where the older kids played baseball and soccer, in the thick clump of trees enclosed by the fence encircling the orphanage grounds. I rose as high as I could get before I got scared and then hung there until the ground started to look a little fuzzy before I came back down. At five years old, twenty feet off the ground was the equivalent of Mount Everest. I had just worked up the nerve to try some sideways shifting when Kurt walked into the little clearing where I was practicing, and looked up at me. Fortunately, I was wearing shorts, rather than a skirt. Skirts were for church and school.

"You hum really loud." He was grinning at me.

"No I'm not." I was indignant, because I knew enough to keep quiet so the kids who might make fun of me wouldn't see me.

"Yeah, you do, but it's not the kind of humming that people can hear."

"That's stupid. How can you hear it if people can't hear it?" I came down a little faster than I intended and my knees wobbled when I hit. Kurt steadied me, and a funny buzzing sensation kind of shocked me where his hand touched my bare arm.

"Like that." He grinned wider, gray eyes sparkling, and rubbed his hand on the front of his t-shirt. "It's okay, I hum too."

"Are you laughing at me?" I had already run into the two chief bullies, Ricky and Donny. They had overheard Miss Abby talking with another houseparent about my reading ability, and came running to inflict their new nickname on me: Lanie Brainy.

"Nope. We're superheroes."

"Huh?"

That was my introduction to the amazing world of comic books and superheroes and mutants and superpowers and saving the world.

We had some simple rules at NCH. Boys didn't go into the girls' cottages and girls didn't go into the boys' cottages between 5 in the evening and noon. Kurt caught me practicing at 10 in the morning, so he couldn't take me into his cottage to dig through his stacks of comic books. He had me wait on the porch of his cottage, Ponderosa, while he ran inside and brought out a handful. Then, we found a quiet corner in the combination social hall/gym/party room in the central administration building, and my education began.

Eight-year-old Kurt was a pretty smart guy, figuring out a theory that explained why he was different, why he could do what he did, and protect his sanity. More important, he discovered guidelines for keeping his "weirdness" hidden and protected, so he didn't get persecuted by the bullies and turned into a tool of the manipulators and users, such as the Grandstones. Or, in the case of the other Lost Kids who didn't hide their weird talents, snatched away without warning. (More on that later.)

He was pretty impressed that I could read already, which saved some wear and tear on his throat. He let me read through the ten comic books he had brought. Fortunately, I was a fast reader, though some of the drawings were pretty distracting. By the third comic book, I felt his gaze boring holes in me, waiting for me to finish.

"Okay," I said, putting down the sixth book. I couldn't take the pressure of him staring at me any longer. "So like we're from outer space and we can do magic?"

"I don't know. I'm the only one I know about. Until you got out of the baby cottage and I could talk to you without the creeps noticing and making a big deal out of." He grinned. "When we do our stuff, we hum. That's how I found you. I already knew you were there, just couldn't find out who you were."

"What do you do?"

"I fix gizmos." He laughed at whatever expression I wore. I couldn't figure out what he was saying. "I can look at something that's broke and I know how to fix it. I can see what's busted. And you know what's really cool? I can make things work without batteries."

Of course, I didn't believe him, so he had to show me. He brought a flashlight and had me take the batteries out. Then he held the long case in both hands, frowned at it, and the light came on, without him flipping the switch on the side. Without the batteries. I nearly dropped the batteries, and for about two seconds I was kind of scared.

That scared feeling was the realization that maybe my kinda-sorta flying *wasn't* something other, older kids could do, that I had simply learned to do early, like reading and tying my shoes.

Then I laughed, because Kurt's superhero power was cool, and it was fun to be able to do things other kids couldn't.

We stayed in that quiet corner of the social hall, talking and figuring things out and going through the other comic books until lunchtime. Our first rule came straight from the comic books: protect our secret identities. If the evil people in the world found out what we could do, then we wouldn't be able to swoop in and rescue people. I was a little hazy on why that was, and Kurt could only explain that secret identities were to protect our friends and families from the bad guys. That kind of made sense, even though at that point the only real, flesh-and-blood bad guys I knew were the orphanage bullies. I was pretty sure the bad guys I saw on TV weren't real. He promised me more comic books to read, so we could figure out the rules together.

One question we really didn't think about until many years later: *WHY were we the way we were, and WHY were we specifically in Neighborlee?*

We split up to go to lunch in our separate cottages and made arrangements to meet up that afternoon, for the mass migration to the city pool. I was really excited, and a little scared. They had a kiddie pool at the city pool, but I wanted to go in the big pool, where the shallow end was a whole three feet. That was an amazing amount of water, in my imagination, since I was used to the inflatable wading pool we used at the baby cottage.

Kurt didn't bring the comic books when we went that afternoon. Paper and pool water didn't get along. We sat on the edge of the shallow end with our legs in the water and talked more. I found out that Kurt and I had something else in common besides humming when we did our tricks. Kurt had been found at the age of two on a park road within sight of city hall, in the middle of a warm snap right after Christmas. No one had come to claim him, either. He didn't match any missing children reports and didn't fit the description of members of a family that vanished from Darbyville, the town south of Neighborlee, just before he was found.

"So kids without anybody can all do tricks nobody else can?" I said, when we compared what little we knew about our similarities.

"Nah, there's a bunch of kids here who just came out of nowhere, but nobody is special like us. We're like superheroes, you know?" Kurt said, after a few seconds of thinking.

It turned out that "a bunch of kids" only meant four other Lost Kids at NCH at that time that Kurt knew of. But he was right. The passage of time, and careful observation and taking notes, revealed that they were ordinary.

A shout of "Cannonball" and hard slaps against our shoulders interrupted our talk. Ricky and Donny, the bullies, jumped over us, hitting us with their feet, and landing in the pool with high, far-reaching splashes.

Those two were a matched set and did everything together. Where we saw one, we saw the other. They were cousins and had been dumped in the orphanage until an uncle in the military came back from active duty overseas.

We got up and moved away when Ricky and Donny stayed right there in the shallow end and splashed us and crowed about "Kurt's got a giiiirlfriend!" Seriously? I was five and Kurt was eight. We were barely aware that he was a boy and I was a girl. The differences didn't matter back then.

The bullies followed us. When we retreated behind the locker rooms, they ran outside the fence and scooped up old pinecones and shells of acorns and other trash that fell down under the trees surrounding the pool. Then they came back and threw that junk at us. Kurt and I ducked for cover and ended up hiding under the picnic table on the far side of the locker rooms, where nobody could see us. With all the shouting and laughing and whistles blowing, nobody could hear us call for help.

"Y'know, this is really stupid," Kurt said after we sat there for about fifteen eternal minutes. "We're superheroes. We should be able to fight back. Those jerks should be running away from us."

"Can you make a machine out of this junk?" I winced when another handful of debris got between the tabletop and the bench by my head.

Kurt grinned. I liked that grin. It was nasty and like laughter was going to explode out of him.

"If you can lift yourself up in the air, maybe you can lift other stuff?" he finally said.

"But I don't know how."

"Come on, don't be a girl!"

"But I am a girl."

He shrugged and his grin went crooked.

"Can any of the superheroes in your comic books do it?"

"Yeah." He yelped as a pinecone got him right in the eye, and slid back farther under the shelter of the table, rubbing his face. "Hold on, I gotta think."

The problem with the comic books was that they showed but didn't explain. Later, Kurt gave me all the comic books where a superhero had telekinetic power. Not that either of us knew that particular word at the time. Usually the only instructions we got consisted of a greenish ray shooting out of someone's head, and blasting a car or tearing a wall apart.

"I don't know," he finally said. "It's kind of like… You know how on TV they show people with superpowers."

"No. We don't get to stay up that late."

"Well it's like—" Kurt scowled and I could almost hear humming, he was thinking so hard. "There was this one TV show where this guy had to learn how to do it and the guy who was teaching him said to think about his power like an extra hand."

"What does that mean?"

"Just think really hard about what you want the superguy power to do, and… I don't know, just think really hard."

I'm still not sure to this day how I made the mental connection, and how I switched over from kinda-sorta flying to grabbing all the trash the bullies had been throwing at us, and with the power of my mind flinging it back at them. With interest. All that really mattered right then was that I did it.

While the bullies ran away screaming and whining, I curled up with my first superpower-induced sick headache, and a nosebleed. That taught me and Kurt a huge lesson.

Actually, a number of lessons. We were too young and inexperienced to put it all into words or separate the factors and different variables. The important part was that we shouldn't try too much or work too hard, when it came to using our superhero powers. Fortunately, Kurt had already figured out another important rule: fuel! He ran to the concession stand and bought two creamsicles and three packages of cookies. He had already learned that using his gizmo talent made him achy-hungry, and if he didn't eat something right away, it turned into a killer headache like I had.

I inhaled the treats, leaving just the one creamsicle for Kurt. By the time Mrs. S blew her whistle to round us up for the bus ride back to NCH, I was feeling almost normal. Once my headache went away and the nosebleed stopped, I felt like I was floating about four inches off the ground. It was a heady feeling of power, to know I had beaten the bullies at just five years of age.

~~~~~

By the time school started, Kurt and I had gone through all his comic books and tried to figure out as many rules as we could. It was a major disappointment to me to learn about all the possible superhero powers that neither Kurt nor I seemed to possess. He believed we'd get more powers as we got older. According to the comic books, we had to be in high school before the big, flashy, dangerous powers showed up. Why they had to be dangerous, neither of us could figure out, except maybe it had something to do with the Army and the Air Force wanting to either blow us up or make us use our powers for them.

There was a word that kept coming up that seemed to be tied in with getting more powers. When I looked up *adolescence*, Kurt and I weren't any closer to understanding what it had to do with anything else. So we had to go to the library to learn more. The NCH library at that time was a large closet next to Mrs. Silvestri's office in the administration building. The bulk of it was a twenty-
~~~~~

volume encyclopedia. We didn't really get anywhere until Mrs. Gilbert, the secretary, overheard us trying to figure things out. She called Mrs. S in a panic, and Mrs. S sat down with us discuss what we were looking for and wanted to know.

She almost laughed at us, but didn't. Then she explained all the chemical changes that happened in the human body during adolescence, which struck both me and Kurt as kind of icky and stupid, but it kind of made sense. Chemicals changed things in the brain, right? The main lesson we took away from this was that we had to wait until we grew up some more.

The important rules were to be careful using our superhero powers so nobody saw us using them, to keep them secret, and to always have extra fuel on hand to keep headaches away, if we had to do something.

Then, we braced ourselves for the biggest change yet in my life: going to school. If we were going to need our superpowers to protect us, it would be at school.

~~~~~

Sylvia Grandstone was in my Kindergarten class. I was already sitting at one of the round tables when she made her entrance. Mrs. S had walked me to my room and introduced me to my teacher, like the other kids' mothers brought them. Sylvia's uncle Rosco brought her because her parents were in London for the theater season. She made sure everybody knew she was staying with her uncle and his two sons. Then she had to tell our teacher, Miss Underwood, all about her outfit, which was an exact replica of her mother's designer outfit.

Finally, Sylvia paraded into the room. She stopped about five steps away from the cluster of four short round tables. She jammed her fists, sparkling with rings and glittery nail polish, into her waist and glared. I watched her out of the corner of my eye while I kept on coloring. The other two girls at my table didn't notice her. They were busy working on a puzzle. The other kids at the other three tables kept working on puzzles and coloring books, for a few minutes longer. Until Sylvia let out one of those high-pitched *hmphs* just like the nasty old women in the grocery store, when nobody would get out of their way before they even stepped into the checkout line. Then some of the other kids looked up. They saw Sylvia. They stared back at her. They went back to their coloring.
~~~~~

My mistake was that I didn't go back to my coloring book and I kept watching her. First lesson: never give a Grandstone an audience. That was what they lived for.

"You're sitting in my spot," Sylvia announced.

"No I'm not."

"That's my spot."

"Your name isn't on it."

"What?"

I pointed at the strips of card stock taped to the table, forming a hexagram in the center of the table, with the names of students on them. "What's your name?"

"You don't know who I am?" Sylvia's voice rose to a shriek, which really wasn't much of a climb, since her voice was already simpering-squeaky-spoiled.

"What's your name? Then I can tell you where you're supposed to sit."

"I want to sit there!"

I raised my hand, waving it to get our teacher's attention. "Miss Underwood, didn't you say we have assigned seats?" Kurt had already warned me that we had to raise our hands before we asked questions in school.

"Yes, I did, Lanie." Miss Underwood closed the door and walked over to my table, now that the last four students had come in. "I put everyone's names on the tables where they're to sit for the first week of school. Just until we get to know each other."

"But that's my spot!" Sylvia insisted.

"No, that's Lanie's spot."

"What kind of name is Lanie?" Her nose wrinkled up and then she tipped her head back so she could look down her nose at me. However, I was taller than Sylvia, even sitting down.

"At least I have a name," I said.

"I'm Sylvia Grandstone." She stomped for punctuation.

"You're over there." I pointed at the table opposite mine.

"How do you know?"

"Because I can see your name right there, in green."

"No you can't! You're lying!"

"Sylvia—" Miss Underwood caught hold of her sequin-covered elbow. "—your spot is at that table."

"Why did you tell her where my spot was?" she demanded.

"Duh," I said. "I can read. Can't you?"

"I'm only five! You can't read either!" She yanked her arm free of our teacher's grip and stomped up to me and got close enough I could feel her breath on my face. I could also smell her. The cloud of perfume rolling off her made my eyes water.

Miss Underwood caught hold of her and led her away to the other table. The four others already at the table looked at Sylvia with that look of dawning fear that Grandstones were very good at inspiring in everyone around them. While Miss Underwood settled Sylvia, the others at my table quickly informed me in whispers just who Sylvia Grandstone was. They'd had the misfortune to be in nursery school with her, and some of them had encountered her nasty bully cousins, Reggie and Freddie. They let me know the Grandstones were rich and mean and always wanted everybody else's stuff. Well, that had been demonstrated clearly enough, with Sylvia walking in and trying to take my place at the table.

Sylvia focused on impressing her tablemates with her belief that the Grandstones owned Neighborlee, and we were duty-bound to obey her and give her anything she wanted. She stayed away from the rest of the class for the remainder of the school day, which was only a half-day. Proof that God was merciful.

Kurt was waiting when I got out of school. Well, to be honest, everybody from NCH was waiting to walk back home for lunch. For the first month, everybody was expected to go back to the orphanage for lunch. That meant I could walk with the other kids and learn the pretty straight route between NCH and the schools. Then in October, everybody else had the option of choosing if they wanted to eat in the cafeteria and play on the playground after lunch, or if they wanted to walk home to eat. I didn't have that choice, as the only resident in Kindergarten. Considering what I had already gone through, just in my first half-day of school, I was glad to be going home already. The thought of having to sit in the huge cafeteria with hundreds of other kids was a little nerve-wracking for me. Especially if there was a chance I would have to sit at the same table with Sylvia.

I waited until the other kids from NCH headed down the sidewalk ahead of us. Kurt didn't seem to mind us being at the end of the line. He stumbled a little when I asked him if he knew anything about the Grandstones.

"Where did you hear about them?" he asked. He groaned when I told him about meeting Sylvia, and told me what a selfish lying jerk her cousin Reggie was, who was in his class. "There are three Grandstones. Reggie and his stupid brother, Freddie, and now Sylvia. Whatever you do, don't tell anybody in your class that you're an orphan."

"Why? Is it a bad thing?" I shook my head, realizing a second later what a stupid question that was. "I mean, yeah, I know it's bad we don't gots parents and everything, but … is it a bad thing that people know?"

"Not usually." Kurt shrugged and he looked around, like he expected someone to be following us. "The thing is … I don't know. It's weird. It's the Grandstones. Reggie was a real slug when we were in Kindergarten, and then he tried to be my best friend for a while, and then he got even worse than he was before. Somebody told me he wanted something, but I guess he figured I didn't have it, so he changed his mind. I bet if Sylvia finds out you're an orphan, she'll want to be your best friend. Then she'll be a total creep later. I don't know why. Usually after you meet her parents." He frowned. "Or maybe it's just her uncle. Freddie and Reggie's dad. He came to school for a program and he talked to me, and then Reggie was a slug again." Another shrug. "I don't know why."

"That's okay. I wouldn't want to be friends with her for anything. I'll stay away from her. She smells awful."

For some reason, Kurt thought that was funny.

Chapter Three

Sylvia left me alone for the first week of school, until Miss Underwood let us move our nametags. She marched over to my table, ripped my nametag off the table, tearing it halfway through between the N and the I, then slapped her nametag down in my place. By this time, I had received plenty of advice from Kurt and Mrs. S and Miss Abby for how to handle even worse bullies than Ricky and Donny. I picked up my nametag off the floor where she tossed it and moved over to the table she had just left.

The funny thing was, everybody at my table pulled up their nametags and moved to other tables, leaving Sylvia completely alone. That worked out, because there were six places at each table and four tables, but only eighteen students in the class.

Sylvia didn't even notice that she had the fourth table entirely to herself until she looked up from taping her nametag down again. Her mouth dropped open and she looked around the room. Then she stomped over to Clarice O'Donnell, who had been sitting next to me at my first table and had taken the same spot at our new table.

"What are you doing over here?" she demanded.

"I want to sit over here," Clarice said, her voice barely above a mumble.

"But I want you to sit next to me." Sylvia reached over to pull up Clarice's nametag, which she had just finished taping down.

"Sylvia, what did I just tell everybody?" Miss Underwood called.

"You said we could sit wherever we wanted now, we can sit by our friends. I want Clarice to sit next to me." Again with the little stomp for punctuation.

"I also said that everyone could make one move. You've already moved to a new table, and Clarice has moved to a new table. No more moving."

"But Miss Underwood, I want—"

"Clarice, do you want to sit next to Sylvia?" Miss Underwood asked.

"Yes, she does," Sylvia said, while Clarice hunched her

shoulders and shook her head. Everybody had been watching in silence until that moment. Then they burst out laughing. Sylvia turned red, darker than her blood-red nail polish.

"The rules are the rules," Miss Underwood said. "Go back to your table, Sylvia."

"But I'm all alone!"

"Yes, and why don't you think about why you're alone?"

"Clarice is stupid and didn't do what I told her, that's why."

"No one is allowed to call anyone stupid in this classroom."

Sylvia spent the rest of the morning standing in the corner, doing her addition worksheet against the wall, with her back to the rest of the room.

I told Kurt what happened on the walk home for lunch. He got that big-eyed, somber look, grabbed my hand, and barely finished saying, "Come on," before he took off running. We went right down the first street past the school instead of walking to the center of town and turning right, to get to NCH. Just after we turned right, we caught up with Clarice and her brother, Chuck. Kurt had me repeat what I had just told him.

"Yeah, she told me," Chuck said. "That was pretty brave, Reesy, not letting a Grandstone order you around."

"But Sylvia never told Clarice to sit with her," I said. "And she never asked her. Sylvia never talks to Clarice at all."

"Grandstones expect people to read their minds and know what they want before they say what they want."

"Gotta have something written there before you can read it," Kurt mumbled. He and Chuck did that stupid boy thing, punching each other in the arm and snorting. "I figure they're gonna come after you, as soon as Saliva tells Reggie." He grinned when Clarice and I both giggled at how he warped Sylvia's name.

The plan was simple—walk with Chuck and Clarice until they got home safely. We didn't really think about the next day, or the day after that. We were just kids. We didn't hold grudges for very long. What we didn't realize was that Sylvia and her rotten cousins weren't "just kids." They were taught from the cradle to hold grudges and to wait years, if they had to, for their revenge. In Grandstone mentality, that meant justice.

Fortunately for us, they also had a very high pride level, and a short attention span.

Before we had gone another block, Sylvia and Reggie caught up to us on their bikes. They rode circles around us, but the sight of four of us against the two of them was enough to stop them from inflicting punishment on Clarice. The four of us kept walking, which made Sylvia and Reggie continually adjust the path of their bikes. On the third circle around us, Sylvia hit the curb crooked and knocked her bike over and fell off. She let out a shriek and Reggie fell off his bike.

"Did you?" Kurt said as we kept walking. He was the only one who looked back. It took me a minute to understand what he meant. I shook my head. "Too bad. That would have been cool."

Sylvia didn't come to school the next day. Her leg hurt too much. Clarice told me that Sylvia's uncle came to the O'Donnells' house that night, accusing them of beating up on her. Chuck had experience with Grandstone lies, so he had already told his father what happened. Mr. O'Donnell told Mr. Grandstone that nobody had touched Sylvia, and if he tried to sue, he would counter-sue and slap a restraining order on Sylvia to keep her away from Clarice.

Clarice actually giggled when she told me that Mr. Grandstone got all weepy and his voice got high. He insisted that Clarice was Sylvia's best friend and she was just so fragile without her parents in the country, she needed her best friend to withstand the torments of the first few weeks of school.

I had to explain what fragile was.

"Daddy explained to me that Sylvia thinks I'm her best friend because I'm too scared of her to argue," Clarice added.

That afternoon, when Kurt got back from school, Mrs. Silvestri called both of us into her office. We had to tell her all over again what happened. Reggie knew Kurt, so when the Grandstones failed with Chuck and Clarice, they tracked us down, to accuse us of beating up on Sylvia.

"I'm proud of the two of you, for helping to defend others against bullies," Mrs. S said. "However..."

"There's always a however," Kurt muttered, slouching down in his seat right next to mine, facing Mrs. S's desk.

She pressed her lips flat and a little snort-giggle sound escaped her. She bowed her snowy head and rubbed at her temples, then sat up and looked at us again.

"Please be careful in all your dealings with the Grandstones. I don't want to have to punish you for doing what's right."

Then Mrs. S proved she was proud of us. She took us to Divine's Emporium for an hour before dinner. She and Angela sat at the little white wrought iron café table and chatted while Kurt showed me his favorite room upstairs, full of bins of bits and pieces of engines and tools and gears and belts. He put together a cute little wind-up car just while we were walking around the room, from the things he pulled out of the bin. We had fun watching it roll around the room on the mismatched wheels, bumping into the walls and bouncing off, until Mrs. S came for us. Angela let Kurt have the parts he used, for the leftover allowance he had in his pocket. Then she gave me a bag with twenty licorice whips in five flavors and told us to keep up the good work.

Sylvia must have been so ashamed of how she messed up, both crashing her bike and failing to get us in trouble, she left Clarice alone. Actually, she spent the next three weeks pretending Clarice wasn't there. Reggie and Freddie didn't come after Chuck or Kurt. However, Kurt reported that the Grandstone brothers asked a lot of questions about both of us. Some of the questions made no sense, like it was important that we didn't have anybody. At all. Why did they ask more questions about Kurt, when Reggie already knew about him? After that Sylvia learned new, nasty words for me, and used them anywhere an adult wouldn't hear her. *Throwaway* was one of the milder taunts. *Reject. Leftovers. Sloppy seconds.*

Since she didn't sit at the same table with me in class, Sylvia made a point of standing at the easel next to me during painting, and tried to spill water or other colors into my paint jars.

After three weeks of warding off Sylvia's sloppy sabotage, I didn't get headaches anymore. New superhero lesson: regular exercise of my moving *trick* helped me get stronger, and better control. My appetite grew. Being a superhero, even a superhero in training, used up a lot of calories.

~~~~~

Charlie and Rainbow Zephyr had come to Neighborlee to live, just about the same time that Pastor Peter Simons, whom everybody called Pastor Rocky, bought the old Wickslow Chapel. Neighborlee Gospel Church had been meeting in one of the community rooms that were available for rent in the old Bucksby
~~~~~

Factory on the edge of town. They had finally grown large enough to buy a building of their own. The Zephyrs were writers, researching the "weird and wonderful and wacky" as they phrased it, and they had decided to start slowing down now that they were nearly forty. "Slowing down," to them, meant having an actual home, instead of living in their van. They bought the Sherman place, a massive old farmhouse and about thirty acres of land on the edge of town. Once they moved in, they joined Neighborlee Gospel Church and joined in the renovations of the chapel.

That took the congregation of NGC most of the summer and into the fall. Pastor Rocky believed that with all that work behind them, and an established base of operations, his congregation had an opportunity for outreach now. One of their first outreaches was to go to the orphanage and spend time with the children. Twice a month, the members of the church came for games and baking and crafts and singing. They found out what the older students wanted to do with their lives, and matched them up with members of the congregation who were doing the same thing, such as accounting, auto mechanics, gymnastics, or teaching.

Rainbow read to us from the most amazing books. Charlie sat on the floor with us, drawing pictures with lighting strokes to go with the stories, or building amazing, impossible buildings and creatures with building blocks. It only took two visits from the congregation, but especially Charlie and Rainbow, for all of us to look forward to our Sunday afternoons with them.

She earned the name of Rainbow because she dyed her hair a different color every time we saw her. She was a curvier-than-average Asian woman with incredible blue-gray eyes. Charlie was a head taller, with a receding hairline and iron-gray hair caught in a long ponytail down his back. They both wore moccasins and jeans with lots of patches on them, and Charlie never seemed to have anything but tie-dyed t-shirts. Basically, they were Hippies, but about twenty-some years out of date. None of us kids cared. We just loved having them around. They were Mr. Z and Mrs. Z from day one.

The fun just got better as we headed for Christmas and they took us caroling and came to make cookies and decorations and crafty little gifts to give each other.

Then the nightmares started.

I never woke up screaming, never talked in my sleep. However, after the third time I jumped out of bed and ran around the room I shared with three other girls, checking to make sure the door and windows were securely shut and locked, people noticed. All I could tell anybody when they complained about me waking them up was that I heard someone trying to get into our cottage.

The girls in my room were nice and didn't tell anybody but Miss Abby. The other girls in our cottage weren't so nice when I got out of our bedroom and checked all the windows and doors. They complained, and word got around. About a week before Christmas, Kurt overheard the complaints and the teasing, and he confronted me.

"Do you feel like a kind of itching in your feet?" he said, when we were tucked up safe in our talking place behind the stage in the social hall. He sighed, more like a groan, and slumped back against the wall. "You know, like when I can feel our superpowers working."

"You can feel them. I can't," I reminded him.

"Yeah, but I'm getting weird dreams too. Is someone trying to get through the walls, scratching at them all the time?"

"It's not people," I told him, my voice dropping to a whisper.

Kurt looked at me very solemnly, looking much older than his nearly-nine years.

We talked about everything we could remember of our dreams, which wasn't much, just the impression of someone trying to get into wherever we were. Kurt was frustrated with me that I didn't get an itching feeling. Then he forgot about that in the surprising discovery revealed by further talking. The itching was always on the same side of the room, when he woke up from his dreams of the intruder. Meaning if he lay on his back, the itching was on his right side, but if he lay on his stomach, the itching was on his left side, and if he was curled up on his side facing the wall, his face itched. The itching was always closest to the outer wall of his room.

Talking didn't solve anything, and didn't do us much good in dispelling the nightmares, either. We both had nightmares that night. On the way to school the next day, we walked at the back of the line so we could have a little privacy to talk. There was only one thing we could think of. Fortunately, it was the smart tactic.

At lunchtime, instead of going back to NCH, Kurt and I ran all the way to Divine's Emporium. Our logic was sound, at least, as sound as two elementary-age children could come up with. We just weren't sure we were allowed to cross that five-lane street without someone who was over age twelve. Still, we had to do it. Miss Angela was the source of all the comic books that Kurt and I used to formulate our superhero rules, and to learn what we could possibly do someday. She was the source of all the wonderful, magical things in our lives. Besides, she had the Wishing Ball, and the clearest thought in my sleep-deprived mind was that I could make a wish and make the nightmares go away.

Angela was spreading cinders on the flagstone path in front of Divine's Emporium, outside of the wrought iron fence, when we ran up the long street. She stopped and put the bucket down inside the fence and then turned and watched us coming, her arms wrapped tight around herself. The closer we came, the sadder her expression grew, so that by the time we were about ten yards away, we had slowed down. The last thing I wanted in the world was to disappoint Miss Angela, and I was sure Kurt felt the same. By the time we got to within maybe ten feet of her, I was wishing I could turn around and run back to NCH and make Miss Angela forget we had come there. She had to know we were supposed to be heading home for lunch, or at least I was. Kurt packed his lunch like all the other NCH kids did in cold or rainy weather, so he could stay at school to eat.

"I'm so sorry," Miss Angela said, and went down on one knee, holding her arms open wide for us. We ran to her and I nearly cried from relief when she hugged us.

"So we're not dead meat?" Kurt said, when she released us and gestured for us to go ahead of her through the gate.

"Not on my watch. No, you two are in very good odor. Although... Well, we'll just have to think of a totally reasonable cover story and make it true. That's one of the laws of the guardians of Neighborlee. While we have many secrets, there are many truths that the ordinary people of this town don't need to know, for their own good and their own mental wellbeing. Can we truly call anyone ordinary who lives in Neighborlee?" She frowned slightly as we trooped up the cinder-strewn path to the front porch of Divine's. Then her frown turned to a smile, she winked, and chuckled as the door swung open while we were three steps away.

"Did you do that?" Kurt said in a loud whisper. "I didn't feel it."

"Ah ha!" Miss Angela nudged our shoulders, to propel us forward through the door. "Did you discover another facet of your gifts, Lanie?"

"What's a facet?" he asked.

"It's like the flat part of a diamond." Yes, I must confess, there was some scorn in my voice. I had a habit of devouring every book I could get my hands on. After I had learned where the tiny library was at NCH, I had read through the entire encyclopedia. Between the start of school and Thanksgiving. That put me in possession of a great deal of scattered, unrelated bits of knowledge, and I felt rather superior every time one of those pieces became useful.

"Hmm, accurate, if not totally… Well, maybe it is applicable. There are many faces or sides or dimensions to what you can do, or possibly could do someday," Miss Angela said. "There are many futures, full of possibilities, and no true means exist to see clearly which one is for sure." She guided us upstairs, to her living quarters on the second floor. Both of us were astonished and enchanted, because it had never occurred to either of us that someone could actually live in the same building as their business.

While we put together a lunch of sandwiches and soup and hot chocolate, Miss Angela made phone calls. First, she called Mrs. Silvestri and told her not to worry. We had made a slight detour and come to see her about advice for Christmas shopping. She promised Kurt would get back to school before the lunch hour was over. Then she called Mr. Longfellow and asked him to come to the shop. Then she called the school and left a message for Mrs. Longfellow, who was Kurt's teacher, and told her Kurt was helping her and Mr. Longfellow, and might be late getting back to class. That was when we learned Mr. Longfellow's first name was Ford. Then she told us to set the table for four.

We were sitting down to the most incredible chicken soup we had ever had in our lives when Mr. Longfellow came into the shop. He ran right upstairs, knocked once on the door of Miss Angela's apartment and walked in before she answered. Then he flung his long rusty black pea coat onto the ottoman, and slid into the fourth chair at the table.

"Hey, kids. How come I'm not surprised it's you?" He winked, and then nodded to Miss Angela.

Ford Longfellow was a familiar figure, since his family attended Neighborlee Gospel Church and helped out with visiting NCH every other Sunday. He was tall and bald with enormous, bushy eyebrows, and his long whiskers were in that fascinating transition between dark red and white, meaning they were all shades of burgundy, gold, and silver. He worked with the older boys who wanted to be mechanics and engineers, and Mrs. Silvestri had introduced him to us the very first Sunday as a tinkerer. He made his living finding antiques for people and renovating furniture and houses. Mrs. Longfellow taught the third grade at Neighborlee Elementary and was in charge of the school library.

Their daughter Portia was maybe in her mid-twenties at the time we met the family, and even then there was something visibly not quite "there" about her. I heard someone refer to her as "flaky." She just seemed to flitter from one interest to another. Part of her problem might have been that she was super-smart, like Mr. Longfellow, but she couldn't focus on anything.

The other Longfellow daughter was Lenore, also very smart, and involved in dozens of things, inside and outside Neighborlee. She had graduated from Willis-Brooks College, was taking a bunch of correspondence courses toward a master's degree, and could speak five other languages. She was a lot of fun when she visited NCH on Sundays, and she was about the only person I had met who didn't seem surprised at my reading level. We got along great, and she helped me convince the head librarian at the Neighborlee Public Library that yes, I could handle books from the adult section.

Then there was Jinx Longfellow. He was in high school. I never did learn what his real name was. Somewhere along the line, he had earned the nickname of Jinx, and it stuck. Nobody could ever explain why he earned the name, because he was possessed of the most incredible good luck, rather than bad.

Mr. Longfellow knew Kurt a whole lot better than me, just because Kurt was allowed to go with the older boys to the mechanics' group on Sundays.

"I haven't asked them yet, but I could feel the weight on them when they stepped onto my street," Angela said. "It must be grave indeed, to recruit them so young."

"Recruit us for what?" Kurt said.

"What Miss Angela said before," I said, putting down my mug of soup. "We're guardians. Right?"

"Very right," she said.

"Kids pay better attention than adults." Mr. Longfellow slouched in his chair with his soup mug cradled in both hands. "Maybe you and I have been so focused on figuring out what's causing all the discord in the air, we've blinded and deafened ourselves. The kids got called up sooner than either of us would like because they aren't distracted."

Chapter Four

"What brought you here to talk to me?" Miss Angela said, when Kurt and I just looked back and forth between the two of them, trying to figure out what they were talking about. It wasn't like they were talking over our heads, but there were so many unsaid things behind their words.

"We've been having dreams about people trying to get into our rooms," Kurt said, when he had looked at me and I looked at him, and we silently agreed he would do the speaking. It wasn't telepathy, but we had spent enough time together, we understood each other well enough to just know without words. He told them about how we were getting out of bed before we woke up, to make sure the doors and windows in our cottages were secure.

"How long have you had them?" Mr. Longfellow said.

With careful questioning, we determined that our nightmares had started the night of the community decorating party at the old Bucksby Factory. Some of the movers and shakers in town had decided the factory should be renovated, one room at a time, using only donations and volunteer labor, to turn it into a community center. The lobby had been refurbished, with a new drop ceiling and new floor tiles and new paint, and the decorating party was a combination of celebration, community event, and promotion to get people excited about the possibilities.

"We've disturbed something, you think?" Mr. Longfellow shared one of those long looks with Angela that adults were so good at.

"I think it's more along the lines of it taking advantage of all the activity, all the emotions being stirred up, the contention and excitement and the vast possibilities and potentials." Miss Angela sighed and frowned a little as she picked up the pot-belly teapot covered in dragons and unicorns, and refilled all our hot chocolate mugs.

"The weak spot is either under the factory, or somewhere in the park nearby." He winked at Kurt. "Son, you have a very useful and convenient talent. Smart of you, picking up the direction the power leaks were coming from."

I almost said "huh?" and Kurt gave me a big-eyed glance, meaning he felt just as lost. We finally realized Mr. Longfellow meant the itching sensation that was always on the same side of the room. What I wanted to know, and what we were both sure we didn't dare ask, was what they meant by power leaks. What had been disturbed? How could emotions wake up something? What weak spot? Was there like a hole in the ground or something in the park behind the old factory building? Maybe there were tunnels and things in the old quarries that had been turned into state park land that nobody knew about, and the tunnels were going to collapse, like the old mines in the TV show we had seen the week before?

We didn't ask, because we were both pretty sure neither Miss Angela nor Mr. Longfellow would tell us. It was pretty clear that while they appreciated our help, they didn't like us being involved. It sure sounded and felt like something just serious enough, I didn't want to know. I mean, I was only five!

"Whatever we do," Mr. Longfellow said a short time later, as he led me and Kurt out to his truck, to drive us back to school and home, "there will be repercussions. Especially if those outsiders are involved. Picking at the shields."

"What matters is that the holes will be plugged, the cracks filled or patched over," Miss Angela said. I saw for the first time the smile that I learned over the years meant mischief as well as dire consequences for anyone who stood against her.

Kurt and I never did hear what they did. The important thing was that I didn't get in trouble for not coming straight home from school. Some of the girls in my cottage were upset that I got to go to Divine's Emporium without them. We took Kurt to school before Mr. Longfellow drove me home. Kurt got back to school with two minutes to spare before the recess bell rang. Mrs. Longfellow was waiting at the side door of the school that opened out onto the parking lot. She stepped out to meet the truck, climbed up on the running board and kissed Mr. Longfellow through the open window. Then she told him to be careful and held out her hand for Kurt's to lead him back into the building.

"Not gonna ask what I'm supposed to be careful about?" Mr. Longfellow asked, as we pulled out of the parking lot and headed for NCH.

"It's grownup stuff, huh?" I said.

"You got it, honey." He winked at me. "Take my advice and stay a kid as long as you can, okay?"

I must have given him one of those "adults are crazy" looks that most kids are so good at. I definitely didn't understand what he could mean. How could I be anything but a kid as long as I was a kid? He burst out laughing. When he dropped me off in front of the central hall of NCH, Mrs. Silvestri was waiting at the front door. He came around to the passenger door of the truck to help me down, because that big, old-fashioned truck was a little high off the ground. Then he tucked some folded pieces of paper in my hand and told me to share them with Kurt, because we had saved him and Miss Angela lots of headaches and we deserved a reward. When I looked later, I found out he had given me five dollars — for each of us. That took care of a lot of Christmas shopping, and sort of smoothed over the explanation Miss Angela had given Mrs. Silvestri, that we needed advice on Christmas shopping. So we really didn't lie.

Maybe teaching us to keep secrets at such a young age wasn't the best sort of lesson, but when it came to defending Neighborlee, and the sanity of the "ordinary" people of our town, it was an important lesson to learn.

Even more important than escaping punishment for breaking several important rules, the nightmares stopped. Completely. Not even echoes of them or fragments.

Later, Angela explained our part in the whole "guardians of Neighborlee" pact that we had signed onto just by acting. She told us that it was like we overheard some criminals planning to do something mean, like chop down the Christmas tree in the center of town, or break into the Project Angel box, where people dropped gifts for needy families. We were just kids, so we really couldn't do anything except tell the adults, so they could catch the people when they followed through on their plan.

Soon after the nightmares stopped, the Grandstones made another attempt to take over the town. Or, from their point of view, take back what had been stolen from their family. According to Sylvia, who parroted whatever she heard her uncle and parents discuss, the Grandstones had built Neighborlee. According to the

Grandstone version of history, they had paid for all the oldest buildings and the surveying for the roads and established the quarries, the first major business, which helped anchor Neighborlee.

A lot of us had very logical questions in response to her declarations. How come the Bucksby Factory was called Bucksby and not Grandstone, if the Grandstones built it and owned it? Sylvia came back with her father's answer. She claimed Neighborlee had stolen the factory that had belonged to her family for generations. She insisted the town didn't even put up a façade or pretense of semi-legal means to declare eminent domain and take over the factory. I asked her what "façade" and "pretense" meant and she couldn't tell me.

Miss Underwood gave us a Neighborlee history lesson. The Bucksby Factory had been sitting vacant for thirty years. The town took it over because a title search had revealed that the owners had no discernible heirs. What stock there was in the possession of anyone outside the family was so minimal that no one could have any claim on the building. All the back taxes, unpaid for decades, put the building squarely in the hands of the local, federal, and county governments. Neighborlee paid some minimal amounts to the county and the federal government to have full control of the property, and took responsibility for security, to make sure no dangerous elements would settle in. The Grandstones didn't have even a shadow of a legal claim on the building or the land, and had never had any claim. Sylvia stood up in class and called Miss Underwood a liar, so she spent the rest of the day in the corner.

Next, the Grandstones went after Neighborlee Gospel Church. On Christmas Eve, their lawyers filed a mountain of paperwork with the county, claiming that Pastor Rocky had illegally taken possession of the former Wickslow Chapel. The actual wording called it "a cult of interfering extremists trying to brainwash the children of the town." The Grandstones' lawyers claimed that the chapel had been built by the Grandstone clan, and it hadn't been intended as a chapel. They had "graciously" allowed a poor, penniless parson to use the building to tend to the spiritual needs of the townsfolk during a time of emotional and economic devastation. Then during a low time in the Grandstone family history, they had been too busy with other problems to evict the parson's son, who had the "temerity" to put his family name on the building and claim it as his property. The Grandstones claimed they regretted having to use the strong arm of the law to take back what was rightfully theirs, but since the people of Neighborlee were so inconsiderate as to withhold their legal property, they were just going to have to act, and air the town's dirty laundry.

They went after the church because the Zephyrs and Ford Longfellow headed the research into town records, to prove the Grandstones never owned the Bucksby Factory. None of them worked for a business whose owners the Grandstones could intimidate, to get them fired. However, they were visible, active members of Neighborlee Gospel Church, so that became the target point to punish them for resisting the Grandstones' latest scheme. Plus, Pastor Rocky found crates of long-missing town records hidden in a secret room in the basement of the Wickslow Chapel.

I was there and a witness to everything because everyone from NCH was at the church on Christmas Eve when the Grandstone lawyers attacked. Or tried to. The congregation had brought a big, fancy turkey dinner to the orphanage, and then took us all to the church for the Christmas Eve service.

We got there in time to see these big black cars tear into the parking lot and try to block the doorway. The problem was that the parking lot had been freshly paved about three weeks before and it was nice and smooth blacktop, still dark, and there was a fresh coating of sleet and snow on it. Those fancy black cars skidded and banged into each other while all of us were climbing out of the NCH bus and all the cars and vans of the congregation and walking to the front door. We got inside while the lawyers were all yelling and blaming each other for the tiny collisions that barely dented their cars, way on the other side of the huge parking lot. Pastor Rocky was very optimistic about the growth of the church. Even though the current building only had room for about two hundred people, the parking lot was big enough for a football game.

So we were all inside and taking our coats off when the lawyers finally got to the door and started banging. Funny thing, nobody had locked the front door, but they couldn't seem to get it open. Kurt and I were talking with the Longfellows and we were close to the door, so we heard all the commotion. Pastor Rocky and some of the deacons went to see what the fuss was, and they opened the door. The lawyers came stomping in with papers in their hands and chains that they wanted to use on the doors to keep people out. Only they couldn't, because we were already inside.

They had filed their paperwork with the county that afternoon, injunctions to keep people out of the building until the ownership history of the building could be properly traced. As we learned later, the people in the county building weren't too happy about that. The county offices were supposed to close at 1pm on Christmas Eve. The Grandstone lawyers walked in the door at five after, and interrupted the Christmas party that was winding down. Plus, the county offices had plenty of experience with the Grandstones and their frequent attempts to take over the town.

Remember what I said about people who ignored the "go away, we don't want you here" vibe in Neighborlee? It drove them crazy-nasty. The Grandstones were just plain nasty people who hung on tighter the more their knuckles got crushed. As we learned years later, they soothed their hurt feelings by spying on Neighborlee and working with some of the people who made the Lost Kids vanish. But this information came many years later, after the Grandstones essentially punished themselves.

The lawyers never got the injunctions and other paperwork filed with Neighborlee City Hall. Even though the legal department was supposed to stay open until noon, that just meant their Christmas party ended at noon. From what I heard years later, someone spotted the lawyers getting out of their cars. The emergency alert system went into effect throughout City Hall. People ran and locked doors and turned the blinds and pulled curtains and turned off lights. Then they hid on the floor behind their desks, holding their breaths and trying not to laugh while the lawyers went up and down the halls, banging on doors and getting angrier and louder, trying to find someone to help them.

So they showed up at Neighborlee Gospel Church on Christmas Eve to chain the doors shut and evict the congregation, even though the county offices told them nothing would go into effect until December 27.

Word got around, and the right people learned what the Grandstone lawyers had done at the county offices. Chief Tanner, a member of NGC, was there with a half-dozen of his officers, also members. Chief Tanner looked like a sleepy basset hound, but even the Grandstone lawyers had a hard time keeping up their bullying tones and self-righteous indignation when he just stood there and calmly waited for them to run out of words.

Kurt and I both agreed, Chief Tanner was our hero. We were there and had front row seats for the showdown.

Within half an hour, Chief Tanner had the Grandstone lawyers sulking and stomping, and sliding on the patches of ice in the parking lot, heading back to their cars. He made it clear that while they were welcome to join the congregation for Christmas Eve services, they had no legal right to bring chains and documents onto the property with the intent to evict people who had every legal right to be there and to use the property they had paid good money for. Then he pointed out that the Grandstones were about ten years too late in showing concern for what they claimed was their property. If they wanted to prove their concern for the neighborhood and the historical value of the building, their first step, as a gesture of goodwill to the town, would be to pay for all the time and effort and resources that had been put into maintaining the property, which had been paid for by the town.

The mere mention of spending their own money to fix up the property was nearly enough to send the Grandstone lawyers running with their tails between their legs.

The Zephyrs got involved again in searching records, pulling strings and using their legal and historical connections. Nobody in town believed the Grandstones had anything to do with the building when it was the Wickslow Chapel. For one thing, it was built to look like and function as a church. Most people believed the Grandstones would burst into flame the moment they stepped foot onto church property. For another thing, every document since the founding of Neighborlee referred to the building as the Wickslow Chapel. For a third thing, Wickslow was the maiden name of Arabella Willis, who founded Neighborlee. Her cousin was a circuit rider preacher who came to Neighborlee to retire from the circuit about two years after Widow Willis brought her band of settlers to the northern portion of the Ohio Territory. The Zephyrs found documentation proving that the Wickslow Chapel was the first brick building in Neighborlee, and the original cornerstone had a date inscribed on it twelve years before any known Grandstone appeared in Neighborlee. The first documented Grandstone was an orphan boy who grew up in a poorhouse and was a generation younger than the Willis twins, so no way did he get to Neighborlee before Widow Willis' cousin built the chapel.

They found all this out in the three weeks between Christmas and when a hearing was held at the Justice Center in downtown Cleveland. The judge wasn't too happy about having to handle the hearing. The other judges who had had to handle Grandstone claims in the past had forced him to do it, because they didn't want to. Whenever someone who had dealt with the Grandstones before sat in judgment on a new claim, the Grandstones and their lawyers started a smear campaign. They claimed the judge was biased against them and tried to have the judgment thrown out. They were partly right. Anybody who had to deal with the Grandstones and their brainwashed lawyers always came away prejudiced against them.

The judge threw everything out and levied a fine against the Grandstones for falsifying documents. Then he added every charge that could be filed without actually saying they were being penalized for being selfish and lying and wasting the court's time.

Chapter Five

The Zephyrs and several other couples who were friends of Miss Underwood volunteered to chaperone the Kindergarten class at a sledding party that Friday the judgment came through. The sledding hill was behind City Hall, along the road going down into the Metroparks. The police department kept fires burning in big metal drums, and the shed used for renting out bikes and skates in the summer dispensed hot chocolate in the winter. Mr. Z went into the maintenance garage to call the church, where many of the older members of the congregation were waiting for word from the Justice Center and Mr. Carr, the church's lawyer. He came running out just as Mrs. Z was climbing on the back of the sled with me, at the top of the hill.

Mr. Z let out a whoop and turned a running somersault right there, just flipping over in the air and landing on his feet. That kind of got everybody's attention. Then he picked up Mrs. Z and kissed her and shouted, "We won!" and they danced around on the snow that was all packed down from sleds and people. Word got around fast after that, and lots of people came over to talk and laugh. Whenever the Grandstones failed another attempt to own the town, pretty much everybody was happy.

Sylvia had made us miserable in class ever since we came back from Christmas break, complaining about "those nasty church people" who stole her family's building. Miss Underwood had been a lot nicer than Sylvia deserved. She only sent the little snot home twice when she called Miss Underwood stupid and said she didn't know the truth about the situation. When the celebrating started and people gathered around to hear the news, Sylvia was there.

Was she upset? That would be an understatement.

Most snots like her would have flown into a rage, maybe had a kicking tantrum in the snow. Grandstones were nasty-smart, and sometimes they even learned from the bad examples and ridiculously stupid behavior of their ancestors. There are five buildings in Neighborlee with dents in the brickwork from when Grandstones tried to punish someone who had foiled their latest scheme. The stories vary whether the attempts were made with a car or a sledgehammer. Those ridiculously stupid reactions of previous generations had ensured that the Grandstones weren't very numerous in any generation, yet as I said, they did learn. Sylvia was a smarter Grandstone, and she waited.

The celebrating died down, as people ran off to get on whatever phones they could find to spread the news. We didn't have a lot of cell phones back then. The Zephyrs hurried over to where I was standing by my sled. Mrs. Z hugged me and apologized. They both laughed when I told them I knew what was going on. We climbed on the sled and screamed all the way down the hill. Mr. Z pulled the sled and the Zephyrs held my hands and we walked up the hill together. We went down twice more, and then someone flagged down Mr. Z to talk about something and Mrs. Z went to get hot chocolate for us.

Then the crimson and gold figure that had been lingering on the edge of my vision attacked. She could finally tower over me because she stood two feet up the slope.

"You think you're so smart!" Sylvia shrieked. Her fists were jammed into her hips, so it made the skirts stick out in the fancy outfit more appropriate for figure skating than sledding. "You think it's funny? Those stupid, nasty, mean people are thieves!"

Then she said other things with words I didn't understand. I had to look them up later. They were mean, derogatory, and even racially hateful. She picked on Mrs. Z for being Asian and called Mr. Z a drug-pusher and a hippie and accused them of being liars and Communist spies and dozens of other things she could only have picked up from the so-called adults in her family.

Sylvia's arsenal of nastiness did have limits. When she started in on her second round, I told her she was repeating herself.

Interrupting a Grandstone wasn't smart. It just increased their speed, volume and pitch, and sometimes added spitting.

The really un-smart part of the whole encounter was that I should have turned my back on her as soon as she called the Zephyrs stupid. I mean, I had a sled right there and I was on the hill. I could have just turned and sat down and pushed. By the time she realized I wasn't listening, I would have been twenty feet away.

"That is enough, young lady," Miss Underwood said, in that tone that was so calm and disappointed, it was scary.

Most Kindergarteners would have stopped short, frozen by guilt, knowing we had made our teacher unhappy.

Sylvia let out a shriek and launched herself at me. Miss Underwood caught her by the collar of her coat. Sylvia had strong legs and a hard push-off, and enough momentum to unbalance them both and send them into the snow.

Miss Underwood got up first, laughing and wiping her face off. She looked around and winked as she gestured for me to get out of there.

All right, so I was a little slow that day. All those new vocabulary words were swirling around in my head, so I was justifiably distracted. I dragged the sled up the slope to Mrs. Z. She was easy to find, with her long hair the prettiest shade of lime green, braided with silver ribbons and a dingle-bell on the end.

"Sweetheart, you have got remarkable self-control." She was coming up to me with a big cup of hot chocolate. "I would have popped that snot after about the third sentence." We walked over to a bench that no one was using. Very rare. "What's her problem?"

"She's a Grandstone."

"Ah." She pressed her lips flat and we sat down and sipped for a few seconds. Miss Underwood and Sylvia parted company, and both vanished into the crowd. I figured Sylvia was going to go look for some adult to complain to and follow through on her regular threat to have Miss Underwood fired.

"Mrs. Z, what's a chink?"

She snorted, and I could have sworn a few drops of hot chocolate came out her nose.

"Well, for one thing, highly inaccurate in this case. I'm part Polynesian, part Japanese. Chink is a nasty nickname for someone who's Chinese." She winked at me and sipped again. "My, what do they teach their children in her house?"

"Sylvia wants to be queen of the whole town."

"That's what I've heard about the Grandstones. I'm sorry you had to pay for what isn't your fight."

"It's about the church, isn't it?"

"That it is," Mr. Z said, settling down on the bench on the other side of his wife. "I was way down at the other end of the run and only heard bits and pieces. That girl saw you with us and figured... Well, she's at least smart enough to know she couldn't take her disappointment out on us, so she attacked you."

"I like your church."

"Good. We sure like having you come."

By this time, school had let out, and older brothers and sisters were showing up at the slope to either join the sledding or take their Kindergartener siblings home. Some of the parents who had been supervising gathered up their children and the sleds that had been loaned out for the afternoon. Miss Underwood got our attention and told us we could take one more run down the hill, and then the party was officially over. The sled I had been using belonged to the Zephyrs, so I thought I would take it to their VW minibus for them. But when I turned around to get it, it wasn't tucked halfway under the bench where I had put it when Mrs. Z and I sat down.

I knew what had happened, even before I looked around and saw Sylvia pulling it, running through deep snow and looking pretty stupid and clumsy. She was going through snow where nobody had walked all afternoon, so it was up past her knees. I knew it was the Zephyrs' sled because it was the only one painted dark blue with silver stars all over it in a swirling pattern.

The Zephyrs were talking to Clarice's mother, and they didn't see that Sylvia had taken the sled, so I went running after her. Sylvia looked over her shoulder, lost her balance and went to her knees. I ran in her footprints, so it was easy to catch up with her before she got on her feet again. I grabbed the end of the sled and yanked it out of her reach before she could find the tow rope in the snow. Sylvia let out a shriek and stood there stomping her feet and waving her fists in the air.

This time, I was smart enough to turn my back on her and just walk away. That wasn't very easy to do, because I was pulling the sled by the back end. About a dozen steps away from Sylvia, I stopped and turned the sled around and grabbed the tow rope. That gave her time to catch up with me, shouting at the top of her lungs that I had stolen her sled. A couple of high school boys gathered around, and some older boys and girls with Willis-Brooks College sweatshirts and jackets.

"Come on, give the crybaby her sled back." A guy built like a football player reached for the sled.

"It's not hers. She stole it, not me."

"No. It's mine! It was my Christmas present!" Sylvia insisted.

"It's the Zephyrs' sled. See?" I turned it around to show the words *Zephyr Special* in swirly letters down one side, with all the streaks that made it look like the words were moving fast. On the other side were their names and address.

The older boys and the college kids just shook their heads at Sylvia. One of the college girls knew the Zephyrs, and said she recognized me from church. That felt good. Sylvia just stood there, shaking and going all white instead of red. When the older kids walked away, I left with them. Like, duh, safety in numbers.

"You just wait!" Sylvia shrieked after me. "You're just a stupid reject orphan kid, Lanie August! Nobody wants you! Nobody's gonna help you when—"

Okay, I lost control. I was ticked. I was tired. I was cold and wet. I was fed up with her shrieking.

I gave her a good, hard shove with my mind, and a visual of a big fist hitting square in her chest. I did it from ten feet away, a new distance record for me, considering all the force of that blow. Sylvia spun around as she went down. I have no idea if I meant it, or it was just physics, but she kept spinning when she hit all that deep, untouched snow on that part of the slope. She rolled downhill and kept rolling, picking up more snow. No, it wasn't like in cartoons where she turned into a huge snowball and then hit a tree at the bottom of the slope and exploded all over.

Close enough for me.

I did push a little too hard, so I went to my knees and pressed my mittens to my temples with a momentary, sharp headache. But I didn't let go of the tow rope, and the Zephyrs were right there almost before my knees hit the snow. They, and about two dozen other people were witnesses that there was lots of empty air between me and Sylvia when she went down. Everyone agreed that despite Sylvia's insistence that I had jumped that distance and punched her in the face, she must have lost her balance at the start of her temper tantrum and fell.

Grandstones, being Grandstones, insisted that Sylvia was the innocent victim, that she had been doing nothing wrong, that in fact she had been bringing the sled back to the Zephyrs because I had been careless and let someone else steal it.

Neither of Sylvia's cousins had come to the sledding hill to meet her after school, like they were supposed to. They lied and claim they were there and saw the whole thing. However, at the time Sylvia was making a lopsided snowball, Reggie and Freddie were at Miller's Diner, trying to steal chocolate malts off a table while the customers were feeding quarters into the jukebox. The two klutzes slipped on the wet floor on their way out the door, running, and soaked themselves. Even better, half of the high school photography club had stopped there after their meeting. They snapped pictures of the two Grandstone snots with chocolate all over their clothes and the big Elvis-face clock in the background, nailing down the time it happened.

Of course, that put me squarely in the center of the Grandstone hate radar for the next few months. Sylvia was on a campaign to break every crayon I used during coloring time, and mix the colors of the paint I was using during art time, and squash my clay figures and pots, and trip me whenever she could. I built up a lot of strength using my telekinesis, just tweaking things out of her reach or lifting myself an extra few inches whenever I had to walk around her in the classroom. We now knew the name for what I could do, because Kurt found the word in the newest issue of a comic book we found at Divine's Emporium.

That was bad enough, but I soon noticed two cars that were always there when I was away from the orphanage. They took turns, but it was always the same two cars. They followed me to school, and home from school. Sometimes when the weather was nice enough to play outside, they were there in the lot across the street. Kurt believed me when I said I could feel people watching me. We knew better than to tell anyone at NCH, but he told Mr. Longfellow. He believed Kurt, and promised that something would be done. By the end of February, the cars weren't there anymore.

Kurt and I were both impressed by some of the benefits of being considered a guardian of Neighborlee, starting with adults believing us when we told them weird things.

Reggie and Freddie joined in trying for revenge, because it was somehow my fault they got caught lying. They gave up their lunch in the cafeteria and their time on the playground to walk Sylvia home from school, so the three of them could try to ambush me. Normally, the Grandstones had someone drive and pick up Sylvia at lunchtime in the winter, but for all of January, she insisted on walking home. Kurt was already walking with me when I went home at lunchtime, because of the cars, but I was especially glad he was there with the Grandstones nearby.

Honestly, Kurt and I had fun for the first two weeks, frustrating the latest clumsy attempt to ruin my day or ambush us on the way home from school. After two weeks, it got exhausting. I didn't feel quite so proud of myself that I was learning to sense looming trouble, such as snowballs coming at me, or paintbrushes full of the wrong color sliding toward my baby food jar of paint. I was learning some fine control with my telekinesis, giving a mental shove just the right strength to ward off the snowballs or paintbrushes or whatever.

Other people noticed, though. Kurt reminded me of our rule not to let people know what we could do, so I couldn't turn snowballs in mid-flight and hit the throwers in the face. I could only tip over Sylvia's jar of paint with my mind, not make her paint her face. Still, there was a lot of noise. Grandstones weren't just sore losers, but loud losers. Then the Zephyrs found out. Maybe Mr. Longfellow told them.

The very next day, they were waiting in front of the elementary school in their VW mini-bus. They had a permission slip signed by Mrs. Silvestri and Miss Abby, saying they could take me out for the afternoon. Yes, in some ways, we were still living in a more innocent time in Neighborlee, that we could do things like that. Besides, I liked the Zephyrs, and honestly, no one would ever have the guts to forge Mrs. S's signature or lie about her giving permission.

I felt kind of bad because Mrs. S didn't think about Kurt leaving school to walk with me. He gave me a weird look, and even talking about it later, he wasn't quite sure what he was feeling or thinking. Except that he wished he could take the rest of the day off and play with the Zephyrs. They drove him home to NCH for lunch, giving him a little more time to work on the engine he was making for his bike, then we left on our adventure. Lunch at Miller's Diner and an hour at the sledding hill, then a visit to Divine's.

We had a fun afternoon. I loved books, and since the Zephyrs wrote books, I thought they were the coolest, smartest people in the whole world. They told me about a book they were working on, and it made me kind of sad to learn that they were leaving to go to Peru for a couple months. Still, it was cool hearing about the plains drawings, the Nazca Lines, that were supposedly put there by aliens in spaceships, and according to some people at the time, used for navigation. The Zephyrs weren't sure what the lines were for, but they were pretty sure that even if they couldn't fly, the people at that time were plenty smart enough to calculate where the lines should go, even if they never saw them. Besides, who could say that they didn't have hot air balloons or the equivalent of hang gliders at that time? Leonardo da Vinci thought up such things, so why couldn't other people? Especially a culture that was able to build the South American equivalent of the pyramids?

That's what the Zephyrs did. They went around the world, investigating the weird and wonderful, the things that people explained away with bizarre theories. They looked for commonsense explanations. Or they dug up all sorts of solid facts on these things and places and events that other people ignored because they were "inconvenient" and threatened theories that were a whole lot more fun.

They laughed at my reaction when they said they had decided to settle in Neighborlee because they considered it the center of the weird and wonderful in the United States, and maybe even the whole world. I felt like my brain had skidded to a halt. What was so weird about Neighborlee? It was an ordinary town. Kind of small, kind of quiet. We didn't have malls or stadiums or racetracks or museums, even though the Neighborlee Historical Society kept trying. Truth be told, Neighborlee could have been considered rather boring, sleepy, and safe. They just laughed when I finally put my reaction into words, and told me they thought I was one of the smart, observant ones who would figure out that things were not at all ordinary or boring in our town, when I was older.

That made me feel good, but didn't quite take away the "huh?" reaction that sort of clung to the back of my mind for the rest of the day. Kurt had the same reaction when I told him what happened.

Soon after that, Sylvia and her cousins gave up their harassment campaign. She found a new target for her ire, a new girl in our class, Fantasia. Yeah—like, ugh, right? Her family had moved to Neighborlee, and she was an even worse snob than Sylvia. Logic dictated that two entitlement attitude snots would stick together and be best friends. Maybe their slow seething rage toward each other for the rest of the school year came from having so very much in common. Rivalry, pure and simple.

Life was easier after that, but the girls in my cottage got jealous, once I started getting letters from the Zephyrs. Miss Abby explained that was because everybody liked the Zephyrs. I got a little confused. Everybody else in our cottage had a relative of some kind, even though they were too old or too far away, and couldn't take them. The point was that everybody else got mail, even if it was just birthday and Christmas cards, and presents. This was the first mail I had ever gotten. I shared my letters from the Zephyrs with the rest of the cottage, and things were okay after that.

Granted, I felt a little bit of resentment. The way I saw it, if the Zephyrs wanted everybody else to know what they were doing, they would have addressed the letter to Oak Cottage, right? I always made sure I read the letter a couple times through before I let the other girls pass it around, but that didn't seem to help much. Honestly, I was only going on six at the time. Cut me some slack for being selfish.

There was one letter I didn't share with the other girls, because it came in a padded envelope, just big enough for a cassette tape, and there wasn't much to the letter. Inside the envelope was a piece of stone, maybe four inches long, maybe half an inch thick, and two inches wide, with all sorts of carvings on it. The whole thing was wrapped up in a layer of what Miss Angela later told me was alpaca wool or fur, then bubble wrap around that, then encased in packing tape with strings running through it. My letter had a dried flower folded up inside it, with a sweet smell like rain that still came from the petals when I touched it. The Zephyrs asked me to take the bundle to Divine's Emporium. Miss Angela would know what to do with it.

I never considered keeping the errand a secret from Mrs. Silvestri, and not just because she had handed the envelope to me when I got home from school, instead of leaving my mail on my bed. There were just some things no one with any brains did, and one of them was keeping a secret like this from Mrs. S. I showed her the letter and the odd bundle wrapped in packing tape. She thought for a moment, then told me to have Miss Abby call her when I got back to our cottage. Then I was to wait for her in front of the administration building at 1:30. It didn't take much thinking to figure out that Mrs. S was taking me to Divine's.

What I hadn't figured out or planned on was that she let me out of the car in front of the wrought iron gate and told me she would be back in an hour. She had errands to run, and she trusted me to be a good girl and obey Miss Angela. She got that solemn, not-quite-a-frown look when she said the last three words. Like, who would be stupid enough to disobey Miss Angela?

Chapter Six

Miss Angela came to the door as I walked up the sidewalk. She waved, and I looked back to see Mrs. S sitting in her car, watching me. I had the weirdest feeling she was making sure I actually got to the front door, like there was a chance something would happen to stop me. Why would she think that? Divine's was probably the safest place in the entire town, even including Oak Cottage with all the doors and windows closed and locked and Miss Abby on duty.

"I imagine you're just eaten up with curiosity over what Charlie and Rainbow sent me, aren't you?" Miss Angela stepped back to let me go past her through the door. She laughed when I just grinned at her and nodded and handed her the envelope.

She gestured for me to follow her, and we went upstairs. Not to the second floor, to her apartment, which I had expected. We went up to the third floor, and she pulled a ring of keys out of her pocket and unlocked one of the doors.

"You do know the difference between secrets that are bad for you to keep, and secrets that are bad for everyone else if you *don't* keep them, don't you, Lanie?" Miss Angela paused with her hand on the doorknob.

"I think so."

"Not that I doubt you, but..." She sighed. "Why don't you tell me the kinds of secrets that are bad for you?"

"Well... When somebody gets hurt, and they tell me I better not tell the teacher. Or Miss Abby. Or you," I hurried to add. That got a twitch of her lips and she relaxed just a little bit.

"This is probably laying a burden on you far too soon, but I daresay destiny has already marked you clearly enough." She got down on one knee so she could look me in the eyes as she talked. "Say someone makes you do something that you don't understand, but you know deep in your heart, it's wrong. You don't want to do it, maybe it even hurts, but that person is much stronger than you, and they tell you not to tell anybody. Maybe they even threaten to hurt you, or people you love, if you tell anyone what they did."

"Those bad people can't find us here, in Neighborlee, can

they?" I must have been scared. I know there was a queasy kind of sensation in my head and my stomach at the same time, and my voice dropped to a whisper.

"Oh, my dear, Neighborlee is such an important place, yes, the bad people can find us. They come looking here to stop us..." She cupped my cheek a moment, and then rose up a little to kiss my forehead. "Yes, there are very bad people in the world. People who want to control everybody else. People who think it's nice to hurt other people, who think it's fun, and tell lies all the time."

"The Grandstones, you mean."

"I'm sorry to say, worse than the Grandstones. They're rather pathetic, and sick in their heads and their hearts, if you really think about it." Another sigh. "I'm confusing you, aren't I? Maybe scaring you?"

"A little bit. But I think I know what you mean. There are some people, no matter how mean they are, no matter how scary they are, I gotta tell somebody what they did. Even if it hurts."

"Exactly." She got up and reached for the doorknob again. "Then there are other secrets that you need to keep because telling other people could hurt them."

"Like when Katie and Liz bought a birthday present for Miss Abby and Sheri told her and ruined the surprise?"

"Something like that. There are surprises that nobody should know about, because they're safer if they don't know." She pulled the envelope out of the pocket in her dress and two little lines appeared between her eyes. "This is one of those surprises. Charlie and Rainbow found something that needs to stay hidden and locked away, to protect people. I'm trusting you to know this particular duty I carry, because when you are older, you will help me protect the things I keep safe here."

"Okay."

She pulled the big, old-fashioned skeleton key out of the lock, made sure I took a good look at it, and that I understood the key with the murky green stone among all the fancy scrollwork in the handle belonged with this particular door. Then she tucked the keys back into her other pocket, turned the knob, and led me into the room. A soft, shimmering sort of feeling moved across my skin, through my clothes, like that first soft breeze of real springtime. I shivered a little, liking it, and looked up to see Miss Angela watching me. She seemed pleased at my reaction.

When she turned the light on, it was a long, thin tube light in the ceiling, covered by one of those curved, antique-looking glass shades in swirls of gold and white and tiny streaks of jade. It stretched the whole length of the room. Shelves filled with wooden boxes of all sorts of sizes lined the room. Some were square, some round like hat boxes, some tall cylinders, some rectangular, some shallow, like shirt boxes, and tiny like jewelry boxes. Miss Angela led me to the far end of the room and picked up a box, about the size of a Whitman's Sampler, that sat open with its lid on its bottom. She pulled a green fountain pen from the same pocket the keys came from and wrote on a label on the side of the box. All the boxes had small ivory-tinted labels with words in green ink, and I couldn't understand a single word on any of the labels I saw.

Then Miss Angela unwrapped the bundle the Zephyrs had sent her, and for the first time I saw the short rod of stone with its strange carvings. She stroked it once with the tip of her index finger, then put it gently inside the box, put the lid on top, and put it on the shelf.

I never saw that stone rod again, but the images stayed clear in my mind. At least, clear enough that years later, when I had access to the right books, I looked for those carvings to figure out what they might be. Since the Zephyrs were in South America at the time, I assumed they would be Incan or Aztec or Mayan or Toltec. The funny thing was, they were a mixture that looked vaguely like the pictoglyphs from those cultures, with a dab of Norse and Egyptian thrown in. And I'm sorry to say, like something I saw on a few episodes of *Stargate: SG-1*.

"Miss Angela," I said, as we came downstairs again and she led me into the main room of the shop, "what if Mrs. Silvestri asks me what was in there?"

"She won't."

"Oh. Okay. But I can't tell anybody?"

"Well..." She stepped behind the counter and gestured for me to climb up the little ladder, so we were eye-to-eye. "I suppose it would only be smart for you tell Kurt. You don't keep secrets, even dangerous secrets like that, from your best friend. Especially when he has been marked just like you, to be a guardian." She smiled, and it seemed to amuse her that I was so relieved to have permission to tell Kurt.

I couldn't tell Kurt about the package until we were walking home from school the next day. That was really the only time we were alone to talk. He wanted to go right to Divine's and look at the stone rod, but by that time we were almost to NCH. He wouldn't have time to go there and back, eat his lunch, and get to school before the lunch hour was over.

A week later, his cottage had an outing and they went to Divine's. Miss Angela took Kurt to see the stone before he even asked. That impressed him even more than the stone itself.

~~~~~

NCH had rules about who was allowed off the grounds alone, and who was allowed off the grounds without adult supervision. Between certain ages, we had to ask the older kids to accompany us. When it came to trips to Divine's Emporium, that wasn't too hard. Some of the older kids didn't like to go unless they had some money to spend, even if it was just a quarter for some of the unique candy Miss Angela stocked that a lot of specialty candy stores didn't even carry.

We all could earn spending money by doing chores, and anybody in middle school and high school could earn money in town, mowing lawns or weeding, raking leaves, helping with spring cleaning, washing windows, that sort of thing. Those who were old enough to get real jobs with a paycheck were to be envied. Some were ambitious enough to get paper routes, with the bonus of being allowed to ride all over town. The *Neighborlee Tattler* sounded like an incredible place to go, and to work, even after a field trip showed me that they didn't print the papers right there in the building like they showed in movies.

Those of us under the age of seven shared bikes, with a few simple rules for who used the bikes and how long they could use them. All communal bikes were stored under lock and key in the maintenance shed. Those over the age of eight, who had proven ourselves responsible in other matters, had the opportunity to own our own bikes, and decorate them any way we wanted. The usual procedure was to start saving up our allowance money as soon as we got tired of having to share bikes with several dozen other children, and the indignity of a boy having to ride a girl's bike or a girl having to ride a boy's bike.
~~~~~

When we decided we needed a bike of our own, we asked our houseparents and they went to Mrs. Silvestri and she went to the governing board. We got our bikes, with the cost of a plain, basic bike paid from a fund maintained by donations from local businesses and churches and civic groups. We were responsible for paying for extras. We earned that money with our chores and jobs in town and by earning good grades.

I explained all that to lead up to Kurt's summer project. I helped him. He loved gizmos, and I just liked hanging out with him and talking about comic books and speculating on what other superhero powers we would find as we got older. Plus Kurt was just more fun than the girls in my cottage. While I liked dolls, playing house was completely out for me because it seemed like all we ever did was chores. Some older girls loved reading just as much as I did. Their favorite thing to do was go to the town park, on the higher elevation looking down into the Metroparks, curl up on a blanket or find a nice, sturdy spot in a tree, and read in utter, blissful solitude. If I didn't catch up with one of them before she left the orphanage grounds, I was stuck, left behind.

Mr. Longfellow had taken Kurt under his wing, ever since we had those dreams that warned him and Miss Angela. Every other week, the two of them would spend a day "gallivanting" as he called it, visiting junkyards and places that sold odds and ends, or just digging through the bins of bits and pieces in the spare parts room at Divine's Emporium. When they went to Divine's, they took me along. I spent several blissful hours digging through the book room, or earning pocket money, helping Miss Angela. We would rearrange shelves or dust, explore the cellar and pull out boxes of hidden and forgotten treasures, to take upstairs, clean up, and put out on the shelves. The cellar at Divine's just seemed to go on forever, with multiple rooms. Sometimes, I'm positive, the stairs went down much deeper than just the ordinary depth of the cellar.

Kurt's big project was to build a motor for his bike. He was constantly looking up books on engines and mechanical design at the school library or the Neighborlee Public Library. I helped him with that. Every visit to a junkyard or the spare parts room or other places was to find parts to build the engine and figure out how to attach it to his bike to make the wheels turn without tangling with Kurt's pant legs, or weighing the bike down so much that it wouldn't move. Kurt's superpower made the motor work just fine whenever he used it, even when all laws of engineering would have declared it impossible, because something was missing. Kurt had dreams of setting up a business for himself before he got into high school, building engines out of spare parts for other kids, and being able to buy his own house as soon as he graduated and was out on his own.

However, he couldn't build and sell engines if they would only work when he was riding the bike. I was his test pilot and assistant. As soon as Kurt stepped more than ten feet away, or I rode the newest version of the bike-and-engine more than ten feet away from him, it died, or fell apart, or in one instance, switched into reverse. Along with experimenting with his prototype engines, we learned a lot about the extent of our various superpowers, too. Before the end of June, I had developed enough bumps and bruises from crash landings, I was ashamed to wear shorts and short-sleeved shirts. I also developed much better control of my kinda-sorta flying ability, to leap free of impending disaster and float down to a safe landing.

That sounds like all we did was work in the tool shed out behind the baseball diamond. Mr. Guilderman, the maintenance man, let Kurt take it over as his workshop. We didn't. There was swimming at the Neighborlee Pool. Hikes in the safe-for-public-access section of the old quarries that had stopped being operated decades ago. Hikes and swimming in the Metroparks, which had taken over part of the old quarries. Then there were trips to the Cleveland Metroparks Zoo, always free on Mondays to Cuyahoga County residents. Usually there was a bus full of kids going to the zoo every other week. Then there were baseball and basketball and football games, either on the orphanage grounds, or the summer leagues, on the Neighborlee Schools grounds. All three schools plus the board of education building were all on one plot of land on the east side of town, which made it very convenient.

My first summer free of the baby cottage was a turning point. Besides laying the groundwork for Kurt's future as an inventor and all-around fix-it man, we read every comic book we could get our hands on, and expanded our rules for survival.

The Sheridans came to Neighborlee that summer. Yes, those Sheridans, of the media conglomerate and numerous other investments. The difference between the wealthy Sheridans and the wealthy Grandstones was the difference between cashmere and burlap. Why did the Sheridan clan come to Neighborlee?

Grandfather Sheridan had once lived at NCH. He got a job delivering papers for the *Tattler*, saved his money, earned a journalism scholarship, graduated high school when he was fifteen, and left town to seek his fortune. He had a soft place in his heart for Northeast Ohio, and especially for Neighborlee. That summer I turned six, the Sheridans were sponsoring five scholarships at Neighborlee High and ten at NCH for those who wanted to get into journalism and broadcasting. At that time, their family empire owned thirty community newspapers and ten radio stations and were looking into the growing cable TV market.

Such a display of wealth, plus the connections with the media, drew the attention of the Grandstones. The Sheridans were "their kind of people," as Roscoe Grandstone declared where everyone could hear him. It didn't matter if anybody listened. The Grandstone clan canceled their usual summer routine of going to Maine as soon as school let out. Sylvia pouted and refused to leave the house until July. She was the only Grandstone who didn't participate in the new sport of "chase the Sheridans all over town and convince them we're best pals."

That turned out to be a blessing for the youngest Sheridan grandson, Daniel, because Sylvia's father tried to match her with him. Seriously, at six and eleven years old? Why do I mention a rich boy who was five years older than me, who I only saw from across the baseball field several times? He comes into my life story much later. Keep this in mind: Grandfather Sheridan was a Lost Kid who displayed no unusual talents, so no one snatched him away.

Back to the whole dynastic marriage scheme: I overheard some of the older girls giggling over rumors that the Grandstones were trying to arrange a marriage between Sylvia and Daniel. Because this was so typical of Grandstones, everyone believed the rumors. They liked money, they liked power, and they liked having the media spotlight on them. If they could marry into money with controlling interest in newspapers, radio stations, and TV, even if it was cable, all the better.

Mr. Sheridan brought the entire clan two days after school let out. Clan, as in him, his wife, two sons, a daughter, their spouses, and five grandchildren. They rented two adjoining, vacant farms on the edge of town. The land was being farmed, but nobody was living in the houses. They rented the Zephyrs' farmhouse, which kind of made me sad. Somebody living in their house made it so much more real that they were gone.

Between the gossip and Sylvia's griping about the Sheridans, I was interested in seeing them. My first chance was at a boys' baseball league game at the middle school. I liked baseball, but watching old Mr. Sheridan and his wife ignore Grandfather Grandstone and his unmarried sister and his two obnoxious sons was much more interesting. It turned out the game had the largest audience in Neighborlee history, because so many people came, anticipating some kind of clash, or at least a big, noisy set-down. The fact that Freddie and Reggie were participating ensured lots of fireworks, Grandstone-style.

Grandstones didn't usually participate in community or summer league sporting events. Not fancy enough for them. They preferred leagues where their children got individual coaching and wore fancy uniforms and had medics sitting on the sidelines. The best we had was a bucket of ice for bumps and bruises, and an off-duty nurse or paramedic who agreed to sit on the bench next to the first aid kit. Instead of uniforms, the players had strips of cloth in their team colors on their right arms. To match the Sheridans' community involvement, the Grandstones dredged up a lot of community spirit. That made Reggie and Freddie utterly miserable. The coaches were even more miserable, because the boys preferred to sit on the bench, in the shade, eating ice cream, while their father hounded the coaches to put them in. Until Reggie or Freddie tripped over their own feet or got hit with the ball.

The Grandstones showed up everywhere the Sheridans went, even crashing a couple of events they hadn't been invited to. No one was surprised when the Sheridans cut short their summer plans. However, not all the blame could be placed on the Grandstones. Kurt and I were there to see something odd happen.

We were included in the Longfellows' picnic the last Sunday in July. We overheard Mr. and Mrs. Longfellow talking with Police Chief Tanner about the Sheridans and the two old men in a dark, windowless van that had been seen around town for a few weeks. Chief Tanner thought the men in the van worried Mr. Sheridan even more than the Grandstones irritated him.

The two old men in the van seemed to be everywhere in town for the last two weeks. The first time they encountered Mr. Sheridan, according to rumors, there was just silence and glaring. Then the second time, he stomped over to their van and pounded on the side until it slid open and he climbed in. He climbed out and stomped away maybe ten, fifteen minutes later. Then after that, every time he saw the van, he herded his family away.

Some people speculated that the men in the van might be government agents or officials and they were checking on Mr. Sheridan because he was involved in something illegal. Looking back, though, I had to wonder if Sylvia had more to do with driving the Sheridans away than anyone thought. Once her parents bribed her into leaving the house, she tried to glue herself to Daniel, showing up everywhere he went in town. I saw her follow him around at one of the summer band concerts in the park. A week later, the Sheridans canceled their summer lease early and left town. I prefer to think Daniel's parents fled in fear.

The timing was good, because the Zephyrs returned to Neighborlee just two weeks later, and they needed their house back. They had finished up their research early, and when Pastor Rocky welcomed them back at the start of the service in church the next Sunday, they declared they'd been homesick. They had put down roots in Neighborlee, and they missed the entire town and especially their church family.

The Zephyrs took me out for my birthday. We went to the zoo and Mrs. Z packed the most incredible picnic lunch. That was when I found out she also wrote cookbooks, all full of recipes based on healing through food. That made a lot of sense to me. Who wouldn't want to eat to cure their colds or their allergies, instead of having to take shots or pills?

That evening, we went to a baseball game. Cleveland played Chicago. The Tribe smeared the White Sox, and Mr. Z said it must have been because we were there, because the Indians hadn't been having such a good season up until that point.

When he suggested that the three of us try to catch as many games as we could for the rest of the season, I really liked that idea. Watching from the seats in the stadium was a whole lot more fun than trying to watch the game on TV at the orphanage. Especially when the girls in my cottage didn't like to watch baseball, so I usually had to watch in the social hall. The problem with that was that the bigger kids would change the channel if I had to get up to use the bathroom, and they wouldn't change it back when I came back. Liking baseball so much was just one more thing on the huge list of all the things I liked about the Zephyrs.

The day was so long, and I was half-asleep on the way home, so it really didn't sink in when the Zephyrs started talking about the three of us being together a lot more. As in me moving in with them.

As in them adopting me.

Chapter Seven

The Zephyrs were smart enough to take it slow, to get me used to the idea. In some ways, though, it wasn't slow enough. Everything happened so fast, and I was so excited to have them back. To be honest, my impression was that our lives together would be all baseball games and Sunday school and spending time at the farm and looking at the pictures they took all over the world. Things went fast because the Zephyrs had actually gotten started on the paperwork and applications for adoption before they went to South America. Plus, they wanted everything settled before school started in the fall.

The downside of the whole proposition didn't really sink in until about a week or so later. Kurt and I hadn't spent much time together before that, because if he was home and working in the toolshed, I was out with the Zephyrs, talking with child welfare people or picking out paint and wallpaper and furniture and things for my room at their house. If I was at home, he was out with Mr. Longfellow. I was so glad that Friday morning when we were both home and working in the toolshed. I could finally show him all the engine schematics and other things Mr. Z had researched and given me to give Kurt, that would help solve some of his engineering problems.

We worked for probably three hours, talking about nothing but the engine and how this time it was going to work, with a couple forays into what it was going to be like this fall, when I was in school all day. We thought maybe we could rig a cart behind his bike, so when the motor worked we could ride to school instead of walking. Then Mr. Guilderman stuck his head into the shed about fifteen minutes before we had to go eat lunch, and told me Mrs. Silvestri needed me to come to the office. Someone from the court wanted to talk to me, a judge's clerk.

"What does he want?" Kurt asked, his voice hushed, once Mr. Guilderman walked away.

"I don't know. Everybody keeps asking the same questions all the time." I got to work getting the grease and grit off my hands with the orange-scented cleanser.

"What kind of questions? Who's asking you questions?"

"All sorts of court people and official kind of people."

"What'd you do?"

"I didn't do anything."

"Then what's going on? Lanie? You didn't tell anybody, did you?"

For a moment, I had no idea what he was talking about. Then I put down the rag I was using to dry my hands and turned around and saw Kurt, his eyes wide with real fear. His voice had crackled with it.

"About...us?" I should my head hard enough my neck actually hurt a little. "No, this is stuff Mr. and Mrs. Z want. They gotta get about a thousand people to let them adopt me."

"Adopt you?" His voice squeaked. "But...you can't. What're we gonna do when you go away?"

Honestly, I hadn't quite made the conscious connection between being adopted and no longer living at NCH. Even after decorating my room at the farmhouse. Maybe I had this idea of sleeping over on weekends and holidays? I can hardly remember what I was thinking and feeling back then, but it was clear I was a little oblivious. Again, because everything happened so fast, at least to my perceptions.

"Go away? I'm not going anywhere!" I started crying, which made no sense, except maybe my subconscious had figured out a few things that my conscious mind hadn't. I was only six, after all.

We didn't have time to really talk, because Mrs. S was waiting for me with the clerk from the courthouse. Even when my world was falling apart around me, it was the worst crime of all to keep her waiting. Kurt caught hold of my hand—his was still dirty and greasy—and led me at a near-run to the main building. He didn't come inside with me. I looked back as the door swung closed behind me and I thought he looked like he was going to cry.

Mrs. Silvestri explained everything that I hadn't caught onto yet, after I had a short talk with the clerk. Considering that the clerk asked me questions like, did I understand that my name was going to change, that I would be Lanie Zephyr now? Did I understand that I was going to live with Mr. and Mrs. Z and we would be a family? Did I understand that if I was scared, if I didn't really like them, if I didn't want to leave NCH, I didn't have to? Did I understand that once I was adopted, I couldn't change my mind later, that it was forever? Honestly? What six-year-old understands what "forever" really means? More important, do adults understand?

I was kind of dazed by the time the clerk shook my hand and congratulated me and said even though the Zephyrs were a little quirky, they were good, solid, kind people and she hoped we would be very happy together. I didn't even ask Mrs. S what "quirky" meant. She took me by the hand and led me out the side door of her office, down the short hall to her private quarters, where she had lunch waiting for us. Then, while I ate, she explained all the little details that had somehow slipped past me. I was going to live with Mr. and Mrs. Zephyr and be their daughter. My name would be Lanie Zephyr and not Lanie August, and I would call them Mommy and Daddy, or maybe Mom and Dad, or whatever we agreed on that felt right. I would have my own bedroom and live on the farm, and I would see all my friends from NCH at school and around town, but we wouldn't live together anymore. I would get to travel with my new parents and see different countries when they went to do research for the books they wrote. She couldn't guarantee that I would grow up like any "normal" girl, because yes, the Zephyrs were a little quirky. However, "normal" wasn't all it was cracked up to be, and she knew I would be very happy, because they were good people and they loved me, and she thought I loved them, too.

"Do you love them, Lanie? A little bit?" she said, when I just sat there with the crust of my toasted cheese sandwich in my hands, looking at her.

"Yeah," I whispered. "I like them a lot. I want to be their little girl—but—but—"

"But what, sweetheart?" She rested her soft hand on my shoulder.

"But what about Kurt?"

"Oh. I thought that might be the problem." She smiled, a little teary-eyed. "Lanie, dear, the Zephyrs know how much Kurt means to you. He's been like a big brother to you, hasn't he? I've been so proud of him this past year, looking out for you like he has. I suppose he's going to be a little hurt when you leave, but you're not going to another country. Just the other side of town."

"Can't Kurt come with me?"

She couldn't answer me. What could she say that wouldn't backfire on all of us later? If she said "no" outright, that would be cruel. If she said that was up to the Zephyrs, that would be putting all the pressure on them. Mrs. Silvestri had had enough experience over the years with other children who had been adopted, or who had been taken away by relatives after a long wait, she knew this was an uncertain time and emotions ran high even for the ones like me, who were in a daze. We would latch onto anything that sounded like a promise or a solution to our problems. Other children had been given a "we'll see" answer and took it as a "yes," and then there was trouble later, untangling all the hurt feelings and misunderstandings.

Maybe it was cruel, but the best answer was not to answer me at all, except to offer me ice cream with peanut butter and chocolate topping and extra whipped cream, and then let me go back to the toolshed, where Kurt was hard at work.

"How're we gonna build a motor for your bike if you aren't gonna be here?" he finally said, when we had worked in silence on mounting the motor on his bike frame for what felt like the hundredth time that summer.

"I don't got a bike."

"You will. I bet they buy you a bike as soon as you're all official and adopted."

"Then I can ride it over here and we can work like always." I rubbed at my eye, which was starting to get teary. A stupid move, since my hands were greasy-gritty again. "I'm just going to live on the other side of town. I'll see you in school all the time."

"It won't be the same."

"Maybe. Who says we gotta change anything?" A tiny spark of anger broke through the thick, muffling feeling in my head. "We're best friends, right? Who says I gotta live here to stay best friends? Or are you scared of being friends with a girl who isn't your sister?"

"You're not my sister now, dummy." Kurt managed a crooked smile at my words.

"We're better than brother and sister, right?"

"Yeah. We're mutants or aliens or something even better, so we gotta stick tighter. Forever and always, no matter what."

So that was how we came up with our blood oath. I think we were both disappointed that when we cut our thumbs to mix our blood, the cuts didn't immediately heal, like in the comic books. If we had been thinking clearly, we really wouldn't have hoped for that, because we had certainly gotten ourselves cut up and bruised many times before. Still, the oath did a lot for helping us both feel better about the imminent separation. We promised we would always be there for each other, we would never let stupid things come between us, like boyfriends and girlfriends and getting adopted, and we would keep our superhero powers secret, never ratting out the other one no matter what people did to us or threatened to do to us or promised to pay us for information.

The adoption wasn't official before school started, but the child welfare people and the school officials were understanding. I got registered with my new name, Lanie Zephyr, and moved in with my new parents two days before school started. I walked into first grade with new clothes and a new name and a vintage Star Trek lunch box the Zephyrs and I found at Divine's Emporium. I got a lot of admiring and envious looks as we hung up our backpacks and put our lunch boxes in our nooks in the back of the room. We didn't get lockers for our coats and other possessions until third grade.

Of course, Sylvia Grandstone was there, showing off her new clothes and bragging about the trip to Alaska she took with her parents at the end of the summer. It was all business, but she acted like they had gone to Alaska just to please her. We had assigned seats with our names written out on big strips of card stock across the front of our desks. She ran around the room, reading off everyone's names and making fun of anyone whose names struck her as weird.

"You're not allowed to be here," she announced, stomping up to where I stood with Clarice and some of the girls I had met up with on the walk from the playground to our classroom door.

"Yes, I am," I said. I was pleased to see that I must have grown an inch or two over the summer, since I could almost look Sylvia in the eye. She was wearing two-inch heels, while everyone else wore sneakers or saddle shoes.

"Your name's not on your desk. We're sitting in alphabetical order." She pointed at the neat rows of desks: four across and five rows.

"Yes, it is." I almost stuck my tongue out at her, but that was something Sylvia would do. We had had a most enlightening discussion in Sunday school just a couple weeks ago on how we didn't want to be like other kids, especially when they did stupid things like sticking their tongues out, or calling people names.

Sometimes it was a pain being more grown up.

"You're just being a snot because Fantasia left town," Sheila McCordle said, her voice kind of whiny and sing-song. She didn't go to our church, so she could stick her tongue out.

Sylvia's face went red and she took a half-step backwards and inhaled sharply and loudly. Then she turned around, her white-blond curls swinging out behind her far enough to threaten my eyes if I had been standing closer. A survival tip was to never get close enough for a Grandstone to punch or scratch, or snatch something out of your hands. Sylvia stomped away.

Then Mrs. Gimble stepped into the room and rang the blue bell sitting on the edge of her desk to get our attention. For such a small bell, it had a loud, deep tone. When she got our attention, she asked us to find our seats. I was in the last row and the far right corner. I got some confused looks and frowns as I walked around the outside of the rows. Our name tags were across the tops of our desks, not the fronts, so only those close to my desk could see my name. We settled down and got quiet, then Mrs. Gimble took attendance. When she called my name, especially my new last name the envious looks were very satisfying. It was kind of fun to realize that a lot of the kids in our class who knew my new parents were a little jealous of me.

Eating in the cafeteria was a new, fascinating experience for most of us. The girls who weren't really my friends tried to dominate the conversation at the table, crowing about how upset Sylvia was that her only real friend, Fantasia, had to leave town. Just when had those two become friends? Some of the stories they told had to be exaggerations. The gist of it was that Fantasia's family didn't like Neighborlee. Her mother said the town was creepy. Everybody laughed and said she was crazy. I couldn't help wishing that Neighborlee would drive the Grandstones away.

Then the topic of our lunchtime conversation turned to me and my new name and family. I was pleased that most of my classmates seemed happy for me. Sylvia couldn't find anything nasty to say to me about being adopted that day, but she had plenty of cruel comments to make later, about me and the Zephyrs. She probably had to go home and get help from her parents, because she couldn't think of anything on her own.

All in all, my first day of first grade with my new name was highly satisfying. Except I didn't see Kurt at all until we were leaving school at the end of the day. He waited for me, which was nice, but then we couldn't really find anything to say except hi and ask if we liked our new teachers. I mean, what could we talk about? We had seen each other the day before, when our church had come for the regular visit to NCH. That had felt a little weird, being the visitor, instead of the one being visited.

Some older boys walked by while we tried to figure out what to say, just at that tipping point of feeling awkward. Someone whistled and someone else squeaked in falsetto, "Kurt's got a giiiiiiirlfriend." Kurt turned red and then he grinned and shrugged and walked away.

I got out of there because I wasn't sure what I was feeling, and I did not want to start crying in front of everybody if that was what that tickling feeling in my head meant.

~~~~~

My new parents made sure that I went to visit my friends in the orphanage on a regular basis. They understood that the children and Miss Abby were my family. I still can't decide if that made it easier to settle in or helped me hold back from settling in and becoming a family with them. Sometimes, especially when the Zephyrs were busy researching a new book and might be gone for the day, I would walk home from school with the other NCH kids. That was a chance for Kurt and me to talk a little, separate from everybody else, and catch up on what new information he had harvested from his comic books. I would settle in the library or in the common room somewhere and work on my homework. Sometimes I would get to eat dinner with either Kurt's cottage, or at Miss Abby's cottage. It was nice.

I didn't call the Zephyrs Mum and Pop, like they asked me to. That must have hurt, and sometimes they looked sad, but they never scolded me, never put a guilt trip on me. They were patient. Well, duh, they were my parents and they loved me. Maybe it was
~~~~~

easier for two people nearly forty to decide to love, than it was for a six-year-old who felt guilty because she had a new home and all her brothers and sisters didn't.

We got through September. The second week of October, Mrs. Z and I headed to Divine's Emporium to work on my Halloween costume. I think she was more excited than I was, until my parents suggested that we invite some of my friends from NCH to go trick-or-treating with us. At NCH, we were allowed to go trick-or-treating on our side of town. The problem was, most of the streets surrounding the orphanage property were businesses, and the residential district was a good twenty minutes of walking away. That was a big chunk of minutes taken out of trick-or-treat time. The Zephyr place was on the far side with all the farms—corn and farmers' market kind of farms, pumpkin and Christmas tree farms. That didn't stop my new parents. They worked out a careful plan of attack, to drive me and my friends to the farthest edge of the residential section, so we could start ringing doorbells as soon as the official "beggar's hour" started, as our teachers referred to it. Then we would work our way back to the edge of the residential section closest to our house. Then we would all go back to our farm and have hot chocolate and donuts before we took the other kids back to NCH.

Once other kids heard me and Kurt and the girls from Oak Cottage talking about the plans, suddenly I had a lot of new friends. Everybody wanted to come with us. That really bugged me, but I wasn't sure why. Kurt neatly solved my problem before I put too much thought into it, referring to them as leeches. When I went to Mrs. Z about it, she called them fair-weather friends and told me if I was afraid of getting the other kids mad at me, I could just say that we had run out of room, there were only so many seats in the VW mini-bus. Which was true.

Then we made our trip to Divine's Emporium for my costume. Funny thing was, the vintage clothing room seemed twice as big as usual. Not ordinary used clothing, but World War II uniforms, poodle skirts, flapper dresses, zoot suits, that sort of thing. Plus, costumes that belonged in Ren Faires. Gorgeous brocades and gossamer and the next best thing to chain mail without being actual metal. Mrs. Z and I spent a good two hours just pulling out one hanger after another and squealing or laughing or sighing over the offerings. So many of the clothes were way too big for me, but that was all right because she needed a costume to go trick-or-treating with me, right?

My costume was a tree faerie. A tunic in multiple shades of brown, rough like bark, with leaves and vines all over it in glittery shades of green. It came with a green wig and a cap that looked like more bark, with dragonflies perched on it. The best part of the costume was the wings. They were nearly as tall as me, and attached under my costume with a harness that kept the wings in place, standing straight up and down, and flapping just a little bit when I walked. My wings looked like a cross between butterflies' and dragonflies', with shimmering shades of blue and green and gold. We walked in triumph to the counter in the main room with our findings. Mrs. Z decided to go as Zorro, including an incredible sabre. I almost changed my mind about my costume, but that sword would drag on the ground the whole time and it was realistic enough to be pretty heavy.

Angela burst out laughing when she saw my costume. She pressed her hand over her mouth and shook her head and sputtered, trying to stop laughing.

"I'm sorry, Lanie. It's not you—I just—I didn't know that was in there. Someone must be playing an awful joke on—" Miss Angela sputtered again.

She and Mrs. Z just grinned at each other while she tried to get herself under control. I was lost, and despite her words I still had the awful feeling she was laughing at me, for picking that particular costume. She rang up our purchases and paused once or twice, while packing everything into costume boxes, to wipe her eyes.

"So help me, Angela, if you don't explain..." Mrs. Z chuckled as she took our boxes. She handed me the box with my costume pieces, and took the long, flat box with my wings, since they were too big for me to carry.

"It's just that the Fae haven't had wings in several centuries. Whoever put that costume on that rack either did it to irritate someone, or as a monumental joke."

"Why?" I had to ask.

"Why did they put it there?"

"Why don't Fae have wings?" I felt kind of stupid asking, but I had to. "What are Fae?"

"Faeries. It's a more respectful term for them, considering all the...well, all the derogatory meanings." She sighed, and some of her merriment left her face.

"But why don't they have wings?"

"I'm not sure, except that it went out of fashion. Maybe they decided they didn't need wings anymore since they don't really spend much time among Humans like they used to. Why not?" she said, when I opened my mouth again. "Well, the world has changed since the days when Fae could travel among us. All the technology. Then there's pollution and other considerations. Besides, the Fae enclaves are really much more suited to them. What are Fae enclaves?"

Chapter Eight

Miss Angela laughed and came from behind the counter, to bend down closer to me. By this time, I was just standing there with my mouth open and a thousand questions and ideas and images swirling around in my head.

"How about we save this conversation for later? Maybe this winter when you're off school and we can just curl up on the couch and talk?"

"That sounds like a lot of fun," Mrs. Z said. "I don't suppose I'm invited?"

"You, my darling Rainbow, are a spy for the enemy," Angela said, her face going prim and somber, but her eyes sparkling like she would start shooting lights from them at any moment.

"What's that mean?" I had to ask.

"The books your father and I write tell all the secrets behind the magic," Mrs. Z said. "Or we would if we actually found all that magic we're looking for."

"The problem is that when you're soaked in magical things, like the two of you are, it's very hard to see other magic." Miss Angela laughed when I just looked back and forth between them, probably with my confusion very clear on my face. "Later, all right, Lanie? Maybe much later, when you're a little older and you've seen so much more of the atmospheric weirdness and magic of Neighborlee, so you have a frame of reference."

With that, we said our goodbyes and we headed out the door.

"Are you really magic?" I had to ask Mrs. Z when we got back into the mini-bus.

The first thought that came to me, as the spinning in my head slowed, was that if my new parents were magic, then maybe they could do tricks like me and Kurt, and I could tell them... I could show them what I could do. I didn't like keeping my superhero powers secret from them. It wasn't right. Nobody had to tell me the rules for being a family, for me to know that.

"It's an old joke, honey, that's all." She pulled out of the gravel lot next to Divine's and headed down the street. "Do you know what hippies are?"

I nodded. I had an idea from things I saw on TV, but I was pretty sure I didn't know the truth. I had heard people call the Zephyrs hippies, but they didn't seem to mean it in a nice way.

"Well, some people mean it as a joke, and others certainly do not, when they say that your dad and I are refugees from the 60s. It's the way we dress, mostly. And this van of ours." She patted the steering wheel. "Charlie got sassy with someone once, when they tried to give us trouble. He told them we really were from the 60s, but we had driven right through a time-warp bubble and ended up twenty years in the future. Some people think that time travel is more magic than science, more fantasy than science fiction. I think that's what Angela was referring to."

"Oh. Okay."

By this time, I had figured out a few things. I could tell when it was smart to put a topic aside for later, until I had learned more or figured things out for myself. This was one of those times.

~~~~~

In Neighborlee, we were allowed to go trick-or-treating even after it got dark. Most communities had started instituting a rule that it started like 6 in the evening, and could only go to 8 at the latest. In Neighborlee, we were encouraged to have fun. Now that I'm older and know a lot more about the world and all the un-wonderful things in it, I look back at our innocence and how thoroughly we were sheltered, and I am amazed and grateful. If everyone could have a childhood as magical as most of us had in Neighborlee, the world would be a much kinder place.

Or a whole lot more insane. Remember what I said about the town driving away people who didn't belong, and how crazy or nasty or both they became if they didn't run for their lives.

Kurt, Stacy, Amira and Tammy came with me and Mrs. Z for trick-or-treating. I had told them about my costume and the room I hadn't seen before at Divine's, so they went there to look for costumes. Kurt was a soldier in camouflage clothes and a poncho. The girls were all princesses of some kind or another. Not Disney princesses, but in big, puffy skirts and long white gloves past their elbows and glittering with glass and rhinestone jewelry, including tiaras. When they told me Miss Angela let them borrow the jewelry and didn't make them pay anything, I wasn't surprised.
~~~~~

We had a good time, just running up to the houses and calling out "trick-or-treat!" and seeing the reactions different people had to our costumes. And then of course comparing the sugary loot dropped in our bags. By the time we got to the end of the first street, we had collected just as much candy as we did any year going with the gang from NCH. That just made us more greedy, more determined to see just how much we could gather in one night. The only thing that slowed us down was the increasing weight in our bags, and the fact that after two hours, we were running out of room for our goodies.

The five of us came down the long, curving sidewalk from the Winkles' house, exclaiming about the big, crinkly balls in orange plastic wrap. Later, we learned those were popcorn balls. Mrs. Winkle made treats like that for Halloween and Christmas. Neighborlee was the kind of town where we didn't have to worry about things like pins and razors or other nasty surprises in homemade treats.

We got to the sidewalk and there was Mrs. Z, almost invisible in her black clothes, except for her smile. A man in a brown dress uniform stood next to her. He frowned a little at us as we gathered around her and held out our popcorn balls, bigger than softballs, and asked what we had just gotten.

She explained what we had and we set off down the sidewalk, aiming for the next house. The man in the uniform hadn't been introduced yet, and he walked with us. He said nothing, and only seemed to pay attention to me, when he looked at anyone, as we walked between houses for the next half hour. He and Mrs. Z talked when we were up at the doors, going through our routine. That much was evident whenever we rejoined them. She didn't seem upset, so I wasn't worried. I just wondered who this man was, because I didn't recognize him from church.

Mr. Z was waiting with the mini-bus when we finally dragged our way down to the end of the last street. By this time, we were all exhausted and our arms ached from the weight of our candy that threatened to rip the seams of our bags. We promised each other we would lift weights and do other things to get stronger and bring pillowcases next year, instead of our bright orange sacks with the plastic handles that threatened to tear free. We climbed into the mini-bus and it felt so incredibly good to sit down. By the tiny interior light, we dug through our bags, checking out everything we had gathered that night. The door didn't slide shut right away. When I realized Mrs. Z hadn't climbed into the passenger seat in front and Mr. Z had gotten out of the van, I looked around.

They were standing on the sidewalk, talking to the man in the uniform and looking a little irritated. I got chilled, because it took a lot to irritate either of the Zephyrs. Then the three of them seemed to notice at the same time that I was sitting there, looking at them. The man in the uniform said something, and they separated. The Zephyrs got into the mini-bus and the stranger walked down the street, vanishing into the shadows between the houses before Mr. Z started the engine.

When we got home more than an hour later, after dropping off the other kids at NCH, the man in the uniform was sitting on the front porch swing. They introduced me to Col. Hayward, and I learned my new parents were not only friends with someone important in the Army, but they sometimes worked for the government.

By this time, I had done some research in the library at school and I knew more about hippies. So it was kind of surprising to learn my parents were doing the exact opposite of running around and trying to tear down the "Establishment." Of course, no one told me anything.

Col. Hayward shook my hand and said he was very pleased to meet me, and congratulated the Zephyrs, then Mrs. Z took me upstairs to help me get out of my costume so I could go to bed. I fell asleep hearing the soft rumbling of their voices drifting up through the floor of my room, which was right over the kitchen where they sat.

~~~~~

We spent Thanksgiving at NCH, which was a lot of fun. Sort of. I was glad to be able to spend the holiday with my friends, but at the same time I had the awful feeling that my parents really wanted to have our first Thanksgiving as a family with just the three of us, or maybe going over the house of friends or even having friends over to the farmhouse. I had the awful feeling that we went to NCH because of me, because I still wasn't able to call my parents Mum and Pop yet, and because maybe they were afraid I wasn't happy.
~~~~~

That's kind of dumb, huh? And kind of sad. And at the same time, kind of nice, because looking back, I can see how my parents were trying hard not to push me, not to put any pressure on me. We were going to be a family someday, and they were sure enough of it to let me figure things out at my own speed.

The pace of family life tripled and quadrupled once Thanksgiving was over. Christmas was always a crazy busy time, especially with kids trying to earn money so they could give all their friends some kind of gift. Miss Angela let me come spend some Saturdays and a few afternoons after school at Divine's, rearranging shelves and washing pieces of glassware and other items that had come into the shop, before they went out on the shelves. I earned money toward presents for Kurt and Mrs. Gimble, and the Zephyrs. I spent it right there in Divine's, following Angela's advice on what would please them the most.

Christmas changed for me that year. It was always a fun time, but this year, my first Christmas with my new parents, the focus shifted from what I would be getting to what I could give, what I could do to help other people. My parents were incredibly giving, generous people. They were involved in two groups that put together gift baskets and collected presents for people who had no one to look after them. We went caroling every other night, and when we weren't caroling, we were sledding. We had the best time hanging lights all over the farmhouse on the inside and the outside, decorating for Christmas.

We put out a nativity scene in the living room, and another one in the big office where my parents did all their writing and research, and another nativity scene in my bedroom. The only thing we didn't put up, by the second week of December, was a Christmas tree. That was a special event all in itself.

We waited until two days before Christmas, then went to Green's Christmas tree farm to pick out two, one for us and one for NCH. I liked the responsibility of helping to pick out the perfect tree for the social hall. Even more, though, I liked picking out our tree. All ours. Just the three of us.

Green's was incredible. It wasn't just the rows and rows of cut trees, but the ability to go out onto the farm and walk down one row of trees after another and pick out the perfect trees. Then Abner Green or one of his sons or grandsons would cut it, right then and there. Spike, the youngest grandson, was in second grade and he kept busy running around with long streamers of twine to bind up the trees. They hauled the trees up to the front parking lot and sprayed them to encourage all sorts of bugs and mice and other critters that had holed up for the winter in the trees to vacate, and then bound them with twine, all ready to put in our van. Meanwhile, we had more fun. There was hot cider and hot chocolate, and a puppet show in the main barn, craft tables to design our own ornaments, a storyteller in one corner, and Christmas carol singing in another corner.

Despite being hippies, my folks wanted a Norman Rockwell holiday. That meant a live tree and all the fun of getting it, plus picking out new decorations. Mrs. Z got kind of teary when she picked out three different "our first Christmas" ornaments. I kind of did too.

I liked the storyteller, except that we came in at the end of one story that sounded kind of sad, where a girl got lost in the snow and never came home. What kind of a Christmas story was that? Then again, I had already been introduced to five different dramatized versions of Dickens' *A Christmas Carole* by the time I hit my fifth Christmas at NCH. After a break, during which about half the audience left, to be replaced by even more people, so the six long benches in front of the stage filled up, the storyteller dove into a new one. This one dealt with the first Christmas, and the animals in the stable where Jesus was born, who were arguing and shoving each other around because everybody wanted the best, warmest, coziest place. Of course, they got really angry when Joseph and Mary showed up and the animals had to all move aside. The meanies took it out on Joseph's donkey.

Then midnight came and Jesus was born. Honestly, where does it say in the Bible He was born at *midnight*?

I only wondered for about two seconds, because the next line amazed me. The storyteller slid down from his rocking chair to kneel on the stage, and his eyes got big and his voice turned to a raspy whisper. Anybody who had been whispering or fidgeting went completely silent and it felt like everybody held their breaths. That was a good trick, whispering to make it harder to hear, so everybody focused and listened harder.

The animals talked. It took a second for me to understand what the storyteller meant. They had been talking up until this point, after all. Then he made it clear: these animals talked with human voices, and they could talk to people, and they got excited and ran around and frightened a bunch of people who heard them talking with human voices.

Then the story kind of broke down. What did they do with the ability to talk? The animals used their new voices to keep arguing, and got in the way of the ones who wanted to tell people that Jesus was born. They finally figured things out and they ran out of the stable to tell other people, and of course dawn came and they went back to making animal sounds.

That was kind of unfair. Unless the animals were being punished for arguing and wasting the magical gift given to them?

The final line of the story caught my attention. *Somewhere in the world, every Christmas Eve, at midnight, animals are given the ability to talk.*

I wanted to ask the storyteller if he knew where it happened, if it was a different place every year, or the same place. He left the stage as soon as the audience finished clapping, so I didn't get a chance. Then the Zephyrs came to get me. They had been talking with some of their friends from church who were on the ministry team working with NCH, so they didn't hear the story. I wondered if they knew it. By this time, I was sure my new parents knew just about everything worth knowing in the whole world. After all, they wrote books, didn't they? Anything they didn't know, Miss Angela knew. Maybe I should ask Miss Angela about the animals talking at Christmas Eve. After all, anything that was magical in Neighborlee was her area of expertise. But did I really want to wait until I could get into Divine's Emporium to ask her?

We packed up the van, with the two trees on top, and headed home. I was silent for about ten minutes, thinking hard, while they chatted about the schedule in the next couple days for delivering the tree and helping out with the gift baskets for needy families in town. We turned onto the street that would take us to our part of town. That was when I dropped my bombshell.

"Mr. Z, can animals can talk on Christmas Eve?"

In the front seats of our VW mini-bus, my new parents exchanged *that* look.

"Lanie, honey," Mrs. Z said, "where'd you hear that?"

I gestured with my thumb over my shoulder at the tree farm we had just left.

"Garrett Olson was telling stories," Mr. Z said. "I haven't thought about that story about animals talking in years." He grinned at me in the rearview mirror. "Wish I had heard that one. Think you remember enough to tell it to me when we get home?"

"I think so."

"That'll be fun."

"Is it true?" I asked after waiting a few seconds.

"Well, Neighborlee *is* the weirdness capital of the world. If animals talk on Christmas Eve anywhere, it'll happen here."

"Have you heard them?"

"Not yet, but I'm still young." He grinned at me again in the rearview mirror, stroked his iron-gray ponytail, then turned his attention back to the snowy street.

At the ripe age of six, I had enough street wisdom to be pretty sure when an adult lied to me. The Zephyrs weren't "most adults." They cared about truth. I knew enough about how they made their living, all the research they did, investigating and debunking things like werewolves and UFOs. So when Mr. Z said *anything* could happen in Neighborlee, I believed him. I was kind of relieved to have him say that aloud.

Maybe their passion for truth made it hard to call them Mum and Pop? Kurt and I had secrets, and we had vowed to keep those secrets safe and not tell anyone. Ever. Not even my new parents.

I didn't put it into so many words, but about that time I was getting a clearer idea of what exactly was wrong, blocking me from settling in and being happy with my new parents. Other than leaving my friends at NCH and not seeing Kurt every day. I mean, how could we study comic books and figure out how to be superheroes if we didn't see each other every day?

Chapter Nine

We got home and made lunch. Then after lunch, we put our tree up. I was kind of astonished to learn the Zephyrs didn't put up a tree last year, after they moved to Neighborlee. Our living room was huge, with a high ceiling, and the corner by the fireplace was the perfect spot for a Christmas tree. It was almost a crime not to have one. Mrs. Z had already bought several boxes of ornaments at Divine's, all individual and mismatched. They were gorgeous. Even more beautiful were the "first Christmas" ornaments she picked up at the tree farm. We had a lot of fun that afternoon, teasing and pretending to argue about where to put specific ornaments, where they looked best, and if we needed more lights and more tinsel.

The only thing we didn't put on the tree that afternoon was the big gold and blue, lighted star for the very top. Mr. Z needed a new ladder. I could have put the star on without a ladder, but according to all of Kurt's and my comic book research, that could get me sent back to the children's home. Or worse.

The next day was errand day, and we headed into town. First stop: the hardware store, for the ladder. I found a toolkit that Kurt had told me about that he wanted. Mr. Guilderman let Kurt use his tools, but Kurt wanted his own tools that he didn't have to fight with the bigger boys to use. Besides, this tool kit had more sizes of ratchets and other parts that the orphanage's shared tool kit didn't have. He really wanted it, and I wanted to give it to him, but I didn't have enough money saved up, even with all my chore money and my allowance, which had been doubled at the start of November.

"What are you looking at?" Mrs. Z said, catching up with me in the tool aisle. I pointed at the box, with all the shiny tools displayed through the thick plastic window. "Honey, your Pop has all these tools at home, and you can use any of them." She laughed softly and winked at me. "As long as we're helping you, of course."

"Not for me. Kurt. He loves building stuff, and the big kids don't share tools. If he had his own set..." I shook my head. "Next year."

"You know what?" She knelt next to me. "Kurt is like a brother to you, so we'll get him something from our whole family. How does that sound?"

"Really?" My voice came out half an octave higher.

"Really." She had tears in her eyes after I hugged her.

The next stop was our church, to help put together baskets of food, clothes, and toys for families in Neighborlee who were going through rough times. At five, we headed for NCH. Even after three months of participating from the other side of the ministry effort, I still felt weird, bringing presents instead of getting them. But it was a good weird.

Kurt met me as soon as we arrived at the social hall. We hadn't seen each other since school let out for Christmas break a week before.

"You been keeping quiet?" he whispered.

I mimed turning a key in between my lips. "I bet I could tell them, though."

"No. We can't trust nobody but each other."

"But they're my folks. They aren't like other grownups."

I almost added that Miss Angela already knew about us. And Mr. Longfellow. Maybe he didn't know I could kinda-sorta fly, but Angela did. They had to know, because we were guardians, right? I bet if Kurt showed them his gizmos that only worked for him, they wouldn't be surprised. I just knew, deep down inside, if I lifted myself up in the air, my folks wouldn't be surprised or scared or angry, like it happened in the comic books.

"They love me." That was the strongest argument I could make. Or so I thought.

"Yeah?" Kurt looked down on me from his nine-year-old superior height and wisdom. "Do you call them mom and dad yet?" He patted my shoulder when I could only shake my head. "It's okay, Lanie. We got each other."

Pastor Rocky, Chief Tanner and Mr. Z had formed a band. Pastor Rocky played drums and piano, Chief Tanner played guitar—acoustic, electric, and bass—and Mr. Z played a whole band's worth of instruments. Three saxophones, an oboe, a flute, a trumpet, a French horn. He also played guitar and piano, but he didn't in the band because the other men did. We had a lot of fun after dinner, singing Christmas carols, especially with a rock beat.

They did a few songs that were their own versions of songs from Mannheim Steamroller's Christmas albums.

While they played and led us in singing, a lot of us sat down at the long tables where we had dinner an hour before, and we decorated Christmas cookies. We had all sorts of colors of frosting and gels in tubes, and dozens of colors and textures of sprinkles, and colored sugar, and gumdrops. We had huge gingerbread men cookies and tiny stars and bells and angels and other shapes. And of course, some of us ate cookies while we decorated them, or just ate frosting. No one got angry at us. Some of the kids got sick on frosting and others just overdid it and curled up in a corner to take a nap and work through their sugar coma. Then there were the kids who got hyper on sugar. They were kept busy singing and playing games like hopscotch and Twister.

When we finished decorating cookies, the littlest kids were carried off to bed, most of them completely asleep. I remembered that happening when I was in the baby cottage, although the Christmas parties were a lot quieter and shorter. Things were certainly more fun since Neighborlee Gospel Church adopted the orphanage as one of their ministries.

We gathered around the tree to hang all the decorations the other kids had been making for the last week—paper chains, popcorn snowmen, foil angels and stars, and strings of popcorn and cranberries. Then we had a short devotional from Pastor Rocky. He read the Christmas story while Mr. Z and two other men fussed with the strings of Christmas lights that wouldn't light up, checking the bulbs and connections. With perfect timing, the lights came on just at the point where Pastor Rocky said the angels filled the night sky over the field where the shepherds were watching their flocks.

After the devotional was over, we had cookies and eggnog and broke up into small groups. The biggest group was around Mr. Leland, who had grown up at NCH and started the tradition years ago of former residents coming back and acting as big brothers and sisters to the residents. He was a great storyteller. Tonight, he said he was going to tell us a story that he hadn't told anyone in nearly fifty years, and it was a true story that took place in Neighborlee at Christmas. That got everybody's attention, and some of the people gathered around, kids and adults, got up to get other people and have them join the story circle. In minutes, nearly everybody in the room was sitting around Mr. Leland.

"This happened back in the bad old days before the Civil War." He looked around the circle, and then he paused and took a sip of his coffee. "I'm proud to say Neighborlee was a way station on the Underground Railroad. You all know what that was?" He looked around again and nodded to a boy near the back who raised his hand.

He stood up. "It wasn't a real railroad."

I didn't know who he was. Before I could turn to him and ask, Kurt whispered to me that the boy had just come to the orphanage about a month ago when his dad beat up his mom. She was still in the hospital, and his father was hiding from the police. I hadn't heard anything like that happening, and when I asked him where, Kurt said it was in Trumpton, on the far east side of the county. I was glad people like that didn't live in Neighborlee.

"And it didn't run underground," the boy continued. "But that would be cosmic, wouldn't it?" He looked like he might smile, but stopped just short. "The Civil War was a big fight between the people who wanted to keep black people as slaves, and the other people who said it was wrong, and that the black people should be set free because they were people too. Anyway, the Underground Railroad was a bunch of people who helped slaves escape and go up north to Canada, because some dumb lawyers and senators and other people in the government said that when a slave escaped, it was the law to give them back to their owners. But Canada doesn't have to listen to the United States, so if slaves got all the way to Canada, they could stay free. So the Underground Railroad helped them hide and get up to Canada."

"What a clear, accurate assessment." Mr. Leland nodded slowly. "You would make a fine historian someday. Thank you so much." He waited until the boy sat down. "Yes, the Underground Railroad helped slaves find freedom. I'm proud to say that many people in Neighborlee at that time, back before the Civil War, before Abraham Lincoln ran for President, were part of the Railroad. Of course, the slave hunters and owners of runaway slaves didn't like Neighborlee. If they chased a runaway slave to Neighborlee, our sheriff and other law officers knew to make themselves scarce, so they couldn't be forced to help track down those poor unfortunates. That was the law back then."

Murmurs and whispers went through the group, and he waited until everyone quieted down again.

"Neighborlee was a wonderful place for the Underground to operate because of the quarries. An important part of my story is that when they were quarrying out all that stone, sometimes the diggers would open up tunnels through the rock. These weren't just crevices, but tunnels big enough for a man to walk through, winding through the stone. People figured maybe they were Indian tunnels, but people who knew about such things went exploring the tunnels and couldn't find where they started. The tunnels just didn't come up above ground, except where the people in the quarries had dug down to them. The old folks when I was your age used to joke about enormous worms squirming through stone, eating through the sandstone like ordinary earthworms eat through the flowerbeds. For maybe three, four years, someone broke through to another tunnel every few months. Then it stopped as abruptly and inexplicably as it started."

"We gotta go look there," Kurt whispered to me when Mr. Leland answered questions from some kids over on the other side of the group.

"Not without adult supervision," Mr. Z said, leaning forward so he could whisper. Both of us kind of jumped a little bit, because we didn't know the Zephyrs were sitting behind us. We looked around and he winked at us. "Some parts of the quarries are dangerous, not good to go alone. That's why they're chained off. Not saying that it wouldn't be all right if we went as a group and looked out for each other. Because kids have been known to vanish without warning, just turned a corner and— poof—gone." His eyes got big as he said it and his voice got quieter.

"Charlie." Mrs. Z slapped his arm.

I could tell just from her grin and the way she wrinkled up her nose at him, and he wrinkled up his nose back at her, both of them were joking around.

"What? I'm just as curious about those tunnels as the kids. Might be our next great book, sweetheart." He sat back. "Whenever you kids want to go, tell me."

"Us," she added.

"Your dad is pretty cool," Kurt whispered, his voice pretty much covered up as Mr. Leland answered the last question and resumed the story.

He had us hanging on by our fingernails in places, and in others laughing, as he told how the Underground Railroad brought a group of slaves to our town just before Christmas. We laughed at how the sheriff pretended to cooperate, while sending the slave hunters off in the wrong directions. We laughed more when an ancestor of the Grandstones got interrupted in her bath when the slave hunters broke into her house. The weather worked against them and worked for the Underground Railroad. The slaves ended up hiding in some tunnels that had been found and expanded under the Wickslow Chapel. The funny thing was, when the slave hunters went to the chapel, the tunnel dead-ended after just a few dozen feet, but an hour later, there the slaves were, snug and dry and safe.

"We gotta check out your church," Kurt said. He turned around to face my parents. "Can we go look?"

"I heard that story a short time after we came to Neighborlee," Mr. Z said. "I searched that basement from one corner to another. Yeah, there's a tunnel, but it ends in bedrock, with no sign of anything filling it in."

"Not even a whole truckload of cement getting dumped in it?"

"Actually, that's a test we never thought to run," Mrs. Z said. That earned a chuckle from Mr. Z.

"Would the people of that time have the chemicals, the engineering know-how, to disguise cement so it looked like untouched granite and sandstone?" He frowned in that way I had learned meant his mind was going off in ten different directions with all sorts of ideas.

"What about from the other end?" I asked. "Did anybody look for the tunnel where it ended up at the river?"

"How about we try to do that this summer?" Mrs. Z said.

Like Kurt said, my parents were really cool. That conversation made me even more certain that it would be safe to tell my folks about the things we could do. I didn't have a chance to talk privately with Kurt about it before the evening ended, but I made up my mind that I would the next time we went to NCH. The way I figured it, my folks knew so many weird and wonderful things, they could help us figure out more superhero powers that we hadn't discovered yet.

When we got home that night, I was half-asleep, worn out and stuffed full of Christmas cookies. I didn't wake up when Mrs. Z helped me into my nightgown and tucked me in, and I was completely asleep before she left my room.

But I woke up as the clock downstairs chimed midnight, and I remembered the story I had heard at the tree farm, how the animals talked in the stable the night Jesus was born.

I believed in magic. With good reason. At my age, there wasn't much difference between magic and what made superheroes super, even though most of the explanations were rooted in some kind of warped, totally unrealistic science. So I crept downstairs, to put on my coat and boots and go outside, and listen to the animals speak in our barn out back. I never made it that far, though. When I reached the living room, I got distracted.

That big, beautiful blue and gold star was sitting there, waiting to be hung on our tree. The ladder was leaning against the wall. I wanted to see that star on that tree. Right away, no waiting until morning. My first Christmas tree all my own.

So I did what any normal six-year-old would do who possessed the ability to kinda-sorta fly. I carefully took the star out of the box, and I floated up and put it on the tree.

In triumph, I moved back about five feet, hovering so I was at eye-level with the star, so I could get the full effect. The Bethlehem star couldn't have looked more beautiful.

"Lanie?" Mrs. Z said, her voice a sigh.

I looked down. I was hovering about two feet above my parents' heads. They just stood there, looking at me.

Worse than being sent back to the children's home, I knew I would be sent to some underground laboratory for testing and study. Kurt's newest batch of comic books had a long story that covered four issues, where the superhero who was a high school kid got caught and locked up and examined.

We just stood — and hovered — there for a few seconds, frozen. Then I noticed something. My folks weren't scared of me. They didn't look angry, either. As I waited, trying to figure out what was going to happen, their astonished expressions changed into smiles. Those proud smiles that I had seen them wear a few times when we did something together as a family.

This was what family did, I realized. That moment of epiphany was due, for the most part, to my being so tired. I couldn't tie my brain into knots with all sorts of counter arguments and second and third and fourth thoughts. The Zephyrs were my parents. Suddenly, the words made so much more sense.

Mum shook her head and held up her arms. "Young lady, what do you think you're doing, flying around the house at this time of night?" She tried to scowl at me, but it was easy to see she was fighting not to laugh.

Pop laughed. "I wish you'd told me before I spent all that money on a new ladder."

"You're not mad?" I let Mum get hold of my nightgown and pull me down into her arms. I felt her heart racing. "Kurt said you'd be scared."

"Yeah, well, it's a surprise, that's all." He tousled my hair.

"Honey, you're our little girl. That's all that matters. Being able to fly isn't that scary." Mum touched her nose against mine. "Some people think I'm kind of scary, dying my hair a different color every week."

"But green is perfect for Christmas, Mum."

We ended up on the couch in a heap, hugging each other and laughing.

Like Pop said, our town was the weirdness capital of the entire planet. Hippies trapped out of time and a little girl who could kinda-sorta fly belonged together. We belonged in Neighborlee, and fit in just fine.

I didn't hear the animals speak that year, and by next year I had forgotten all about the idea. If the animals ever did talk on Christmas Eve, they probably did in Neighborlee, because that was just the kind of thing that happened in our town. Bottom line: I had enough magic in my life, I didn't need to prove it for myself.

Chapter Ten

Pastor Rocky participated in our investigation of the tunnel under our church. He took it one step better, contacting a friend who had a friend who could get seismic or radar or other kinds of tests of the soil and bedrock all around the chapel, looking for crevices and tunnels and any anomalies. The official reason for doing the testing was preliminary work in anticipation of building the first of several planned additions. Neighborlee Gospel Church was growing nicely, even faster than anyone had hoped when the original members bought the building.

The testing didn't find anything. If there ever was a tunnel, it had been filled in so solidly, with rock the same density and mineral content as the original rock, the most advanced equipment couldn't detect the difference.

When the weather got better, we packed up the VW bus and headed to the quarries.

Originally, the quarries that had given Neighborlee its stone and its financial foundation covered nearly as much ground as the town itself had, at the turn of the previous century. In the 60s, about two-thirds of the quarries had been taken over by the park system, a combined effort of the county and the federal government. The river was expanded and re-routed, and several of the quarries were filled with water, turned into fishing and swimming holes. Trees were planted and nature was allowed to take over. The other third was left alone. The park service and the police shared responsibility for patrolling the quarry trails and keeping the steeper roads or the ones leading to dangerous sections chained up to keep people out, so they wouldn't get hurt.

That didn't mean people couldn't and didn't get in. Mum and Pop took the official route and asked for permission to explore and bring in equipment. They requested and got maps of the old tunnels and old pits and the places known to be dangerous. Plus, letting the officials know we were going in there meant someone would check on us, wouldn't run us out, and would be ready to help if anything went wrong.

Nothing went wrong, of course. That was just how things went in Neighborlee. Those who followed the rules, who waited their turn, who got permission, who acted responsibly, rarely if ever ran into problems. The ones pulling pranks and doing stupid things, breaking the rules, essentially saying with their actions that the rules didn't apply to them -- they got into trouble. That was a comforting thought, and one to hold onto when it took far too long (in my estimation) for karma or justice to catch up with the jerks and creeps and selfish twits.

We spent at least one weekend every month exploring the quarries, mapping the tunnels, and taking samples of the rock and water and eventually the plants that started coming up when the weather turned nice.

Then Col. Hayward showed up. He followed us when my folks drove me to school on Monday morning. It was a rainy March morning, typical for Northeast Ohio. Wait ten minutes and the downpour would either stop or turn into a blizzard. Mum and Pop had plans to do some major shopping and then hole up in our house for as long as it took to do the final polish on their newest book, comparing hundreds of Bigfoot-type legends around the world. I was looking forward to helping, because they said my spelling was so good, I could be a proofreader.

They decided to drive me to school, and promised to pick me up if the weather was still lousy when school let out. The Colonel must have been coming up the street and saw us when we left the driveway to head for school. He pulled up behind us while I was climbing out. I saw him and I thumped on Mum's door and pointed while he was still opening his door to get out. She saw him, sighed, but didn't look upset or scared or angry, so I didn't think anything about it. She kissed me goodbye and told me to have a good day, and waited as the Colonel walked up to the van. Pop climbed out and came around to the passenger side. The three of them were standing on the curb, talking, when I looked back just before going into the school door.

They picked me up after school as promised, but instead of settling in for that massive rewriting and retyping session, we headed for Downtown Cleveland to expedite my passport. Col. Hayward wanted my folks' help with something sensitive and secret, dealing with the government more than the military, and they weren't going to England and then Venice without me.

Yeah, England and Venice, at six years old.

Like Kurt said from the beginning, and said many times since, my parents were and are pretty cool.

We went to Venice because some artifacts found in a grave in England were similar to something that had been found in a grave in some catacombs under the largest island in the chain of islands that made up the city. Seriously? Catacombs, dug underneath a city that was built on water? That was just asking for trouble.

The trip only lasted three weeks. I got to visit museums and go sightseeing in England with a young Air Force lieutenant who didn't wear her uniform because she didn't want to attract attention. She was fun, but only until she asked a lot of questions about my folks and got snippy because I didn't have any answers. That happened around the fourth day. That night, I told Mum, and she got that look on her face that could only be compared to a mother wolf whose baby was threatened. Really cold and stern and kind of exhilarating, because I knew she was angry for my sake. I spent the next day with my folks, looking at a grave from pre-Roman Britannia that had been uncovered while digging a foundation for a building that would jointly house some military operations for both the U.S. and England. I knew how to stay quiet and pay attention, and most important, stay out of the way and the notice of other adults.

Mum gave me chores to help them out. They bought me my first camera and first micro-recorder while we were in England. My job was to take pictures of all the people they worked with and try to record conversations, especially the ones full of big words that I didn't understand. That was much easier than trying to remember all those words for later, to ask my folks to explain.

While the grave was interesting, I thought Venice was much more interesting. There were places where the buildings looked like they came right up out of the water, and other places where the islands were a little more evident. I just kept looking around and trying to figure out how they built this entire city so it seemed to float on the water. Pop stood with me for almost a whole hour, watching a repair crew attach huge air bladders to an old building to hold it up out of the water while they worked on the foundations with scuba gear. The gondolas and gondoliers were interesting, but didn't make up for the smell of the water. I was going on seven, but I could figure out that the water had to be disgusting, that the sewers had been emptying straight into what was technically their streets for hundreds of years. Ick.

I was ordered never to discuss the results that justified the trip, but there were a lot of anomalies, anachronisms having to do with dating of various artifacts. The similarities between what had just been found in England and what had been found thirty years before in Venice promised to either explain one or the other, or make the whole situation even murkier. What it had to do with the military, and why Col. Hayward turned to my parents instead of more well-known, better-respected members of the academic community... Well, I can guess, but again, this is something I can't discuss. It's classified.

We were well into April and much nicer weather when we got home. I had done my homework and had my assignments ready to turn in when I returned to school. My classmates either ignored me, were upset with me for some reason, or they bombarded me with questions about the trip. It was kind of fun being pseudo-popular, until some people asked the same questions multiple times. Like they expected me to give them a different answer each time? Maybe they thought I was lying and they wanted to catch me contradicting myself? The only one who was really glad to see me, and who I was really, honestly glad to see, was Kurt. He was bursting with news.

With nicer weather, we were allowed to eat lunch outside. The elementary school kids couldn't go past the boundaries painted on the playground. Each year was a different color, and this year was an orange that made my eyes hurt. Kurt came to the door of my classroom when the lunch hour bell rang and waved until he got my attention, when I was retrieving my lunchbox from my nook. My teacher gave permission and we ran down the hall and outside as fast as we could.

"Those weird old men came back," Kurt said. "You know, the ones who gave that rich old man a hard time last summer," he hurried on, before I could ask. "You know, those people the Grandstones were trying to suck up to?"

"Oh, yeah. They ran away. Wish the Grandstones would."

"They're just stupid." Kurt snorted, He looked around, like he was afraid someone would try to listen in on us. "And you know what else happened? Rodney disappeared." He dropped down on the edge of the planter box that bordered that side of the playground nearest to the street. He sighed when I just looked at him, completely lost. "Don't you know who Rodney is?"

"Is he the really tall, skinny kid with the hair that's almost white?"

"Yeah, him."

"What do you mean? Like... Is he invisible?"

"That'd be cool." He laughed and waited for me to sit down next to him and open up my lunchbox. "Nope, those old men were hanging around out behind the baseball field and the maintenance shed. They hacked off Mr. Longfellow something fierce. He saw them when he came out to look at my engine—I think we finally figured out how to keep it working even when I'm not using it. He got really mad, the kind of mad where he doesn't talk at all, he just gets red, and he headed off across the field. All I saw were two people in dark clothes, but they looked like suits, you know? Then before he came back, I heard an engine and saw this long, dark car, driving away."

"They were driving a van last year."

"You're right." He frowned and thought for a minute or two. "Anyway, I think they were spying on Rodney."

"For what?"

"You know that fire behind the stage when we were taking the Christmas tree down?" Kurt leaned closer and his voice dropped to a whisper. "I think Rodney started it."

"They sent him away for that? Why? He's a nice guy. Not like those jerks who keep picking on the little kids."

"He doesn't play with matches or lighters or anything, and he was like ten feet away when the fire started. He just—" Kurt spread his hands, shrugging. "He made the fire start. Like how we do things," he added, dropping again to a whisper. "I felt the buzzing humming kind of stuff. There were like six fires after you left, and everybody has been talking about them. The funny thing is that right before each of the fires started, somebody was picking on Rodney or they got him really mad, or they were picking on someone he likes."

"Wow! So he's like us."

"Yeah, and two days after I saw that car and Mr. Longfellow

scared them away, somebody showed up and told Mrs. Silvestri they were relatives and they took him away."

"Well, that's nice for him. He's lucky."

"Lanie!" Kurt squeezed his sandwich hard enough it squirted mustard and he had shreds of ham on his fingers. "Rodney is a found kid, just like us. I know because he told me. So if he's a found kid, then he doesn't got any family."

"So those people who took him are lying?" I felt a little breathless. "You think those old men took him? They found out about the fires and they came and watched him, and then they took him away?"

I completely lost my appetite. Kurt could only shrug in answer. We agreed to be even more careful in hiding what we could do. We didn't want to get taken away. Rodney was twelve or thirteen. He was just the right age for superhero powers to start showing up, according to the comic books.

Of course, Kurt and I had discovered our *tricks* a lot younger than twelve, before adolescence showed up. Maybe the old men who took Rodney got their rules from the comic books too. So maybe they were only looking at kids who were in adolescence and making mistakes with their *tricks*, meaning we were safe? By the time we got to be twelve years old, we would have lots of practice hiding what we were, what we could do.

On the other hand, we might have a whole lot more superhero powers showing up when puberty attacked us, and maybe they would be harder to control than fixing gizmos, detecting other kids who were weird like us, or could kinda-sorta fly. We might have just as hard a time controlling those new *tricks* as Rodney had. And look what happened to him.

Somehow, investigating the tunnels in the quarries just wasn't as much fun as it used to be. On the plus side, my folks trusted us because we had proven we didn't do stupid things and take dumb risks. That summer, they gave me my own bike and told me to be careful when we went exploring, and make sure someone knew where we were going. They also gave me lots of warnings of danger signs of what kind of people to avoid, as we went adventuring all over town. Otherwise, they didn't lay a lot of rules and regulations on me.

I didn't realize until later that they had actually put a very effective leash on me, to keep me from doing stupid, reckless, dangerous things or breaking unspoken rules: They gave me a journal of my very own, just like the journals they kept as they traveled all over the world. They asked me to record what I did, what I saw and heard, the things I thought about, the things I learned. They told me someday I might want to write a book about my life, and they thought seeing through my eyes would help them with their own research and writing. Essentially, asking me to write down what happened during my day kept me from making really dumb or rebellious choices, because I didn't want to do something I didn't want them to read about later. It never occurred to me *not* to write down all the things that happened in my life.

Kurt picked up the journaling habit, and my folks got into the habit of giving him a new journal when they gave me a new one. We wrote down all our thoughts about our powers, all the rules we gleaned from the comic books, all the pluses and downsides to having different powers. Yeah, like we could have any influence on what powers we would develop in the future? We just recorded anything we could think of, any patterns, some clue to help us find other kids like us. Safety in numbers, although we weren't exactly thinking in those words and terms. Our first good choice was to guess and hope that the age differences between us were kind of set. Three years between me and Kurt, and he was nine and Rodney was twelve when Rodney showed his fireworks talent, so three years. Maybe the next person to show up would be three years younger than me?

~~~~~

The summer I turned eight, there were two children, a boy and a girl, who graduated from the baby cottage. The boy went to Kurt's cottage, which made it easy for him. It wasn't so easy for me to keep track of the girl. If she had gone to Oak Cottage, I would have been able to at least check on her when I visited Miss Abby and the girls I used to live with. The best I could do was try to walk by the Kindergarten room at school and look for her. Kurt reported that he didn't feel any buzz, didn't hear any humming when he was around either the boy or girl, walking to school. Of course, that could just mean they weren't doing anything with their super powers—if they had any.

Maybe our theory wasn't as strong as we wanted it to be. It
~~~~~

wasn't like we could go around asking questions. That would break so many other rules we had made up to keep ourselves safe. At eight and eleven, Kurt and I had plenty of experience in what adults would do if they thought we were doing something strange or suspicious.

A couple times, we talked about asking my folks if they would help us. After all, Mum and Pop had proven trustworthy when they found out I could kinda-sorta fly. They were more than willing to help Kurt and me spend more time together so we could compare ideas. Pop drove us to comic book stores, even as far as Columbus, to find more sources for information on what superheroes did and why superheroes were super. Maybe, since they were researchers, no one would think it strange if they asked questions like, how many children at NCH were found kids, lost kids, and how many had just been misplaced or temporarily placed by relatives, and they were waiting to go home to their families or relatives. Kurt pointed out that Charlie and Rainbow Zephyr, known investigators and debunkers, asking questions, would just focus the attention of the wrong people on the orphanage. If the Zephyrs were interested, other people would get interested

I was glad I had never told Kurt about Col. Hayward showing up and being a friend to my folks. When we went to England and Italy, all he or anybody else in Neighborlee knew was that they were investigating something for a friend. Then, when we got home, people only knew that the investigation didn't pan out. Kurt might panic if he knew that anyone in the military knew my name, much less that someone in the military knew Neighborlee existed, and had actually come into the town.

We considered asking Miss Angela for her advice, but we were busy with the start of the school year. Kurt still had to get permission to go anywhere off the orphanage grounds by himself. I could go to the shop on my bike, but I didn't want to go without Kurt. Besides, as much as we loved Divine's, and we trusted Miss Angela, sometimes the shop could be a little frightening. Especially when I walked in and could feel something had changed, a room was larger, or a new room had appeared since the last time I visited. Or in the case of my Halloween costume that first year, Angela looked surprised to see it or discover it. Divine's Emporium was her store, and her home. Shouldn't she know everything inside, and everything that happened inside it?

Then we had other things to think about. The Grandstones were at it again. This time, they claimed the land under Neighborlee Gospel Church belonged to them. Now their story was that the Willis family, who settled Neighborlee, had borrowed money from them and had paid it back by signing over the deed to the land. It had already been proven that they didn't build the original Wickslow Chapel, but the land was something else entirely. Some historian had produced a deed they claimed proved the land was theirs, along with more historical documents claiming they owned a part of the Neighborlee quarries.

That was an ongoing battle since the turn of the last century. The Grandstones made regular claims to ownership of the quarries. The intensity of the fight to prove their claims stepped up when the quarries were taken over and converted to park land. They wanted to be reimbursed by the state and the park system. Every generation, they made a new effort to sue the town for not protecting their property.

The Grandstones made another claim on the quarries, then insisted the sandstone of the original Wickslow Chapel had never been paid for. They then filed a lien on the building, and added decades of interest, and then brought in a new lawyer. The Grandstones went through lawyers and law firms faster than losing colleges went through football coaches. The new guy brought up all sorts of legal precedent that made Neighborlee Gospel Church responsible for the unpaid interest. He twisted legal precedent to claim that by buying the land and building, our congregation was in essence the heirs of the original owners of the building, meaning we had inherited the debt.

Mr. Carr, a member of our church and our lawyer, brought in his firm. Carr, Cooper and Crenshaw was "the" law firm in Neighborlee. The case and the claim started dissolving almost from the moment CCC got involved. The Grandstone lawyer quit after only two weeks. Gossip said he had resigned his law firm, and applied to join the bar in another state.

Neighborlee was so used to this that the general feeling of satisfaction didn't last very long. The entertainment factor had just worn out.

Later, I wondered how the Grandstones could keep spending

so much time and money in these futile attempts. Where did the money come from? They owned massive orchards and their so-called estates, but nothing else in Neighborlee. Except, of course, when they actually bought some land on speculation. Most of those speculation plots ended up failing, and they sold the land at a loss.

Like I said before, people who ignored the "go away, we don't want you" subliminal messages got really nasty and went crazy. The Grandstones were genetically programmed for crazy.

The upshot of this was, about a week into October, I learned Sylvia Grandstone was once more out to pound me. Why?

The renewed attempt to take over Neighborlee Gospel Church, and how neatly it was foiled once again.

Chapter Eleven

Sylvia snarked about it on the playground at lunch. Because I went to NGC, she got in my face about us stealing her family's heritage. The thing was, she still couldn't spell *heritage*.

Dummy me, I told her they were stupid to fight our church because God was on our side. Then I added that they should learn from the devil, who was still fighting God and losing. Everyone laughed.

Kurt overheard Sylvia plotting with her cousin, Reggie, to ambush me after school. His newest gizmo let him eavesdrop in the lunchroom, focusing on one table at a time, even from the other side of the room. So, with fair warning, I walked to Neighborlee Children's Home after school with Kurt to avoid them. I hadn't ridden my bike to school that day because it was at church, decorated along with five other bikes, to pull a float in the youth club parade from our church to the community center that was slowly taking over the old Bucksby Factory.

We cut through the NCH playground after getting Kurt's homemade, motorized BMX bike so he could drive me home. We came around the corner pushing his bike, which purred like a just-fed tomcat and saw Felicity Sinclair, the girl who had graduated from the baby cottage just before school started. She stood to one side of the playground, where the blacktop dipped down and formed a huge crescent-moon-shaped puddle. In the winter, it was usually a miniature skating rink, and the daredevils would take a running start and jump and slide on it. The ice was thick, strong enough to hold them and hold up against the abuse.

Felicity stood there, bent over, staring at her reflection in the puddle. She had her fists clenched and she scowled at herself.

"She's humming," Kurt said.

"Humming? Like our kind of humming?" I wiggled my fingers, and he wiggled his back.

Like, cool! One of our theories had been proven right, and there was somebody else like us, with the three-year age gap.

Felicity's hair was *blue*. It changed from straight to corkscrew curls in two minutes flat, while she stared at her reflection in the playground puddle, and we stared at her. Tiny flickers of color sparkled around her hair, shifting through the spectrum so fast it was hard to determine what colors they were.

"That is seriously cool," Kurt said.

I barely heard him. My stomach knotted in sympathy as taunts rang across the playground, proving that we weren't the only ones to see her experimenting with her hair. I was just about her age when I figured out not to play with my talents in public. Obviously, she hadn't learned that other people couldn't do the same things she could, or the truth of the maxim we learned to put into words a few years later: *different is dangerous.*

Not that something different from us could be dangerous, but that *being* different would be dangerous *for* us.

Felicity stood up straight, and her skin reddened as tears filled her eyes. She took four stomping steps toward her tormenters. I recognized most of those kids. Those few seconds when Kurt and I just stood there, we took a sickening drop. We plummeted from the wonder of seeing Felicity's superpower down to the proof that our precautions and rules learned from the comic books were too right. The hairs stood up on my arms.

"Stupid bullies." Kurt looked at me, and I knew what he was about to say, just from the agony and fear and fury sparking dark in his eyes, and the way his mouth flattened and his shoulders hunched.

We had to do something. But what?

Felicity had stopped, while a few of the other kids moved closer, and their voices got loud. Some of the older girls didn't follow them, and a few of the boys said to leave her alone. There weren't many out on the playground yet, this soon after school. Lucky for all of us. Maybe seven girls, a third of the children on the playground that afternoon, continued toward Felicity, asking if the circus was in town and what planet she was from.

Good question, which we saved for dealing with seriously later. Maybe we were from another planet. Just as possible as being mutations or escaped genetic experiments.

"She's humming again," Kurt said. "Louder." He pointed, his eyes getting wider.

Sparks danced across the top Vs of the chain link fence. Then they leaped across the top bar of the swing set and slid down the bracing bars of the slide and swing set. A fizzing haze of sparks erupted from Felicity. A moment later, the girls taunting her ran shrieking, with sparks the size of my fists dancing on their zipper pulls and the rivets in their jeans.

Kurt's bike shrieked. A swarm of sparks spun around the engine like sharks in a feeding frenzy. The engine died with a loud *clatter-clank-snap* and that burned hair smell filled the air.

"She killed it," he whispered, with a horrified, wide-eyed look.

"She's like us," I said, as Felicity went to her knees in the puddle. She looked just as sick and terrified as Kurt did.

I took a step toward her, but he didn't follow. I looked back, trying to keep an eye on Felicity at the same time. It kind of made my head hurt — that particular ache that happened when I pushed my telekinetic/kinda-sorta flying talent too hard. Kurt stood there, holding his bike, his shock and dismay shifting to sick fury.

"She's like us," I repeated, yanking on his sleeve. If he hadn't raised his head from the scorched ruin of that engine we had both worked so hard on, I might have grabbed hold of his ear to make him look. "She doesn't know the rules. She's just a little kid. We gotta get her out of here. What if those guys who took Rodney find out?"

That got him moving again. Kurt had made the rule that if we ever found people like us, we had to protect them. Despite his dead bike, we had to follow the rules.

We ditched Kurt's bike, got permission from Miss Shonda, her housemother, to take Felicity with us, and walked to Divine's Emporium for candy and a long talk. I called home to let Mum and Pop know I would be late. I had to leave a message.

Felicity's hair turned back to straight, glossy mahogany, and her skin tones returned to coffee-and-cream within three blocks. By that time, we had asked enough questions to determine what we already were pretty sure of: she was another Lost Kid, like us. Abandoned in the middle of nowhere as a toddler. In her case, she had been found by Francine Green, daughter-in-law of Abner, of Green's Christmas tree farm. We learned years later that Francine wanted to name her first daughter Felicity, but she and Simon only had boys — six of them, ending with Spike.

"Do you know how you do that?" I asked, after we explained

that most people we knew of couldn't change the color or texture or length of their hair without going to a beauty parlor, and that was why the older girls made fun of her.

"I just think real hard an' it happens," she said with a shrug.

"Is that how Mystique does it?"

"I'll have to buy more X-Men comic books to find out." Kurt dug in his pocket and jangled the change. "I don't have much allowance left."

"I have a quarter left from the money Mum gave me for the bake sale." Right then, those brownies I had devoured at lunchtime sat kind of heavy on my stomach. While it was nice to have a metabolism that burned up sweets faster than I could inhale them, sometimes being a sugar fanatic could work against me. Especially when some extra money would have been helpful to get more research material. "Maybe we can get the books on my folks' credit."

"You'll have to tell them why."

"Well, duh!"

"What if you have to tell them about us, to explain?" Then Kurt got that sick look in his eyes again. "You told, didn't you? That's why your dad helps us get more comic books. He's researching us like they research their books!"

All this time, Felicity just looked back and forth between us, those frown lines around her mouth and between her eyes just getting deeper as we confused her more.

"I didn't tell. They caught me flying. And it didn't freak them out at all. They think it's cool. They think I'm cool."

"You can fly?" Felicity said, her eyes getting big and round and she kind of smiled, sort of lopsided.

"You told," Kurt mumbled.

"I did not!"

By this time, we had stopped and Kurt was kind of leaning in toward me, so that even though I was about half a head shorter than him, we were sort of nose-to-nose. Fortunately, there was no one on the street. We had entirely forgotten about the need to get off the street and out of sight of certain nasty people who wanted to pound on me.

"Lanie—"

"My folks would never tell anybody. Besides, those comic books I got at Christmas? Pop bought them, special. He thinks that you're helping me figure things out, not that you're a superhero or mutant or whatever thingy too."

"What can you do?" Felicity asked, when we stood there just glaring at each other. It was a good thing she asked, because I was getting that sick feeling of fear in my stomach.

"I can fix things, make things work, engines and machines and stuff, when they shouldn't," Kurt said, relaxing and stepping back. He still kept his gaze on me. "Broken stuff, too."

"Like your bike," I said.

"Yeah, it's not really dead." His shoulders relaxed a little. "But just when I was getting it to work when other people were riding."

"Can you really fly?" Felicity said.

"Kinda-sorta," I said, and was able to breathe a little easier.

"Show me?"

So I showed her, rising up about five feet off the ground. I could have gotten away with two feet. Five feet would have been hard to explain away if there were people on the street or someone had looked out their front window at the wrong time. God or just the general atmospheric weirdness of Neighborlee was definitely looking out for us that afternoon, that we weren't caught. Then again, someone might have seen us and just didn't pay attention. I noticed that sort of thing happening a lot over the years in our town. Sort of a "ho, hum, so what else is new?" attitude, where strangers to town would freak out and either check their glasses, ask if their lemonade had been spiked, or call the FBI.

Felicity was properly impressed. She wanted to know if I could do loop-the-loop and other flying tricks. We started walking again as we tried to explain that the extent of my flying was to go straight up as high as I wanted, hover, and then come back down. After some experimenting two summers ago, I could take a running leap and glide for a long time. I couldn't do maneuvers like an airplane or any number of flying superheroes.

"So are you broken?" she asked, looking back and forth between us.

We kept her between us, walking down the sidewalk. It was fortunate that no one was on the sidewalk all along the route we took to get to Divine's. We were so intent on our conversation that we wouldn't have seen anyone in time to separate and let them have part of the sidewalk. We might have been overheard. Not that anyone would have noticed or taken it seriously, since we were only three kids, ages eleven, eight and five. Then again, with the general background weirdness of Neighborlee, someone might have at that.

I looked at Kurt and he kind of grinned at me. I knew we were having the same thought, even though, after much experimentation, we had proven neither of us had any kind of telepathic abilities. Which was disappointing. That particular talent could have saved us trouble and problems in later years.

We stopped again, which wasn't smart. The longer I took getting home and away from the more traveled streets in town, the easier it would be for Sylvia to find me. Of course, we weren't thinking about spoiled brat snot nemeses at the moment.

"Maybe not really broken," Kurt said. "I mean, we're still kids, right? We just haven't figured out all the… I don't know… Like the controls? Maybe all your controls haven't been turned on?"

"But maybe you can work the controls." I took a couple steps back from the two of them. "Should we try?"

He shrugged. Felicity grinned at us. Maybe she was picking up on the things flashing between our heads. Maybe she had telepathic powers and didn't know it yet. Anything was possible, now that we had found a third member of our little tribe of mutant-genetic-experiment-alien-visitor-freaks. Besides, the fact she was smiling now, when she had been so somber and fidgety and afraid just a little while ago, kind of encouraged us to try.

I lifted myself just a few feet this time. Enough to let us hide what we were doing if someone stepped out of their house or someone drove down the street or came around the corner of the sidewalk. We were starting to pay attention to the world around us again. I hovered. Kurt closed his eyes and clenched his fists.

The air thickened and tightened around me, like an invisible envelope, so light that I had never felt it before until it tightened up. It felt like a noose snare catching a rabbit that hopped into it on a forest trail. Before I could react to that sensation, I spun around three times. Not fast at all, but since *I* didn't do it and didn't expect it, the first rotation wrung a squeak out of me. Then the second time I caught Kurt staring, his mouth dropping open in total delighted shock. The third time, he tipped his head back and let out a whoop. His concentration must have broken, because suddenly the tight, enclosing sensation — not unpleasant, not suffocating or squeezing, just weird — evaporated. I dropped. It wasn't that long of a drop, and I caught myself about a foot off the ground, for a slightly slower landing.

"Well that was interesting," Kurt murmured, and shivered a little. The good kind of shiver that he got when he was nearly buried under an avalanche of ideas.

Felicity just laughed and clapped her hands, and demanded that he make her fly. It took a little talking to convince her that if she couldn't do it to begin with, Kurt couldn't give it to her. Just like he couldn't make a toaster give him ice cubes, even though he had been able to make a broken ice dispenser at school give him ice cubes.

Fortunately, Felicity didn't challenge us on that, because honestly, we were making up the rules and figuring things out as we went along, just following our instincts. There were some things the comic books couldn't teach us. We did feel pretty sure that Kurt could only take over or change talents that someone else was using. We proved that in short order by him trying to make me fly when I wasn't, and then trying to make Felicity's hair change color and then create a miniature electrical storm. No luck.

We started walking again, and Felicity wanted to know how we knew so much. Who had taught us? We explained about the comic books, and for a second I thought we'd get back into the argument about telling my parents about our superhero powers. Kurt seemed satisfied that they only knew about me, and not about him. Maybe the increasing need for more comic books to help us figure out Felicity convinced him. If she could change her hair, would she maybe be able to change her entire appearance when she got older? That could be majorly cool. And dangerous.

"You think Miss Angela will have the issues we need?" I said.

"If there is one, she'll have it."

That was the magic of Divine's Emporium. Whatever we wanted or needed, it was there.

Of course, then Felicity wanted to know who Miss Angela was, and we were both a little stunned to realize that she hadn't taken the trip to Divine's Emporium on her fifth birthday like we had. With a little questioning, we found out that Felicity had a bad cold on her birthday, and it had been raining, so she hadn't gone. That wasn't fair, we were very sure. Definitely, we had to make sure her first trip to Divine's Emporium was extra special. That required as much candy as we could get between the remainders of our allowance, which meant we would get the comic books on my parents' credit.

We were so busy telling Felicity about all the treasures at Divine's, we didn't hear when Sylvia and Reggie caught up with us. Right at the corner where we were about to turn down the quiet, dead-end street overlooking the park, where the shop sat. One stroke of luck: Freddie wasn't with them.

"Where do you think you're going, Lanie Zephyr?" Sylvia snarled. "You are so dead!"

"Ignore her," Kurt said.

We kept walking. Felicity looked over her shoulder at the two Grandstones in their fancy clothes and fancy bikes, and she reached up to hold our hands.

All Grandstones hated being ignored. Sylvia went into her usual tirade about throwaway kids and rejects. Felicity's hand trembled in mine. Then Reggie joined in, showing off the new filthy words he had learned. When we didn't stop, ears burning, he caught up and rode circles around us.

What happened next ... to be honest, I really didn't *think*. Maybe the Grandstones had a superpower, too: the ability to *stop* someone from thinking clearly while they got up to full steam with their nastiness. I saw a thick stick lying in the gutter and yanked on it with my mind, pulling it toward me. Straight into Reggie's spokes. He shrieked like a girl and tumbled into the same gutter. Like most Grandstones when someone stood up to them, Sylvia shrieked about what her lawyer would do to us.

Kurt and I laughed, because we didn't *touch* the stick that got stuck in Reggie's wheel, did we? Of course, *proof* and *truth* meant nothing to the Grandstones. Sylvia kept threatening us as she glided along on her bike while we continued walking steadily toward the sanctuary of Divine's. Then she returned to threatening my church. Then NCH.

Chapter Twelve

Felicity's hand shook more, and got cold, and I felt little pinprick bites of what had to be her EM sparks caught between her skin and mine. It was kind of ticklish, and gut instinct told me not to let go of her hand. But when Sylvia said her uncle owned a bulldozer and she was going to take it and come knock down the orphanage in the middle of the night, common sense kind of deserted all of us. Later, we laughed at ourselves, because the whole mental image was ridiculous. Even if the Grandstones did own heavy machinery other than fancy cars, Sylvia couldn't have reached the controls for it. None of that mattered to Felicity, who didn't know what liars Grandstones were. All she knew was that this mean girl was threatening to knock down her house.

Shrieking, "Shut up! Shut up!" Felicity yanked her hands free of ours and pressed them against her ears.

Howling filled the air. And barking.

From every direction all across town, dogs came running.

They circled Sylvia and Reggie, barking. She pedaled for her life, fleeing, shrieking at the top of her lungs and threatening to sic her lawyer on the dogs. He raced after her, cursing at the dogs chasing them. The dogs howled and barked and leaped and ran circles around them. As the whole strange, churning group went around the corner, Sylvia and Reggie screamed and shouted louder than the dogs.

We stood there, our mouths hanging open, and couldn't do anything until the echoes of that chaos finally faded. Then we laughed, kind of breathlessly. Felicity dropped down to land on her bottom, half on the curb, and slid down to the street.

"Cool," Kurt said, when it was just the three of us again. "Hey, Zap, what else can you do?"

Felicity shrugged. She looked wobbly, just like I got when I "lifted" too much with my mind.

"That's okay," I said, and took her hand. "We're still figuring things out, too."

Kurt didn't buy those comic books. An ice cream sundae big

enough for the three of us to share was much more important. Miss Angela welcomed Felicity as if she had been expecting her. She took her on a tour of the shop, then let her pick out two pieces each from five different jars of candy, for free. She seemed to approve of Kurt and me taking Felicity under our wing.

We didn't tell her what happened, and we didn't talk about it while we were in the shop, but Miss Angela seemed to know. Kurt thought maybe she had been looking outside when Sylvia and Reggie came after us. She definitely would have heard all those dogs barking and howling and those two snots screaming as they fled. Whatever she knew or saw or heard, she suggested a slightly different route going home, when we left.

Just to be on the safe side, I stayed back a few seconds, when she was showing Felicity around the shop. I made a wish on the Wishing Ball, that we wouldn't get in any trouble over what had happened. I wished double-hard that Felicity would be safe and nobody would treat her weird, and she wouldn't mess up and change her hair where people could see her do it. We didn't need those two old men in the van to see her and take her away.

We stopped on the corner by the Mall. That was what we called the business and shopping district of Neighborlee, east of the municipal area with city hall and the city park and the service buildings and such. We had to wait for the light to cross the street to head home. This late in the afternoon, the school crossing guards had gone home. Plus we had time to start thinking about what we would do when we had to separate, me to walk home and them to go the other direction to NCH. Kurt didn't want to let me go the rest of the way by myself. Just because Sylvia and Reggie had raced away screaming and crying, that didn't mean they wouldn't come back, looking for me. There was always the chance they would come back with Freddie, or one of their fathers, or one of their servants, or one of the men who drove their big fancy cars for them.

"Now would be a really good time to learn to do something new," Kurt said, as we watched the traffic rumbling past us.

"Like what?" I sighed and looked across the street, and the orphanage buildings barely visible against the horizon line. "Go invisible? Learn to run really, really fast?"

"Too bad you can't zap things like Felicity."

That earned grins from all three of us.

"Can't you just fly home?" Felicity said.

We were still explaining the rules to her, how it was life and death to us to keep our powers secret, when Mum and Pop drove by on their way home from a research trip to the University of Akron. Time and again, my folks proved that whatever someone was looking for, they found. It all depended on what someone *wanted* to find.

Mum and Pop saw us and honked as they drove past on the far side of the street. We had a really cool horn on the VW. It played *Ode to Joy*, and Pop had figured out how to keep the song going, instead of just playing the first five or ten notes. If he kept hitting the steering wheel, and there wasn't anyone on the street to get upset or feel threatened, he could go through the whole first verse.

"Problem solved," I said, and jumped up and down, waving in response to Pop waving at us.

"Who's that?" Felicity asked.

"My parents."

At the next street, they turned around and came back to the intersection and honked again, two more pieces of the song. Despite the light changing and the "walk" sign flashing, we stayed on that side of the street and waited.

"But—" She frowned. "I thought—" She sighed and hung her head a little.

"Yeah, I used to live with you guys. They adopted me."

"Are they nice?"

"Lanie's parents are super cool," Kurt said. "They know she can fly and it's okay with them. They're about the only people in town who it's safe to know about..." He gestured among the three of us. Felicity's eyes got big, then she smiled tentatively.

Her eyes got bigger, if that was possible, when the VW pulled up past us and turned into the driveway. Right there on the corner, there used to be a gas station, but the company had gone out of business. Neighborlee took over the property and filled in the hole where the tanks used to be, and turned it into a little park, with some benches and all sorts of flowering planters. At Christmas, businesses put up decorated trees, with their names on plaques. The money they paid for that little bit of advertising and PR went into the town Benevolent Fund. There was also a big brick wall with a lighted community bulletin board on it.

The important thing was that there was still a driveway so cars could pull in and pick up people waiting there, or drop them off, and not block traffic. So that's what Mum and Pop did.

That day, Mum's hair was electric blue, and she had played with dying her eyebrows and lashes, so they were hot pink. Her long smock top was paisley in those exact same colors. Pop had a camouflage billed cap on, and a camouflage jacket over his standard tie-dyed shirt, in matching shades of green and brown, and mirrored sunglasses. I guess they looked odd to someone who was seeing them for the first time, but they were my parents and they didn't look weird to me at all. I have to admit, though, I came near to holding my breath as I waited for Felicity's response once she got a good look at them. She came through. Her eyes stayed big, but she grinned and didn't hesitate to give her name when Mum slid out of the mini-bus and hugged me, then Kurt, then greeted her and asked her name.

Pop figured out right away that something had happened, before he even asked what I was doing there when he expected me to be home, doing my homework. Sometimes I wondered if maybe my folks had a little bit of superpowers themselves, because so many times they just *knew* things. They weren't on the order of *knowing* that Miss Angela had, where it seemed like she could read minds and see into the future. It was more than their incredible powers of observation and flawless logic, and more than the ability to make highly educated guesses. They could out-Sherlock Sherlock Holmes every time.

"Grandstone trouble?" Pop said, as he came around the back of the mini-bus and shook hands with Felicity, finishing the introductions.

"That's just part of it," Kurt said.

"Part?" Mum stepped back and tipped her head to one side, and then she grinned. "The Musketeers have their third, I'm guessing." Then she laughed when Kurt and Felicity both gave me puzzled looks. "You can explain who the Musketeers are, later. Let's get these two home, all right?" Without waiting for a response from any of us, she bent down and caught up Felicity around the waist and lifted her up into the van. Felicity was tiny, even for a five-year-old, and she weighed hardly anything back then. Kurt could have driven both of us on his bike without any problem. If he had had a basket on his bike, Felicity could have sat in it, while I sat on the seat and he stood up on the peddles.

The most astonishing part of the day came when Pop was waiting to pull out into traffic. Kurt told *everything* that had happened to us, starting with my argument with Sylvia on the playground. Pop laughed at my smart-alec advice to take a lesson from Satan losing all the time. Mum sighed and shook her head, but at least she smiled. Then Kurt explained how he heard Reggie and Sylvia were going to ambush me, and our plan to get me home fast on Kurt's bike. That got us out into traffic and heading past the Mall. We were stopped at the intersection, waiting to make a left-hand turn, when he told about seeing Felicity changing the color of her hair. I nearly choked, because Kurt was always warning *me* to keep things secret and safe and not trust anyone. Sure, he had told Felicity that my parents were cool about our superpowers, but just an hour ago he had still been in a snit, thinking I had spilled the beans.

We reached NCH and sat in the parking lot while Kurt finished telling the whole story, ending with leaving Divine's and trying to figure out how to get me home safely. Mum and Pop traded one of those long, silent-speaking looks.

"You wonder sometimes, sweetheart, how hard God laughs when we make plans?" Pop said.

Pop was kind of a philosopher, and I was getting used to hearing things like that. Honestly, that was pretty mild, compared to some other things he has said over the years. Kurt and Felicity just gave me those looks I had already figured out meant they were lost. I would have to interpret and explain some time later.

"We didn't pray right, when we decided to slow down and get off the road," Mum said, and they reached across the open space between the front seats and held hands for a moment. Then she turned a little in the seat so it was easier to look at the three of us, sitting on the front bench. "We're so proud that you three trust us with your secret. You never have to worry that we'll tell anyone, unless you give us permission first. Any questions, any problems, don't ever hesitate to ask us."

"What we need is a better, faster, more private way to communicate, if an emergency or anything comes up," Pop said. "How about you make that a goal with your inventions, Kurt?

Create phones that are small enough to wear around your neck like jewelry… Oh, I know, like a Dick Tracy watch-phone. Some way we can get hold of each other and help in an emergency, without having to go searching for a payphone."

That got Kurt all excited. He liked challenges. Mobile phones were starting to get popular around about that time, but they were big and clunky and not really reliable in the mountains or far away from the transmitter towers. Pop was probably thinking more along the lines of the communicator pins that they used on the new Star Trek series. What was really great, and impressed Felicity a lot, was that it was just understood that my folks would be there for all three of us. They weren't going to be like a lot of grown-ups, expecting that we turn ourselves in to higher authorities and report what we could do, like someone else would report if they found an assault rifle or a bag of stolen money.

We made plans, really quickly. If we sat for very long, someone would come out to ask what was going on. My folks added to rules for keeping us safe. I trusted them enough that I didn't ask if they were going to say anything to Col. Hayward. Of course, I never thought to ask if maybe he knew already.

From that day, our morning routine readjusted. I changed my route going to school, so I could meet Felicity and Kurt. The Neighborlee schools being on one big plot of land meant we didn't have to go in different directions when we were all in different levels of schooling. With three years between our ages, that would have made sticking together and communicating a little harder. Just like Kurt had done with me, we would take Felicity back to NCH at lunchtime, to have more talking and plotting time.

That afternoon, after we dropped off Kurt and Felicity, and we were heading home, I had some time to slow down and really think about what had happened. It was nice to know there were more of us, and Kurt and I had guessed right, about the pattern. Would there be another one of us showing a talent in three years? How come the three of us showed our powers earlier than "normal" for superheroes? Maybe we weren't really superheroes. Sure, I could kinda-sorta fly, Felicity could call dogs to come protect her, and Kurt could borrow my flying ability. I couldn't see any of us appearing in comic books, doing what we did. Maybe that was a good thing?

"What are you thinking, honey?" Mum asked, when we turned onto our street.

"What did you pray about, that you didn't pray right?" I asked after a moment of thinking. I couldn't exactly tell them that I was glad I would never appear in a comic book, could I?

Pop laughed.

"God has a pretty strange sense of humor, sometimes," he said, slowing to turn down our driveway. "He likes to make us think about how we pray, and what we pray for, and the things we say. He wants us to be careful, and He wants us to be wise, so when we make promises that are just plain reckless and thoughtless, sometimes He makes us live up to our word."

"Like what?"

"Oh…" He sighed, brought us to a stop behind the house, and put the VW into park before he turned to look at me. "Like someone gets himself into big trouble, and promises God that if He'll get him out of that trouble, he'll never do something ever again, like swear or steal or whatever. Or he promises God he'll do something, like become a preacher or give all his money to missionaries or something like that. When things calm down, he starts regretting what he promised. The problem is, now he's got proof that God came through, so if he's smart and if he wants to be able to look himself in the mirror every morning, he's gotta fulfill his part of the bargain. Make sense?"

"The trouble comes when it's something he doesn't really want to do," Mum filled in. "He likes drinking or smoking or swearing, and he likes his money, and he doesn't want to become a preacher, because again, if he's smart and if he has any honesty at all, he knows he'll make a terrible preacher."

I thought about that for a little bit as we got out and crossed the gravel yard to the kitchen door. "How come he doesn't just tell God he made a mistake and he's sorry, and can he do something easier?"

"Ha!" Pop bent down and hugged me hard, and then picked me up and spun me around, setting me on the top step. "I tell you, if kids were in charge of the world instead of adults, we'd be a lot better off. Logic, pure and simple."

"Did you make a promise to God you really didn't want to keep?"

That got more laughter from him, and a loud sigh and a grin from Mum. We went inside and hung up our coats in the mudroom off the kitchen.

"No, honey, I didn't make a promise to God that I didn't want to keep. The thing is, when your mom and I decided to settle down, slow down… I can't really say we got off the road, because we do still travel. We decided it was time to find a place where we belonged, a place to come back to." Pop pulled open the refrigerator and looked inside. "Leftover buffet tonight?"

He pulled out all sorts of containers and put them on the long table made for ten that filled half the big farmhouse kitchen, and kept talking. Mum and I got to work either putting containers in the microwave or dumping them into pots and pans on the stove, and setting the table.

"We had run into Angela years ago, looking for books for research. She had the books, but we had to prove to her we deserved to look inside them." He sighed, and for a moment, he looked tired and his eyes grew distant. "There's some knowledge that shouldn't be saved anywhere, with the risk of the wrong people finding and using it. At the same time, it has to be written down somewhere, held prisoner, so to speak, so it doesn't just float around the world, where the wrong person could find it."

My expression must have been pretty confused, with some fear mixed in, because Pop sighed and came over to kiss my forehead and for a few seconds his smile looked strained.

"Don't you worry, sweetheart. Neighborlee is the best place in the world for secrets and for protecting everybody inside it, as well as the rest of the world outside it. You don't need to know, and I hope you never need to know. That's something important your mom and I had to learn. Focus on the job the good Lord gave you to do, and don't worry about anybody else's job, anybody else's burden, unless God tells you to help them. Make sure it's God telling you, and not some egotistical, inflated sense of importance. Some people aren't happy unless they're miserable, with the weight of the world on their shoulders, when God never told them…" He sighed again, only this time he was definitely laughing at himself.

"The gist of the story," Mum said, "is that we forgot to be specific and put details into our prayer, when we asked God if it was time to retire, if He would let us retire. We asked Him if it was all right if we could come back to Neighborlee, because we felt more comfortable here than we've ever felt anywhere — or any 'when' — in the whole world. We knew Angela and liked her, and what's more important is that she liked and trusted us. Over the years, she's trusted us with some things that needed either hiding or uncovering, and we've done the same with her."

"Oh!" I nearly dropped the handful of silverware I had just taken out of the drawer. "That stone thing you sent back from when you went to Peru. You had me give it to Miss Angela. That kind of things, to hide with her?"

"Exactly." Pop pulled a container of kung pao chicken out of the microwave and set it on the table. "God has given us a talent for finding things that maybe other people shouldn't, so we can put it away where it can't be found. And if it has a tendency to be found, to want to be found... Well, we give it to Angela, and she deals with it. Nobody and nothing in this world dares disobey Angela."

He laughed when I nodded, feeling a slight shiver at the utter stupidity of disobeying her. I had never made her angry or even disappointed her, but I had seen glimpses of ice in her eyes, heard it in the tight notes of her voice, when someone else angered her. That was not a good thing. Ever.

"What all this is building up to," Mum said, as she took a saucepan of chicken chili off the stove and put it on a hot pad on the table, "is one really thoughtless line in our prayer. We asked God to make us useful, here in our new home."

"What's wrong about that?" I climbed into my chair and gave it a mental shove to get it closer to the table.

"That's like signing a blank check, and just dropping it in the center of town. Anybody who finds it can fill in whatever amount they want, and because you signed it, you really can't argue about whatever they take."

"Oh." That idea churned through my head as they finished putting our conglomeration of leftovers on the table, removing lids and dropping serving spoons into containers. "But God isn't mean. He won't hurt you, right?"

"That's where His sense of humor comes in. If you give God a blank check, He's going to have fun surprising you, and turning you inside out sometimes." Pop slid into his chair at the end of the table. "It'll be scary and wonderful and you'll grow, and it might hurt, and sometimes you'll get mad at Him for doing this to you, because you didn't consciously sign up for all of it. But He's God, right? So you really can't fight it, and you just have to hold on tight and trust Him. Right?" He held out his hand for mine. Mum sat down across the table from me, and she took his other hand.

"Right." I bowed my head while Pop prayed.

It wasn't a long prayer. Mum always said that long prayers were for Bible studies and devotions and church, and God wanted us to enjoy our food, so dinnertime prayers should be short to keep it from cooling off or warming up.

"So what did God give you to do, Pop?" I said, almost as soon as we opened our eyes again.

Chapter Thirteen

"Honey," Mum said, eyes sparkling, "He gave us you, and now your two friends, to help you grow up safe, and learn to use what you can do."

"If that isn't scarier and more important than running the country or building an atomic bomb or finding a cure for cancer," Pop said, as he slid two cheese pierogis onto my plate, "I don't know what is."

The great thing about my folks was that they weren't like other adults, meaning they didn't step in and take over and give us a plan of attack for figuring out what we could do and how we should do it. They saw themselves in an advisory capacity. They were smart in knowing that if they sat back and let us think for ourselves, we were more willing to go to them with theories and questions and problems and things we didn't understand, and more willing to take advice. That didn't mean they left us completely alone. I got lots of questions when I came back from spending afternoons and all day Saturday with Kurt and Felicity, yet at the same time they weren't intrusive, Inquisition-type questions. More along the lines of wanting to share our fun.

I'm sure a lot of people would be astonished by what could be seen as a laissez-faire attitude toward the training of three semi-pseudo-superheroes. That was proof enough God had chosen my folks specifically for us. We didn't waste time going through a rebellious phase or trying to be secretive, or waste energy thinking up lies. Plus, when we got into trouble, my folks didn't waste time and energy lecturing us. They dove in and helped us hide what happened or cleaned up the mess, and then sat down and talked through everything, to figure out what went wrong. Of course, that didn't mean I didn't get a lecture once in a while. They were my folks, and they expected better of me. They expected me to be smart and careful and know right from wrong. When it came to figuring out what kind of superheroes we could be when we grew up, they left that to us.

After all, we were the ones with the instruction manuals—as in

Kurt's comic books.

Come to think of it, Pop got a kick out of finding new comic book stores and every subscription and new series, and being our financier by paying for them. On the condition that he got to read the comic books too, of course.

We went to ground, so to speak, as soon as Felicity joined us. Meaning I spent a lot of time at NCH with Kurt and Felicity. Mum found a child seat to put on the back of my bike, so Felicity could ride with us, so we got around faster, and didn't have to spend time walking with the other kids from the orphanage. That let us talk freely about what we had thought about or learned since the day before. That kept us off the streets and out of the clutches of the Grandstones.

Sylvia was in my classroom, but that wasn't as much torture as someone might think. The other kids, for the most part, couldn't stand Sylvia. So if there were a bunch of them around when she picked on someone, they didn't let her get away with it. As we got older, they grew less afraid of what the Grandstones would do to them if they didn't knuckle under. Or they decided it was smarter to support the Grandstone version of reality.

~~~~~

Building up to Halloween that year, Felicity brought up a question that had been sort of hovering at the backs of our minds for a couple years. We had been too busy to broach it, or maybe a little uncomfortable about it.

"Superheroes have costumes, right?" she said, after we had spent most of our homework time on the front porch of her cottage, drawing pictures of what we wanted to be for Halloween, and then trying to figure out how to get the pieces and parts.

We already had permission for Kurt and Felicity to come trick-or-treating with me, with Mum and Pop escorting us, and we had been playing with several group costume ideas.

"Yeah." Kurt had that puzzled half-grin he wore a lot since he became outnumbered by girls. He reached for his backpack and pulled out a handful of comic books and spread them out. "You think we should be superheroes?"

"No, I mean, don't we have costumes? Aren't we like them?"

"We're kids," I said. "Those are grownups."

"So we can't have costumes until we're grown up?"
~~~~~

Kurt's puzzled look smoothed out into his thinking look, where I could almost hear the gears whirring and sometimes smell smoke coming from his ears. He emptied all the comic books out of his backpack and spread them across the floorboards while he looked through them. The funny thing was, he didn't even take them out of their bags, he just looked at the covers, tossing one aside after another. Felicity and I sat there, crayons in our hands, watching him. Then he shoveled everything back into his backpack and held up one finger, meaning to wait, jumped off the porch, and ran across the quadrangle to his cottage.

"Did I make him mad?" Felicity said.

I shrugged, and we got back to work, sketching ideas. By the time Kurt came back, we had come up with a costume that all three of us wore together, basically a three-headed monster. We were giggling and adding things like pitchforks and flamethrowers, to drive away the bullies who would try to steal our candy. Kurt jumped up onto the porch and upended his backpack, spilling comic books across the floor again.

These were older ones, odd ones, single stories and not in a series, or so old that the rest of the issues in the storyline couldn't be found yet.

"Kids," Kurt said, holding up the top few comic books from the pile. "Not like us. They're in high school, but kids have costumes too. And cool names." He tossed us the comic books, and we looked at the covers while he dug through the pile. "Here. Superman when he was a kid. He had a costume."

"Yeah, but didn't his parents on Krypton give him his costume?" I had to ask.

"Not all the time."

"What do you mean, not all the time?" Felicity said, her voice rising to a squeak.

"There are a bunch of different stories, and when you see Superman on TV and in the movies, the story is different all the time." Kurt slumped against the post holding up the front of the porch. "This isn't working. I thought we could get answers. All the super-kids are in high school, and I bet somebody gives them their costumes and names. They're all in a school for superheroes, or adults find them and teach them. They're not alone like us."

"We're not alone. Are we?" She looked scared for a few

seconds.

"Nope. We have each other." Kurt looked a little angry, but that was just his determined, taking-responsibility-for-littler-kids expression.

"So we have to just sit here and wait until some grownups with superhero powers find us and give us our names and our costumes?" I said. That certainly didn't sound fair.

"I don't see why. Nobody gave Batman anything. He did it all himself."

"Batman isn't a superhero. He isn't," I hurried on, when Kurt opened his mouth to argue. "He's got no super powers. He's not from another planet or magic or a mutant, and nobody gave him any magic tools. He's just rich and smart and he has a lot of cool weapons and things."

"That's his super power," he insisted. "Rich and smart. And lots of gizmos."

"You can make the gizmos," Felicity offered. She looked a little depressed.

"Yeah, but most of them don't work when I'm not using them."

"That's good," I said. "Then nobody can steal them from us. They only work when we're using them against the bad guys, and if the bad guys take them, it won't do them any good."

That idea sort of cheered up all of us. It was kind of cool knowing that the villains would never get the advantage of us. That afternoon, we made a pact to concentrate on learning what we could do, and leave costumes and cool secret identity names for later on, like middle school or even high school. Nobody would take seriously a superhero who was only four feet tall and wasn't allowed outside after dark.

We also agreed that we had to take on more chores, to earn money for parts for Kurt's gizmos. He needed to concentrate on inventing something that actually worked. Mr. Longfellow, who was mentoring him, would help him sell the gizmo, so he could make money and become rich. Then we would use that money to build a cool superhero hideout and fill it with more tools and parts, to build more gizmos for the war against the bad guys.

At ages five, eight, and eleven, the plan seemed perfectly logical, perfectly feasible, and we had all the time in the world to accomplish it. We certainly weren't in any hurry. And besides, we had homework to do, and Halloween costumes to make.

We did agree on one concrete thing, before I had to go home for dinner. When we got old enough, we would explore the quarry tunnels again, and make our superhero hideout there. Nobody would ever suspect, because after all, the roads were chained and nobody ever went into the dangerous areas. At least, so we thought.

~~~~~

We ended up asking Mum to adjust my faerie costume for Felicity. Kurt went as an engineer from Star Trek, and some of the older boys at NCH teased him about putting a target on either his forehead or his back, because Redshirts were always doomed to die in each episode. I found a vintage dress in one of the back rooms at Divine's and went as Louisa May Alcott. I had to carry a beat-up copy of *Little Women* to show to the people who said, "Huh?" when I told them. That got very old, so by the time we finished the first street of trick-or-treating, I left the book with Pop, and just told people I was one of the original settlers of Neighborlee. It was a little depressing, realizing how illiterate some of the people in our town were.

That year, another room had been opened up at the old Bucksby Factory, in the slow-moving process of turning it into a community center. To celebrate, the Chamber of Commerce sponsored a party after trick-or-treating ended. When we walked in the door, Miss Angela was helping at the punch table to the right of the door. She gave me one of her rare nods and smiles of approval. Why? I had convinced Felicity that, just as Angela had told me several years before, real Faeries hadn't had wings in centuries. Besides, it was easier for her to walk around without worrying about her wings dragging on the ground.

We made the rounds of the carnival-style games in the larger room, throwing bean bags or rings or plucking plastic ducks from a wading pool or bobbing for plastic apples, with numbers on the bottoms that determined our prizes. Miller's Diner had a grill set up outside the front door and provided everyone with fresh-grilled hot dogs and cups of hot cider. Stephanie and Mr. Miller were working behind the long serving table set up inside the lobby, and I nearly shrieked when they kissed, during a lull between customers.

"What's wrong with two people who are in love kissing each
~~~~~

other?" Miss Angela said, coming up behind me.

Her timing was perfect, because I was about to run to Mum and point out what I had just seen. At the age of eight, I had very strong ideas of what was right and wrong. Since Stephanie worked for Mr. Miller, it just seemed to me they shouldn't be kissing. Certainly not in public. Like, ick, gross.

Miss Angela laughed and bent down closer, so we were nearly talking in private. "For your information, they just got engaged. Very romantic, too. He gave her a pumpkin to carve, but it was already cleaned out, and inside was an engagement ring."

I told Mum, and she hurried over to hug Stephanie and congratulate her. I got away from the lobby until I could shake off the oogy feeling. Mr. Wellington, a history professor at Neighborlee High, was giving tours of the factory, telling about the factory's history and talking about the plans for renovations. That sounded interesting. Besides, he was a graduate of NCH, stayed in Neighborlee, and got his teaching certificate at Willis-Brooks College. He visited at least twice a month with other orphanage graduates and made history sound interesting, so I knew he was a good storyteller.

When the tour group of eight got to the second room off the restored lobby, which was the locker room, something weird happened. As far as I could tell, I was the only one who saw the green, glow-in-the-dark gas that seeped up through the cracks in the tile floor and streamed out through the vents in the rusty old locker doors. I watched those streamers swirl around for a few seconds. They turned into tentacles like an octopus, except without the suction cups, and reached across the room to us. Nobody reacted. Not even Mr. Wellington, when one of those tentacles curved around his shoulders and flicked at his coat.

I was pretty sure nothing was going to happen, because the greeny-glowing tentacles were transparent. Common sense said they were just gas. Except would gas act like that? There wasn't a breeze in the room to explain the movement if it was just gas.

One tentacle wrapped around Mr. Wellington's throat, and he choked. I opened my mouth to scream.

The tentacles vanished, just popping out of existence in silence. Mr. Wellington went on telling funny stories. The men and women who had used this locker room, during different phases of the factory's history. The different things that had been manufactured here, depending on the economy or what was needed in the rest of the country.

Nobody else seemed to have seen the tentacles, otherwise they would have said something, right? Of course, I saw them, and I didn't say anything, so how could I be sure? The freaky thing was that Mr. Wellington seemed to forget he was choking, the moment the tentacles vanished. As if he hadn't really felt them, or hadn't been choking at all.

So what had I seen, if what I saw didn't happen?

When in doubt, go to Mum and Pop. They investigated the really weird, after all.

I found Pop first and got him to step outside with me so we could talk in private. By then I knew enough to avoid people overhearing when I reported something. He let me get to the end of the story, and then he asked questions to get the details solid.

We were still talking when Kurt came looking for me. He had that weird look on his face, like he was feeling a little embarrassed and a little scared. He held out his hands and rubbed his fingers together. Our signal that he had felt something. Usually it was one of us using our superhero powers, but how could that be, since neither of us was doing anything?

"Where's Felicity?"

My first thought was that Sylvia and her gang had cornered her when we weren't around to protect her. She might be scared for a few seconds, but then she would get angry. When Felicity got angry, lightbulbs popped. Three days before, someone wanted the purple paint she was using during art time. When she wouldn't hand it over, he poured green paint on her. Felicity's EM burst killed Miss Underwood's electric pencil sharpener. It gave off black smoke and part of the plastic casing melted. I could imagine the disaster that would result from her getting angry here, with all the strings of lights for decorations, the smoke machines and the sound system playing haunted house soundtracks.

"She's okay. We were getting snow cones when I felt it, so I know it wasn't her. Did you do anything?"

I shook my head, while Pop got that thoughtful look.

"What?" Kurt looked back and forth between us.

"If you saw something that didn't happen," Pop said, "maybe

that's because it hasn't happened *yet*."

"So Mr. Wellington *is* going to get choked tonight?" I certainly didn't like that idea. I liked him.

Kurt wanted to know what we were talking about, so I had to go through the whole story again. He thought it was pretty cool if I had a new superpower and could tell the future.

"Powers like that are double-edged, kids, and I'd be very careful," Pop said. "Usually God gives people glimpses of the future to help them prevent something, or prepare for something. I think the first step is to find Andy Wellington and warn him."

"Pop, nobody is going to believe me," I said.

"Yeah, you're right. So let's get somebody he will believe." He held out his hand for mine, and Kurt hurried to keep up with us as we went looking for Angela.

Nobody ever disagreed with Angela.

Chapter Fourteen

We had to search for Angela, which was a little frightening because I imagined those tentacles coming after Mr. Wellington the next time he went into the locker room with a tour group. Tours took place every twenty minutes, so in another ten minutes he could be dead! When we found her, she was in one of the rooms off the office, talking with Stephanie. Pop and Kurt and I stopped in the doorway, as soon as we saw she wasn't alone. Miss Angela looked at us, looked at Stephanie, and for a second she kind of slumped, like something heavy rested on her shoulders.

"That's confirmation, I think," she said to Stephanie. She put on that gentle smile that always promised everything would be all right, and gestured for us to come in. "Stephanie is a guardian, so whatever you two have to say, it's safe to say in front of her."

"Is my Pop a guardian?" I had to ask.

"He's *your* guardian, and that's more important. While we regretfully must keep all sorts of secrets in our duties, you must never keep secrets from your parents, Lanie. I refuse to encourage or allow that."

I felt a lot better about that, because it had just occurred to me that while my folks knew I could kinda-sorta fly, and they knew about Kurt's talent with gizmos, and now Felicity and her lightning bursts, the whole thing with us helping Angela protect Neighborlee might not be part of the deal. Sure, they sent things to her to guard in the shop, but what if they didn't know everything else?

"Now, what has happened?" She settled down on one of the crates someone had stashed in the office during the party. The rest of us found seats as Kurt spoke first.

"The weird thing is that it didn't feel like when one of us is doing something," he finished up. "Lanie and Felicity hum, and it's nice humming, and the sound gets deeper and sounds like guitar chords if they do it long enough. This was bad humming. Buzzing and..." He shuddered and looked a little green. That scared me. "Slithery."

"Ah." Angela and Stephanie exchanged looks. Grownup looks,

that said so much and was always frustrating for us kids when we weren't part of the conversation.

"Tell her, honey," Pop said. "I think Lanie is starting to have visions. Precognition or something else, who knows?" He put his arm around me. That made it easier to explain what I had seen.

When I finished, Stephanie and Angela exchanged one look, and then they hurried out of the office. The three of us followed. I felt relieved, and yet I felt like crying at the same time. We came out into the lobby. Just down the hall, I saw Mr. Wellington leading the next tour group into the locker room. Angela stayed out in the hallway with her hands pressed against the doorframe, while Stephanie followed them into the locker room.

"Wow." Kurt held out his hands. "Prickly hot buzzing. Big."

A *snap-buzz* sound filled my head, and for a few seconds an ugly greenish glow spilled out of the locker room. I had the weirdest impression that Miss Angela stood there in the doorway to block it. The glow changed, to the same color as the tentacles.

"What's going on?" Pop whispered, as I slipped my hand into his.

"You can't see it?"

"Nope." He squeezed my hand, and I felt like crying.

The *snap-buzz* sound stopped and for a second there was a ringing in my head. The glow vanished, like a door had been slammed shut. Stephanie stepped out of the locker room. Angela linked arms with her and they came back to us. Pop recruited Kurt to help him, and he left me in charge, to watch over the two women when they settled back into the office. Angela looked tired and Stephanie was pale for a few seconds. I wasn't sure what Pop wanted me to do, except maybe just watch them. They were both looking closer to normal when Pop and Kurt came back with a tray of drinks and a tray of cookies and hot dogs.

Stephanie's hands shook as she came close to snatching a hot dog from Kurt. She took two big bites and hardly chewed at all before swallowing.

"You've been through this before?" Stephanie said.

"Something similar, so I know the signs. I'm of the persuasion that God gives us special gifts for specific purposes, and we expend physical energy in the battle of good against evil. So, you need to eat." Pop settled down on the crate next to me and put an enormous cookie in my hand.

"What happened?" Kurt said.

"Neighborlee is like one of those little paper reinforcing stickers that you put on filler paper in a ring binder," Angela said. "Our town is a patch on a weak spot where evil tries to break through. This battle against evil, against invaders that would suck our world dry of all joy and light and life, has been going on for so very long. When nasties try to come into our world, people with extra gifts are raised up against that need, as Charlie said, for a purpose. Stephanie has the ability to, shall we say, throw plaster or tarpaper on the weak spots where things try to leak through."

"Was that it coming through, the tentacle thingies?" I said.

"Something was preparing to penetrate." Stephanie winked at me as she popped the last bite of hot dog in her mouth, chewed three times and swallowed. "It wasn't very happy when I stepped into the room and coated the walls to block it."

"Did you make that green light?"

Angela sat up straight, her eyes getting wider and her mouth flattening into something very solemn. She exchanged one of those looks with Pop, and then asked what he and Kurt had seen during the very brief battle. Kurt reported what he felt, and Pop put his arm tighter around me when he said he didn't see or hear anything unusual, except the two of us reacting to what Stephanie and Angela did. He held me while Angela questioned me on what exactly I had seen.

"It's a bad color," Stephanie said, echoing what I had said.

How exactly could I explain, with an eight-year-old's vocabulary and limited experience, a color that I knew was sick and poisoned and just plain evil, like death waiting to fall on something and smother the life out of it? Yeah, I can find those words now, recording my memories many years after the fact. But back then? Not so easy.

"For me, it's a smell, and sometimes I get vibrations like Kurt. Ford has dreams, most of the time, that help us pinpoint where something might emerge. I wonder why he didn't have any warnings this time around," she continued.

"We rarely get warnings all at the same time," Angela said. "You know that. Besides, I am very certain this isn't one of the enemy's regular attempts. It was so easily defeated—" That earned a snort from Stephanie. "All right, more easily defeated than usual, less effort on your part, because it hadn't built up to the usual level of strength and vitriol it flings at us."

"If that's the same monster trying to come through," she whispered. "For all we know, there are dozens, hundreds of nasties waiting to break through. Maybe they take turns, maybe they battle each other to take advantage of the next window of opportunity."

"That may be, but I am encouraged that each time we win the battle of defense, we grow stronger and the barrier we hold up against invasion grows stronger as well. Soon, the nasties will be limited to piercing the wall between dimensions and realms through guile, rather than force." Angela broke the cookie in half and handed it to her. Stephanie snorted again and devoured it. "As I was getting ready to say, I think there was no plan, no preparation to invade this time. All the people here tonight, the excitement of the children, the attitudes and imaginations focused on otherness and all the silly and too-close-to-the-truth stories of Halloween… I think that generated energy to attract its attention."

"So you're basically saying that everybody coming here tonight put out milk and cookies and opened the window and invited the big bad wolf to come in?" Pop said.

That got soft chuckles from both of them, and Angela nodded. "Very succinctly put, Charlie."

"So we can't never have this place like Mr. Wellington was talking about?" Kurt said. "No community center, with gyms and a movie theater and a mechanics club and other things? Because getting people in here will be like bait?"

Angela's smile turned a little sad. She put her half of the cookie down on her lap and held out her hands to Kurt. He responded, putting his hands into hers.

"The most important rule, in this battle you were drafted into before you were born, is that there are no set, concrete rules. Just guidelines. Clues. Patterns to look for and try to follow. Now that one invasion has been defeated, it will be years until something tries to come through at this place again. All we can do is be vigilant and prepared, staying constantly alert and sensitive, and ready to work together." She pressed his hands together between hers. "You are our monster detector. You can feel energy being used, not just among your friends and teammates, but the invaders trying to come through. Early warning is the best defense. Whenever the time comes, those who are part of the defense will hear or see or feel or dream the clues we need. The most important thing is to go on with life as usual, do you understand?"

She waited until Kurt nodded, his eyes big and solemn and trapped in her gaze. "We will enjoy life and we will follow our dreams. We will not let evil make us hide and live in fear, and sit still and die inside, just because someday we might have to battle and we might get hurt. You two did so very well tonight. You helped to defend our town, and this building, and the people who were here tonight, *because you paid attention*. You used the senses the good Lord gave you, and you used your brains and your common sense. The best way to defeat the nasties who try to hurt us is to go on with our lives and live without fear, live with joy, and be ready. Can you do that?" She sighed laughter when Kurt nodded hard, and kissed his forehead.

Then it was my turn. Angela told me to pay attention to what I saw, whether I was awake or sleeping, and very importantly, never try to control the visions I received. They would come when the time was right, when they were needed. Perhaps like the dreams Mr. Longfellow had, my visions were like eavesdropping on the nasties as they made their plans, so I should never think that anything was set in stone. When I told her that I wished I could hear Sylvia Grandstone's thoughts whenever she planned something nasty, so I could warn people to get out of her way, she laughed and hugged me, and told me to think really hard about what that would be like. Then she laughed more when I wrinkled up my face and stuck my tongue out, disgusted by the idea of constantly having Sylvia's whiny voice in my head.

~~~~~

Kurt became nearly obsessive about detecting when one of us developed new talents. To the point Felicity got fed up with his grumbling.

One afternoon in late November, we came back to my house after sledding and enjoying the heavy snow that threatened to continue until mid-summer. Kurt wanted to dive into a new stack of comic books Pop had found. Felicity slapped her little hands down on the stack. She leaned over Kurt, who was sitting down — the only way she could look him in the eye, at that point.
~~~~~

"What do you need a new super power for?" she demanded. "You've got all of them."

Kurt looked at me, visibly clueless. I just shrugged, instinctively understanding what Felicity meant, but a step or two behind in figuring it out.

"It's like wanting to own a bunch of books," she said, stomping back to the neon yellow beanbag chair that was her domain when she was over our house. "What do you need to do that for, when you can go to the library?"

"Oh." He hunched his shoulders and slouched a little in his chair. "Guess she's right, huh?"

"No guessing." I looked at Felicity and crossed my eyes at her. The next moment, we were giggling. Kurt joined us a few seconds later.

After that moment of lucid thinking and five-year-old common sense, we turned our attention to figuring out the limits of our talents, and specifically Kurt's limits. How close did he have to get to us to borrow our specific talents?

By our first Christmas together as a trio, we established, after much experimenting and generating headaches, that Kurt had to be within about ten yards of us to borrow. He also had to be able to see us. Even if we were only separated by a wall, with only five or six inches between us, it wouldn't work. As the years went by, that distance grew to several dozen yards, and Kurt could access without needing to see us. First, he learned to do it with his eyes closed, then on the other side of a wall in the same building, then standing outside and "feeling" for our talent through walls of brick or wood, and even through solid ground. But that was in the future.

Just like with learning to do anything, the more we did it, the better we got, so we took opportunities to practice. Experimenting taught us that some talents were easy to borrow. We didn't have to be using them for Kurt to borrow them. Others, though, had to be active before he could touch on them and borrow them. For instance, Felicity didn't have to be calling the dogs for Kurt to borrow her talent. On the other hand, her EM bursts had to be on the verge of exploding before Kurt could catch hold of the energy she was generating and try to control it. That was a problem, because Felicity's EM energy erupted when she was really scared or really furious, or just plain startled, so she reacted without thinking. When that happened, Kurt didn't have a chance to try to turn it off. The best he could do was try to direct the explosion away from the assumed target. He couldn't borrow my kinda-sorta flying ability unless it was active and could only use my telekinesis at the cost of a massive headache. That didn't mean we didn't keep experimenting and testing. After all, we were still kids. With time would come wisdom, experience, and greater strength.

~~~~~

The first Saturday in December was the annual decorating party at Divine's Emporium. That year, Angela's friends Will and Phil showed up. I learned later their full names were Wilfred and Philomena. They were grownups, but it sure looked to me like they were having a lot more fun than even us kids.

Two odd things about them, that I kept to myself and didn't mention to Kurt or Felicity, because they didn't notice. I didn't ask Angela about them until years later.

First, when Angela handed out the ornaments that looked like miniatures of the Wishing Ball, she didn't give one to either of them. Neither one seemed even a little hurt that she left them out. It wasn't that anyone got to keep the ornaments. The tradition was to make a wish and then hang it on the tree.

Second … I was very sure that both Will and Phil had pointed ears. Not the drastic points like those really bad rubber Spock ears or faerie ears that show up at Halloween for costumes. These were delicate, matched their skin tones, and looked real. Neither of them did anything to make their ears visible, like tucking their hair behind their ears. They didn't make an effort to try to hide their ear points, either.

I hung around them as much as I could, and tried to get close enough to get a clear view, to make sure that I really did see what I thought I saw. Phil caught me staring at her and she just grinned and winked at me, and then she put a finger to her lips to signal me to be quiet. I had the distinct impression she was glad I saw the ear points.

So I didn't mention what I saw to anyone else. Other people were talking and laughing with Will and Phil, a lot closer to them than I got, and nobody seemed to notice.

What else could it be but the weird kind of invisibility or instant amnesia that sometimes seemed to sweep through
~~~~~

Neighborlee? People didn't remember the odd things that had just happened in front of them. Like the girls who were taunting Felicity on the playground never seemed to remember that she had zapped them. Pastor Rocky was talking to Will, and I figured if he didn't see his ear points, either they were invisible to most people or Pastor Rocky wasn't bothered by them. Of course, I knew already he was on the side of the good weirdness that prevailed in Neighborlee.

Besides, Angela attended our church. Maybe not every Sunday, but she came often enough that she had lots of friends among the congregation. I figured her friendship with Pastor Rocky and the leaders of our church was a good sign that the guardians of Neighborlee were on the right side of the war between good and evil.

Bottom line: there was something odd about Will and Phil, and I needed time to figure them out. They were friends of Angela, so they were ... well, I couldn't really say Angela was "safe," any more than Aslan was "safe," but I could be sure they were good.

~~~~~

The three of us had a major run-in with the Grandstone cousins on the sledding hill the weekend after New Year's. They were out to punish the rest of the world because they didn't get what they wanted for Christmas. It was a yearly occurrence.

Kurt had been working in the shop at NCH and with Mr. Longfellow, and developed a sled that steered better than the standard ones most of us had. He also created adjustable runner blades, so that when the snow was really soft and the runners tried to sink in, he could widen the blades. Kind of like snowshoes for sleds. That day the Grandstones attacked was one of those really soft, fluffy snow days. About five inches of it had fallen between the end of school on Friday and when we got up the next morning. The only people able to go down the hill for the first half hour or so were the ones with saucers, because the standard sleds just sank in and wouldn't go.

Mum and Pop wanted to see Kurt's adjustable blades in action just as much as I did. We put the blades Kurt gave me for Christmas on our sled, then picked up Kurt and Felicity and met the Longfellows at the hill. A bunch of kids from NCH came later to join in the fun. Mr. Longfellow had built two sleds, four-seaters,
~~~~~

using the adjustable blades he and Kurt created, and Kurt had his two-seater sled. We got to work having fun. Since the saucer sleds and cheapy plastic toboggans had been going down the hill and packing the snow down a little bit, other people were starting to go down on their ordinary sleds. Nobody really noticed us, other than the way we could weave from side to side, and even make some pretty sharp curves. Then the snow started up again, about forty-five minutes after we got there. Thick snowflakes, big, fluffy, really dry, and refusing to pack. Soon the only people sledding were on the saucers and toboggans. And us.

People noticed, because in a crowd of about fifty people, there were only six saucers and two toboggans, leaving almost two dozen ordinary sleds stranded at the top of the hill. Even through the thick, swirling snow, people could tell the difference. When they came over to figure out what let us sled when they couldn't, that was the start of Kurt's fame as the Handyman. At that time, though, nobody used that name. What mattered was that Mr. Longfellow had a reputation for tinkering and playing with gizmos, so people naturally thought he was the source of the miracle sleds. He set them straight, letting everybody know the adjustable blades were Kurt's idea and Kurt's design. All he had done was provide the tools and materials, and some guidance based on experience.

Kurt and Mr. Longfellow got some tentative orders for the blades to put on other people's sleds, and several people recommended they think about patenting the sled runners, or figuring out something that would snap on over regular sleds. Mr. Longfellow wasn't too interested in making money, but Pop pointed out that it would be a good idea for Kurt's sake, just to protect his invention and keep others from stealing it. Besides, Kurt needed to plan for the future. A little bit of money put in the bank now would grow and pay for college and give him something to start from when he went out on his own.

That was the great thing about Mr. Longfellow. He was always interested in looking out for other people. Plus, the fact he was another Lost Kid created another bond between him and Kurt. Before he left the sledding hill, he and Pop had a battle plan for investigating just what it would take to patent the sled blades. Plus, they wanted to get them into production even before the patent was approved, to take advantage of what remained of the sledding season.

When most of the people on the hill took off to get lunch, the Longfellows left too. They had to go out of town for something. They left their sleds for the NCH kids to keep using, with the understanding that my folks would take them home with us to store until their family returned from their trip. There were maybe a dozen kids from the orphanage, plus me and my folks. We stayed and kept sledding, while other people pretty much gave up and didn't come back after lunch. Even the people selling hot chocolate and snacks closed up the little snack hut and went home, because so few people were there. It was like the hill belonged to the orphanage kids. Mum and Pop didn't really like leaving us alone. Whitney Elbrook was the oldest, at fourteen, and if anything was going to go wrong, it would be when no adults were around. Still, they had errands to run, and it was nearly one in the afternoon, and nobody had had any lunch. Pop ran up the street to Divine's and asked Angela if she would come and supervise, while he and Mum went to see about feeding us.

About two minutes after Mum and Pop left, the Grandstones showed up.

Chapter Fifteen

The first I knew of it, I was climbing back up the hill, dragging our family sled, with Felicity and Gracie Curtis stumbling through the snow drifts behind me. We were all laughing and out of breath and crusty with snow from falling down so many times. While my sled had the adjustable blades, it didn't have the superior steering of Kurt's and the Longfellows' sleds, and one time we completely wiped out. But that was half the fun.

I got to the top of the hill just as the other three sleds were heading down, and there were Sylvia and Reggie and Freddie, scowling and watching from their one-man sleds, which were nearly buried in the snow. The dummies insisted on putting their sleds down in the untouched piles of snow to the far right of the hill, instead of the track that had been worn in the slope by the constant use of our sleds. That was the Grandstones, intent on being different from everybody else, refusing to do what everybody else was doing if they hadn't set the pattern first.

Gracie, who was ten, was usually pretty smart, but even though she saw in two seconds that the Grandstones were stuck in the snow, she wasn't smart enough not to laugh. That got the attention of all three of them. Even people as egocentric as the Grandstones could see that we were sledding successfully. In their viewpoint, it was unfair that others succeeded when they were having trouble. That meant *we* were in the wrong. That meant they had the right to either stop us from having fun, or take away our toys. Reggie and Freddie were older than all three of us. They stomped over, as best they could until they got out of the high snow, and surrounded us. They also knew staging — something that was probably taught to the Grandstones from the cradle. They stood higher on the hillside than us, giving them even more of a height advantage.

"It's my turn now," Sylvia announced, and held out her hand for the towing rope.

Like I was going to hand over *my* sled to her? Especially since this was the same sled we had fought over three years ago?

"Go use your own sled," Felicity said.

Gracie was silent, and creeping backwards to put us between her and the Grandstone boys, even though she was older than me. I found out later she was a regular recipient of the mental torment the cousins put other kids through in school. They pretended to be friendly as long as there was some benefit, like candy, allowance money, or a new toy. As soon as the candy was eaten or the money spent or the toy broken, they turned on their former new best friend. In Gracie's case, she was so smart she was regularly flattered and taunted, to get her to do the Grandstones' homework for them, until she finally got fed up and said no. Then they resorted to tripping her in the halls and stealing her lunch. They went into her desk when she was away from it, ripped up her homework and broke her pencils and crayons.

Other students saw what they were doing, but most kids in their classes either made a habit of looking the other way or refused to get involved. The Grandstone boys were very skilled with their fists, or setting up boobytraps that couldn't be blamed on them without a photo as proof. Gracie had no one to stand up for her, no one to testify to the teacher that she didn't spill glue all over the inside of her desk or that she did bring a lunch but it had vanished. I learned all this later. All I knew right that afternoon was that a girl who was older and taller than me was using me as a shield.

"This is my sled." Sylvia chuckled. "Now."

"Then how come it has my name on it?" I said, and bent down to scrape the snow off the top, so the silver lettering with gold trim was visible against the rich blue background: Zephyr Special.

Sylvia stomped her feet, which didn't have much effect in all that snow. She pouted and turned to Reggie. I made the mistake of looking at him, so Freddie had his opening to lunge and snatch the rope from my hand.

Felicity let out a shriek, but before the subliminal powering-up whine of EM could even start, Sylvia threw a huge glob of snow in her face, filling her mouth and eyes and distracting her. I threw myself down on the sled as Freddie tried to run. If Kurt had created the brake that he had been talking about for the last two weeks, it would have been easy to stop him, essentially jamming a spike down into the snow, until it hit frozen dirt and anchored the sled in place. My weight slowed down Freddie, along with the difficulty of running in the snow. Reggie jumped on me and pushed me off the sled. I rolled a few times, getting snow in my face and down my neck, and my stocking cap came off.

By that time, Kurt had come up the hill with the two first-graders who had been riding with him. He shouted at them and lunged, but he had the same trouble going uphill in deep snow. Sylvia shrieked at him to leave her cousins alone and went screaming, calling for her father. That reduced the numbers of attackers, but I was effectively blind. Kurt was racing after Freddie, and made the crucial mistake of leaving his sled in the care of the first-graders. Reggie grabbed his sled while I was getting to my feet and drying my face.

"Lanie! Fly!" Kurt shouted, as he floundered through deepening snow, only gaining a step on Freddie for every five or six they took.

We had practiced enough that my reaction was automatic, despite our constant recitation of the most important rule: *don't show what we can do, keep our superpowers secret.* I lifted myself just high enough that my boots were on top of the snow. Kurt immediately lifted and he stretched his arms in front of himself like Superman flying. Doggone it. *He* could really fly. That just wasn't fair, because he was borrowing *my* talent, but I couldn't fly like that. Not without a running start, and then it was still more prolonged gliding than actual flying.

In two seconds, he had caught up with Freddie, knocked him off his feet and rolled him downhill, so he kept rolling and getting covered with snow. Freddie screamed like a girl for all that he was ten. I settled down into the snow, but tried to keep myself hovering a little bit so I could move faster as I ran. Kurt and I wasted time enjoying the sight of Freddie whining and floundering through the snow, and continuing to slip and slide, the harder he struggled to get on his feet.

Then Felicity caught up with us, and the two first-graders' shrieks finally got our attention. They pointed to where Reggie was fleeing, dragging Kurt's sled. At least Reggie had the sense to use the packed track through the snow. He was racing toward the adult figure coming through the blowing snow with a little figure in crimson. Sylvia.

"See here, little boy," Mr. Grandstone bellowed, as Kurt caught up with Reggie and snatched at the back end of his sled, to stop him from going any further. "We do not like bullies or thieves."

"Then are you going to spank Reggie and Freddie?" Kurt barked back at him. He dropped down on the end of the sled and grabbed onto the side handles, making it impossible for Reggie to try to tip him off.

"You've got a lot of gall," Mr. Grandstone growled, and stomped up to tower over Kurt. He ignored the rest of us catching up with them. "Of course, what can you expect from the trash that end up at that sorry excuse for an institution?"

Sylvia giggled, wriggling with the intensity of her delight. I knew right then where she got most of the nasty things she and her cousins said about the orphanage kids. From her father. It was clear to me that she had told him Kurt was an orphanage kid.

"At least I don't go around beating up on kids that are littler than me and stealing their sleds!"

"Stealing? Sylvia, darling, did you or the boys steal anything?"

"No, Daddy. These brats tried to steal Reggie's sled. He just took it back. Like you always tell us, we have the right to defend ourselves," Sylvia said, her voice turning into a syrupy coo. Then she stuck her tongue out at us.

Right about then, Freddie caught up with us, bellowing about a dozen kids picking on him and punching him and throwing him down the hill. He staggered over behind Mr. Grandstone and dropped to his knees, gasping as if he had run a mile in two minutes. The melodramatic baby. Through all this, Reggie kept trying to upend the sled and tip Kurt off it. Mr. Grandstone swore at us, and bent down and picked up the sled, knocking Kurt into the snow. Then he drew back his leg to kick at him.

"Hold it right there, Stephen Grandstone!" Angela appeared through the blowing snow with a suddenness that made all of us jump back a step.

Mr. Grandstone stopped so abruptly, he fell. Almost as if something had yanked on the leg he had lifted. He landed on the sled, hard enough that two wooden slats cracked.

"Shall we talk about gall?" She glided over the drifted snow as if she walked on grass. "Kicking a defenseless child? Or how about your nephews, picking on children smaller than them, to steal their sleds? Or how about your spoiled daughter, demanding that the other children hand over their sleds because she doesn't have the intelligence to make her own sled work?"

That got giggles, and I looked around to realize that most of the other kids were gathering around. Mr. Grandstone struggled to his feet, and in the process overturned the sled. The extra-wide blades with the adjustable fins were easy to see.

"What's this?" he said, his self-righteous snarl fading into the same greedy interest I usually saw on Sylvia's face. He stood up, lifting the sled for a closer look at the blades.

"It's mine." Kurt reached for the sled, and Mr. Grandstone lifted it higher and turned around, yanking it out of his hands.

"Give it back," I said, and yanked with my mind.

The sled went straight down, with another loud cracking sound. I used enough force, it broke the slats that had been cracked by his landing on them. That was bad. On the plus slide, the left sled runner slammed down hard into his boot. He hopped away, cursing, earning giggles and gasps from the other kids.

"Thanks," Kurt said under his breath, glancing over his shoulder at me. Then he grabbed at his sled, yanking it out from under Reggie's greedy fingers.

"One for all and all for one," Felicity said, stepping up next to me.

"What did you do to my daddy?" Sylvia demanded, stomping up so she was almost nose-to-nose with me.

"She didn't do anything," Angela said. "Did anyone see Lanie touch the sled?" There was a general chorus of "no" from everyone standing around us.

Sylvia's eyes got big and her face changed from angry red to pale fury, then back to red. She let out a shriek like a tea kettle and stomped away, heading back to the big bulk of car visible through the blowing snow. Reggie and Freddie just stood there, glaring at us. When their uncle got his hopping and cursing under control, their glares turned to smirks.

"I want another look at that sled," Mr. Grandstone said, while limping back over to us.

By this time, Angela stood with me and Felicity on one side of her and Kurt on the other, our sleds safely tucked up behind us, and all the other kids gathering around.

"Why?" Angela said.

"I've never seen anything like it. The design... Who designed it? The money-making possibilities, especially in weather like this. The adaptability. The possibilities. I want to talk to the designer."

"That's me," Kurt said, jabbing his thumb into his chest.

Mr. Grandstone tipped his head back and laughed.

"Pull," Kurt said, leaning forward enough to meet my gaze, and tugging on the scarf that had come unwound from his neck.

Well, duh, I knew he didn't mean *his* scarf.

I pulled with my mind on Mr. Grandstone's scarf. That weird echo feeling inside my head was stronger than it had ever been, showing Kurt was borrowing or piggybacking on my telekinesis. At the same moment, Mr. Grandstone stopped laughing, one hand going to his throat—honest, I didn't mean to choke him, but that was what happened—and he leaned forward so far that he overbalanced and fell. All of us jumped backward and out of his way as he went face-down in the snow.

Kurt went white and stumbled a little bit and I felt kind of twisty-queasy in my stomach and the back of my head. Both of us had pushed too hard, used up too much energy or power or whatever was happening. About the time Mr. Grandstone got up off his knees, wiping the last of the snow off his face, Mum and Pop returned with long trays of hot chocolate and hamburgers.

My folks weren't born in Neighborlee, and they weren't Lost Kids, but they had the parent instinct ten times stronger than anybody I had ever seen. Mum knew the moment they stepped out of the mini-bus that something was wrong. She also had the same ability as Angela, to run in the snow as if it wasn't there. She got over there and down on one knee in front of me and cupped my face between her hands, and she knew I wasn't feeling good. Then she looked at Kurt, and moved on to glare at Mr. Grandstone. Maybe it was just common sense, or a very good, educated guess, that whatever had made us sick, it had to do with a new Grandstone attempt at ruling the world.

Even more important, my folks had a communication link that didn't require telepathy. They proved just how strong and clear it was right that afternoon. Pop called everybody over to get their lunches while the food was still hot, while Mum and Angela bundled me and Kurt and Felicity into the mini-bus, along with our sleds. Pop got hold of the Longfellows' sleds and dragged them over to safety. Of course, it helped that Reggie and Freddie were busy trying to help themselves to the food, and then Sylvia came running, screaming in fury at being left out. Did she honestly think someone was obligated to go over to the car where she was pouting, and offer her something to eat?

Mr. Grandstone stomped over to the mini-bus while Pop was loading the Longfellows' sleds on top, and demanded again to get a look at Kurt's sled. Then he saw the same runners were on the big four-man sleds, and tried to pull one out of Pop's hands while he was lifting it up.

My Pop has got to be one of the gentlest men in the world, but the Grandstones had the amazing ability to bring out the lion in him, and get him to shoot lightning bolts from his eyes. Well, not literally, but close enough. Mr. Grandstone shut up and took a couple steps back, and didn't interfere as Pop finished loading the sled. Pop didn't have to say a thing.

Felicity did most of the talking on the ride back to our farmhouse. Kurt and I were both headachy and in no mood to talk. When we got home, Pop called the Longfellows and left a message on their answering machine to warn them. He and Mum agreed that it would be smart to keep the sleds at our house—all the sleds—just in case. Also just in case, he called Chief Tanner and reported what had happened, focusing on the Grandstones accusing me and Kurt of stealing their sleds. Chief Tanner already knew, because Angela had called him. Then Mrs. Silvestri called to check on Kurt. Some of the other kids had made it home by then and reported that Kurt got sick after Mr. Grandstone and Sylvia and her cousins were picking on us. She got the whole story and agreed that Kurt and Felicity could both stay overnight. She agreed with Pop to ask Mr. Guilderman to put a lock on Kurt's workshop and make extra rounds. Just in case Reggie and Freddie knew that much about Kurt to know about the workshop.

It was a good thing Pop called Chief Tanner. When the alarms went off at the Longfellows' house, in Mr. Longfellow's workshop out back, the Chief was already in the neighborhood. He caught sight of the long black car, the expensive foreign model that only one family in town owned, fleeing way over the speed limit. He didn't give chase. Chief Tanner knew about the booby-traps Mr. Longfellow had set up around his shop and house when the family was out of town, including very messy and smelly bombs.

When Reggie and Freddie showed up in school Monday morning, they still had traces of purple enamel-based paint in their hair.

Stephen Grandstone had a reputation for being a genius in business. After that first encounter with him, we learned that actually meant he was a genius at stealing other people's ideas and twisting the truth to bully people into giving him what he wanted. In this case, he recognized the brilliance of Kurt's invention. He also knew the wisdom in a good defense coming from being on the offensive from the beginning.

I guess that just proved that the Grandstones constantly had something to defend, because they were always offensive.

Chapter Sixteen

Mr. Grandstone proved he had a good eye for inventions and clever things, especially gizmos that would make money. He kept trying to get hold of Mr. Longfellow and even slithered his way into Mrs. Silvestri's office, trying to get in to talk to Kurt and look at the sled runners and the adjustable blades. Nobody was stupid enough to help him, even when he offered some of the older boys at the orphanage twenty dollars each to steal Kurt's sled so he could look at it. His penny-pinching habits tripped him up there. The boys knew better than to take his money, and they reported his offers to Mrs. Silvestri. Then they admitted that if he had offered them fifty dollars each, they might have considered it. Except for the fact that the offer came from a Grandstone.

There was a long, established history of the Grandstones cheating the people who helped them steal from and cheat other people in town. Although, it was often hard to learn about it until years afterward. Most people were ashamed to confess they had let the Grandstones use them, especially when they had ample warning from the stories of previous generations. When Mr. Grandstone asked for help stealing Kurt's sled, those boys were smart enough not to. With the Grandstone history, logic said Sylvia's father planned to patent the design of the runner blades and then accuse Kurt of stealing the prototypes. Even if those boys hired to steal from Kurt weren't really his friends at NCH, most people liked him. More important, even if those older boys hated Kurt, nobody was stupid enough to do something to anger and disappoint Mrs. Silvestri.

Mr. Longfellow got to work and registered the design. Just to avoid a lot of legal problems, because Kurt was underage and a ward of the state, the blade design was registered under both their names. Then, with a big label that declared "patent pending," he and Kurt went to local sporting goods stores and toy stores and offered the blades on a consignment basis. They sold as fast as the shop class at Neighborlee High could make them, and there were even orders piling up.

Kurt's reputation as an inventor and designer and someone smart enough and brave enough to stand up to the Grandstones, even the adults, was made that winter. He made enough money from those blades to set up his own bank account. Once he had the account, he got the idea fixed in his head about saving for the future. He wanted to have a place of his own, to take care of himself when he graduated from NCH. He didn't want to go through the halfway house transition stage of living in the dormitory at Willis-Brooks College, but have an actual apartment. Kurt turned into a saving machine. Correct that. A saving monster.

Felicity and I caught the bug, when we realized the power of money to finance dreams. We needed money for parts for his gizmos, and to furnish our superhero headquarters when we got older. While my allowance was pretty generous, there were still ordinary expenses of growing up to consider. Things like candy and books and comic books and ice cream sundaes at Divine's or Miller's Diner. School supplies beyond the basic necessities, like deluxe colored pencils and scented markers or stickers. All the little bits and pieces that nickel-and-dimed our money away.

So, we got chores whenever we could. Mum was a little leery of me getting a paper route at age eight, going on nine, but Pop thought I could handle it. Especially when Kurt created a catapult that attached to my bike, with a spring mechanism that was powered by the movement of my pedals. I rolled up the newspapers and fed them into the chute. As I pedaled past the driveways, I hit the trigger with my left foot, while my right foot adjusted the angle of the throw. On our side of town, houses were set far enough apart and far enough back from the street I had plenty of practice adjusting my control of the launch height and angle, without worrying about hitting windows, or getting the newspaper on the roof. We had such a low population density that a lot of kids were reluctant to take that route. The *Neighborlee Tattler* came out twice a week. The number of houses that took half an hour of walking in the more densely populated part of town took two hours on my side. Before Kurt got to work inventing.

After a month of delivering just to our street and the two on either side of us, Kurt's newspaper catapult made it possible for me to take on two more routes. Plus, he made some more money by selling the catapult to other kids who delivered for the *Tattler*, when they saw how well it worked for me. And yes, Mr. Longfellow took care of applying for a patent for the catapult. Some of the other once- and twice-weekly newspapers in the county were interested in it, because they depended on kids to deliver for them. Fewer carriers to deal with, faster delivery times, more money per carrier with less work or time taken out of each kid's day all added up to a pretty popular concept.

Funny thing was that the big, daily newspapers weren't interested. They had adults delivering for them. The numbers made it economically feasible for them to use cars and drive down the street, tossing the newspapers from their cars or jamming into the personalized newspaper boxes. I knew better than to try to put the *Tattler* in those boxes on my route. The boy who had the route before me quit after one rainy day when he did that. He was bombarded by calls from his customers, complaining that the man who had the route for the daily paper followed the boy about five houses behind him and pulled the *Tattler* out of the boxes. Not only did he pull our newspapers out of the box, but he threw them in the ditch full of running water.

After only a month of practice, I got pretty good with the catapult so that I could get the newspapers up onto the porch. That meant my customers got the paper on their doorstep, under the shelter of the porch. They didn't have to walk down their long driveways, sometimes in the rain, and pull the newspaper out of the box, like they did with the daily newspaper. They also didn't have to deal with the plastic sleeve.

So, by the end of the summer, Kurt had more money coming in, and I was ready to set up my own bank account. Since Neighborlee did a good job of clearing the streets, even with the worst that Northeast Ohio winter weather could throw at us, I rode my bike and used the catapult on all but the worst snowy winter mornings. Kurt kept joking about building me a little canopy for my bike, like those bubble umbrellas that were see-through, with a little windshield wiper, also powered by pedaling, to use in rainy weather. I knew he was joking because he never got around to actually making it. Kurt wasn't the kind of guy who made empty promises. He always followed through.

Backing up the story a little bit: That spring, we learned that Kurt's making-broken-gizmos-work-only-for-him talent had some advantages to it. Namely: keeping people from confiscating or taking credit for his work.

Kurt turned twelve in May, and that meant he was allowed to get chores in town. That took a little bit of pressure off and reduced the pool of NCH kids who wanted to earn allowances, who weren't allowed to go into town to work. Kurt couldn't get a paper delivery job because kids in the residential section of town were more eager to get those routes. There were routes further out on the opposite edge of town, but Kurt would have to bike half an hour or more to get there.

So, he decided to mow lawns. While many people had lawnmowers of their own that the kids could use, most people who hired others to do the work didn't. If Kurt wanted to get clients, and convince them to use him instead of a professional service, he had to provide his own lawnmower. The gas and oil would be the easy part. Getting an affordable lawnmower was difficult.

Well, that would have been difficult for other boys at NCH. Kurt did have his growing savings account. I was paying him five cents on every dollar I earned from the newspaper route, to pay back the materials and his time in creating the catapult. Pop thought that was only right, and I had to agree with him, because Kurt made my job easier and I was earning a whole lot more money, faster. I would have paid him more, but I was also earning commission by bringing clients to Kurt to build them catapults. Yeah, we were learning business principles and life principles while we built up our savings to obtain superhero equipment.

Kurt didn't want to spend his money and wipe out his savings account to buy a new, or even a reconditioned lawnmower. He went to the junkyard and got the pieces and parts of five different lawnmowers. He spent more money on the spray paint to spiff up his Frankenstein lawnmower creation, and the supplies at the stationery store to design and print up his business cards, than he did for the pieces and parts. Then he had me and Felicity do some research on combustion engines and the owners' manuals of a dozen different models of lawnmowers.

Here was where Kurt's genius came out. For the first time, he *deliberately* created a gizmo that nobody else could use. Most of the time, he would create something cool and it worked perfectly, until he let someone else try it. Then something would go wrong half the time, or something would break, or the invention would just plain refuse to work when he wasn't touching it, or within twenty feet. Kurt spent more time figuring out what was missing or stuck and making it work for other people than he did coming up with the design in the first place.

Mr. Pucket, the shop teacher at Neighborlee High, who also taught beginner's shop one day a week at the middle school, didn't know if Kurt was just lucky or a troublemaker. While something he made for class worked when he was using it, often it wouldn't work for Mr. Pucket. Or what was even more mystifying for him, an examination of the inner workings would prove to anyone with engineering knowledge that it couldn't possibly work, period. Yet Kurt always made it work.

Fortunately, Mr. Pucket was born and raised in Neighborlee, not like some of our teachers, who came from surrounding communities. He knew to work around some of the things that would make outsiders scratch their heads and wonder if they needed to get their glasses checked or change their prescriptions. Mr. Pucket went to Mr. Longfellow, and the two of them were giving Kurt engineering books and tutoring way above his grade level. They knew genius and talent when they saw it.

All this was pointing Kurt toward a very lucrative career as a repairman and inventor, and custom designer of things that people needed. Despite all that, the spring he turned twelve, Kurt was still mostly frustrated because so many things just refused to work unless he was there, touching them, or at least looking at them.

Pop joked that Kurt proved animism was real, because anything he repaired or built took on enough awareness to refuse to work for anyone but him. In the case of the lawnmower, that worked for Kurt's benefit. He adapted an electronic ignition from one broken lawnmower and put it on an older, sturdier lawnmower, so he didn't need the pull-rope ignition. He widened and lengthened the body of the mower, and installed five smaller blades underneath, instead of one in the center, making it easier to trim into corners. He had a little trouble with the timing of the gears, so the blades would overlap their cutting areas without knocking into and nicking each other, but I swear he enjoyed the challenge. Kurt couldn't get away with discarding the gas tank, but he was able to put a lock on the tank so no one could fill it without his knowledge or permission.

That was very important. Some older boys who had graduated years earlier came back and gave advice and warnings for those venturing out into the "mean streets of Neighborlee" to get their first jobs. The most important warning was to make it hard for others to borrow their tools and equipment without permission, and try to put everything back without anyone noticing. Meaning those who wanted to earn some quick money mowing lawns or doing bike messenger work or delivering papers or pizzas, but didn't want to buy a lawnmower or other gardening tools or a bike or scooter, and didn't want to pay rental. The kind of people who maintained it was easier to ask for forgiveness than to ask permission.

Mrs. Silvestri tried to raise everyone to be polite and responsible and considerate of others. Yet in each generation there were always a few who felt the world owed them, since they were orphans or underprivileged or some other excuse. That attitude always struck me as hypocritical when they applied the "It's my right, because I'm an orphan" excuse for committing crimes against other orphans. So, Kurt's priority was to make sure other boys couldn't borrow (steal) his lawnmower without his permission, and try to cover their tracks by putting gas back in the tank, so he wouldn't guess what had happened.

Along with the lock on the gas tank, Kurt installed a dead battery on the lawnmower. Then he made it nearly impossible to remove without causing damage to the casing or using special tools. Even if they managed to take the lawnmower while there was gas remaining in the tank from the last time Kurt mowed, they wouldn't be able to start it. Only he could. With just a firm grip on the controls built into the handle.

What was really cool was that without even intending to, and without using parts from a lawnmower that had the equipment for it, Kurt made his lawnmower self-propelling. So all he had to do was hold onto the handle and steer. It moved ahead for him, going up hills without any effort. Felicity and I thought that was the absolutely coolest thing we had ever seen. Yes, we got a chance several times to see Kurt's lawnmower in action. On the really big jobs, we came along and earned money by helping to sweep the clippings off driveways and sidewalks and empty the collection bag in the compost heaps or garbage cans. Kurt was nice like that, giving Felicity a chance to earn some money of her own, even though she was only six.

We had proof that he wasn't being totally paranoid about his lawnmower, and deliberately designing it so no one could use it but him. The first time was when he came to Vacation Bible School with me and Felicity and a bunch of other kids from NCH. We walked back to NCH for lunch, and then had plans to go to the pool for the afternoon. We passed a big house that first day of VBS, and saw a bunch of high school and college boys, who had started their own lawn service business for the summer. They were still unloading a trailer attached to someone's pickup truck, and several of them were gathered around a piece of equipment. Someone looked up and saw Kurt walking by, and they recognized him.

"Hey, you're that kid who helps Mr. Longfellow, aren't you?" one of them called. "You're good with machines and things, right? Want to take a look at this?"

He turned out to be the boss of the new company. He was a sophomore at WBC, with two of his buddies, and they had hired a bunch of high school boys to work for them.

Kurt told me later that he had met them a couple times, when he was helping Mr. Longfellow rig a trailer hitch and build a trailer for their lawn equipment. So he recognized them, too, and when he started across the lawn to help, I followed. Felicity kept walking because she had spilled paint on her t-shirt during craft time and wasn't satisfied with how it had washed out. Yeah, at age six she was already worried about fashion and how she looked.

One of the high school boys finished unloading a wheelbarrow full of tools from the trailer. He turned around, saw Kurt, and cursed really loud. Then he dumped the wheelbarrow and cursed some more as he scrambled to pick up the dropped tools. The others gave him one of those, "What's his problem?" looks, and then the boss started telling Kurt the problems they were having. They couldn't open the gas cap to see how much gas was in there, and no matter how much they pushed the electronic ignition, they couldn't even get a hum out of it, much less start it. They had unfastened and refastened all the connectors and looked underneath and couldn't figure out what was wrong.

By that time, they had stepped back from the lawnmower. I

recognized Kurt's lawnmower, because I had helped him paint it. It was really cool, navy blue with red swooshes along the sides and a checkerboard pattern across the front that on closer inspection turned into a bunch of interconnected K's and H's — his initials. I looked at Kurt, he looked at me, and then we both turned to the guy who had dropped the wheelbarrow.

He was one of the older boys at NCH, someone who had just come to live there a year ago. I didn't hang around with the older boys, so I had only seen him a handful of times. I didn't even know his name, just the labels Kurt hung on him. *Arrogant jerk* and *Grandstone-wannabe* were the nicest of them. That last told me all I needed to know about his attitude.

"It works fine." Kurt grasped the handle and squeezed. The lawnmower started up with a roar that turned into a purr — without him bending down to even touch the ignition button.

Then to confuse the team of lawn guys even more, he let go of the handle. That should have stopped the engine right there, because of the safety features built into it. The lawnmower kept purring like a big, happy cat. Well, why shouldn't it, when Kurt was right there? He pointed at the guy from NCH, who was backing away and doing an awful job of it, tripping over the wheelbarrow and then a couple bags of mulch. "This is my lawnmower, and he stole it from my workshop at the orphanage."

Of course, the jerk denied it, calling Kurt a liar. That was the wrong thing to do. I got mad and gave the lawnmower a good hard mental shove, so it rolled toward him. He screeched like Sylvia Grandstone having a snit. Kurt laughed, and he must have kept the lawnmower moving, because it chased the jerk about ten feet before it stopped and the engine died. Then Kurt turned it over, to show his name and address painted on the underside.

We were there for another half hour while he told his growing crowd of admirers how he built the lawnmower. Some of the college guys on the crew thought it was a pretty cool design, with multiple, overlapping blades. Kurt got a job as maintenance man for their equipment. The jerk who stole his lawnmower kept claiming he had permission to "borrow" it from Mr. Guilderman, until finally the head of the company told him to shut up and leave, because he was fired. The deal was that he had the job if he provided his own lawnmower, and since it wasn't, he didn't.

~~~~~

Things quieted down a little bit over the next few years, meaning the Grandstones weren't quite as nasty in school. Once the boys moved on to the middle school, Sylvia didn't have backup during recess or after school for any threats she made during class. Kurt, Felicity and I usually went back to NCH after school, tried to fit in some practice and testing time, and did our homework together before I rode my bike home for dinner. If it wasn't for our regular testing and stretching of our talents, we might have decided that maybe we were imagining things, such as the monsters trying to get to Earth through Neighborlee, and the magic at Divine's Emporium. Just because life was quiet didn't mean it wasn't busy.

My folks took me to Australia, the summer between my fifth and sixth grade years, and we spent it researching aborigine legends and rock paintings. Kurt teased me that I had picked up an accent when I got home just a week before school started. Felicity zapped my portable radio and my cassette player without meaning to. None of us could decide if she was happy to see me, or angry that I had been gone for so long. It took us all of September to get back into our routine and that comfortable sense of unity, us-against-the-world. Felicity had gotten closer to the girls her age and Kurt had spent more time with the guys his age, when he wasn't working and inventing with Mr. Longfellow.

By mid-October, though, we were back in the groove and delighted to discover that Kurt had developed a sensitivity for Felicity's oncoming EM bursts, so he could almost get a grasp on the power and at least try to give it a sense of direction. He could piggyback on her connection with dogs, but there was something about the experience that repulsed him, so he never really tried to control them. We figured it kind of made sense, since he was more in tune with gizmos and machines and mechanical things. I had plenty of solitude, away from spying eyes, and lots of wide open spaces in Australia to practice my kinda-sorta flying. While I couldn't leap into the atmosphere and do all sorts of fancy flying like Superman, I had more control. I could take a running leap and keep going as long as necessary, and I was better at picking up heavier objects and taking them with me.

I wasn't quite up to flying to school. I couldn't go high enough to keep from being seen and recognized by people in town. Besides,
~~~~~

if I got too high, I might get caught on radar by Cleveland Hopkins or the Akron-Canton Airport, or even the Air Force base in Dayton.

My telekinesis was a little stronger, and a little more finely controlled, meaning I could pick up around fifty pounds with my mind and move it around for maybe ten minutes before I got a headache. Or, with something smaller, I could move it for a longer period of time. It was helpful with housecleaning, because I could lift things off the floor and hold them up while I vacuumed, or hold all the items on my desk up in the air while I dusted, and then put them back down exactly where I wanted. One really cool trick that made my parents laugh was my ability to write with a pen or chalk on a surface on the other side of the room. What we would use it for, we had no idea. Of course, we were still kids, so did it matter right then if our talents were particularly useful?

Our theory about a new Lost Kid with superhero powers was dealt a painful blow that year. Kurt was fourteen, I was eleven and Felicity was eight, but there was no one graduating from the baby cottage into the general Neighborlee Children's Home population that fall. We agreed that we might be wrong about thinking someone showed up every three years. Still, it was disappointing.

As later events proved, magic or superpowers didn't always stick to patterns and rules. We blinded ourselves with the rules we made up, and just about the time we had a hint that we were wrong, the opportunity and the person who made us suspicious vanished from under our noses. Well, to be totally accurate, from under Kurt and Felicity's noses. I wasn't around the orphanage grounds enough to be responsible for spotting new members of our ranks.

With the new school year, we had more concerns to take up our attention and energy. For one thing, Sylvia Grandstone and I were moved over to the middle school for sixth grade. Kurt moved to the high school, since he was in ninth grade. Felicity was left behind in the elementary school. None of us liked that. At all. On the plus side, though, Sylvia was still muzzled and subdued because she was even more separated from the backup of her cousins in her bullying activities. We had recess by grades, which meant Reggie and Freddie weren't there to follow through on her threats. Sylvia insisted on wearing shoes with heels high enough to give her nosebleeds, so she had to be driven to and from school. A reprieve for everyone. Sylvia learned not to make threats that she couldn't follow through on. I would like to say that she learned some valuable lessons the next couple years about getting along with people and at least pretending to be nice, even if she hated everyone around her, but I can't.

While I developed the ability to discern if someone was lying to me during eighth grade, it usually required being in physical contact with the person I was testing. Even standing close enough that our bare arms touched was just a little too close to a Grandstone. Not the kind of sacrifice I was willing to make, even in my most altruistic dreams of being a superhero. So I had no idea what Sylvia was thinking as she learned to wear a veneer of politeness and interest in other people's feelings and endeavors. The only thing I could be sure of during that time was that Sylvia learned to be a convincing actress.

So, since the three of us had different school schedules, we didn't meet up to ride to school together. The starting and ending times for all three schools were staggered by about half an hour, with the high school starting and ending earliest. It took us a few weeks to get into a pattern. Usually Kurt went to Mr. Longfellow's shop after school or visited one of the hardware or junk stores. I would go to the library or Divine's. I got into track and basketball in middle school. Once I became the sports reporter for the school newspaper, I went to the *Neighborlee Tattler*'s office after school to turn in the mockups for the next edition, to be printed. When Felicity got out of school, since the elementary school started last and ended last, we headed to NCH or the park, where we could talk and do homework and have some small bit of privacy.

Around the middle of October, most of our energy turned to the biggest upcoming concern: Halloween.

Kurt at fourteen, the big-time high school guy, claimed he disdained costumes. Since he still wanted candy, he agreed to go trick-or-treating. Neighborlee hadn't put an age limit on trick-or-treating yet. He couldn't decide what to be, probably because he was paralyzed by the certainty the other guys in his grade would laugh at him if they caught him working on a costume.

I switched back and forth among Robin Hood, Tarzan, the Green Hornet, and Zorro often enough to be dizzy. Zorro had the coolest costume, in my opinion, so I decided to be Zorro. Plus, no shopping was needed, because I could borrow Mum's old costume, with only slight adjustments.

Felicity had no idea who to be, because she wanted to be so many things. We headed for Divine's Emporium to create a costume. Whatever we found, we knew it would be perfect, because that was always how it worked out, under Angela's watchful eye.

We waited until we had a whole Saturday afternoon to browse and consult with Angela. Besides, we were all so busy with school activities, we hadn't had more than flying visits with her since I got back from Australia. I rode my bike to NCH, and the three of us decided to walk. If we found costumes for Kurt and Felicity, there might not be enough room on the bikes to carry the pieces home. Besides, walking would give us more time for talking. On the way to Divine's, we resumed our new favorite debate: Were we mutants, escaped lab experiments, or aliens? Did we come to Earth in the same spaceship, or separately? We were just kids, but we knew better than to ask any adults, except my parents. While I loved Mum and Pop dearly, they frustrated us because they always came up with more research and possibilities instead of giving us a definitive answer. And wasn't that what parents were for?

Pop sometimes made me want to scream when his semi-standard response was, "We live in Neighborlee, the weirdness capitol of the U S of A. Anything is possible, kids."

Chapter Seventeen

At Divine's, other kids were looking for pieces of costumes, so we couldn't discuss our dilemma with Angela, either. The normal weirdness of Neighborlee meant the things we found kind of coincided with what we were discussing. Kurt found fishbowl-style helmets in a room off the pieces-parts room that he always visited. Three helmets, slightly different sizes. They weren't diving helmets, though they did sort of resemble old-style diving suits. They had grids for speaking and breathing, and little antennae poking up from the back collars, and it was easy to imagine battery packs and radios attached to them, to hang down our backs. At the same time, I found a large variety of jumpsuits in silver-toned colors—pale green, lavender, gray—that would look great as spacesuits. Once I dug them out and started checking sizes, Felicity went running to the room where Angela kept things like boots and hats, gloves, purses, and other accessories. She found tall back rubber boots and matching gloves in enough varying sizes, it didn't take long to find boots and gloves that fit the three of us.

Before I knew it, we had three spacesuits. Felicity thought it was cool and was all gung-ho. I was still kind of leaning toward going as Zorro, especially since I could play with Mum's cool sword all night. To be honest, I really hoped Reggie Grandstone would show up and try to take candy from littler kids, so I could carve a Z into his backside. For Zephyr, of course. Still, being a spaceman was just as cool. We had never done a group costume before, and we weren't quite sure we wanted to. It was one thing for half the town to think the three of us were something of a team, but it was another thing altogether to give them solid evidence. Besides, Kurt was still iffy about wearing a costume. Miss Angela let us put aside our tentative costume selection and for the first time I could remember, we left without having our costumes set in stone.

The spacesuit costumes seemed to nudge us toward agreeing that we kinda-sorta preferred being aliens. Being escaped breeding experiments or mutants of one kind or another kind of had a taint of being not quite right. Like maybe something was wrong with us, and it wouldn't show up until later, or maybe at the wrong time. Being space aliens answered so many questions, because after all, it kind of implied there were more like us. People and places where we belonged and were considered utterly normal. And besides, the thought of a spaceship zipping down from the sky someday and carrying us away was pretty cool, too.

The next day wasn't a visitation day for Neighborlee Gospel Church at the orphanage, so Pop suggested we take Kurt and Felicity out to lunch with us after church, even though neither of them wanted to go to church with us. Both of them felt comfortable enough with my folks to continue the conversation about being aliens. We decided that since we were all found at different times, and not together, maybe we came down in escape pods, or maybe we were sent to Earth at different times to rescue us from something. Chances were good, according to our logic, that maybe our spaceships were hidden somewhere. After all, a descending spaceship might escape radar, but the chances of discovery and capture doubled on the return trip, leaving the atmosphere. If we came by interstellar lifeboats, they might still be in the area. Finding our ships, even if just the wreckage of them, would prove what we were, and answer lots of questions. For all we knew, there would be a means of communication with the home planet or the mothership. That made sense to us.

Mum and Pop just did like they always did when we got off on our tangents of speculation and dreaming. They asked questions and gently challenged our theories and helped us find the gaping logic holes big enough for the *Enterprise* to fly through, and yet avoided controlling our thinking or destroying the fun. And yes, it was lots of fun.

When we decided to focus on seriously hunting for our spaceships, Pop just said, "Where do you plan on looking? Even in Neighborlee, it's good to take precautions. You still gotta be careful not to push people over their weirdness limit and get them calling the authorities."

We thought that over until we came up with a plan. Several things that happened in the next two weeks influenced us.

First, we discarded our spaceman costumes as being too obvious. Kind of like hopeful bank robbers going around in prison uniforms and wearing booking numbers around their necks. Why advertise what we were? Divine's had a whole room full of army surplus gear: clothes and camping equipment, radios and folding stools and cots and shovels and tents, and even more than we could ever need. The camouflage gear really caught our attention. Not only would they make cool costumes, so Kurt wouldn't feel like a baby if someone saw him, but we could wear the pieces other places and times. Most important, while we were exploring the forests and quarries and farm fields around Neighborlee, looking for some signs of our spaceships or alien communication equipment, the camouflage would help us not be so visible. We felt kind of official and grownup.

Next, the youth group at my church had a movie night, and showed *E.T.* From the moment E.T. gathered up the pieces for his communication equipment, to contact the mothership, Kurt seemed to vibrate from the intensity of his concentration. We found an old videotape of the movie at McGill's Drugstore for a dollar. Kurt must have watched just the assembly and attempted communication sequences fifty times over the next few days.

Two days before Halloween, Kurt showed us his newest gizmo, which he called the Intergalactic Telephone. We immediately shortened it to the IGT. Besides sounding really cool and secretive, it also made talking about it easier and safer, in case anyone overheard us.

Then the last event that helped us with our plan, our first foray into getting a definitive answer to what we were — or weren't — was a series of stories over three issues of the *Neighborlee Tattler*, recounting various legends of extraordinary weirdness occurring in Neighborlee through the centuries. They had the story of the tunnels in the quarries that we had heard at a Christmas party at NCH, and hiding escaped slaves in them. Stories of people vanishing in the quarries or around them. Strange lights in the skies in the northwest part of town, the area of the quarries and the Metroparks. There were more stories, including legends of magical people who glowed in the dark or flew without wings or who appeared where lightning bolts hit the ground.

The stories that caught our attention happened in the quarries. Really, it just seemed so logical, in our viewpoint. The quarries were the best place to make our first attempt at contacting the mothership, or maybe the home planet, or at least finding signs of alien technology hidden in the tunnels. There were supposedly hundreds of holes, dug during the years of quarrying sandstone, that had been filled in. Who knew what might be buried in them?

Besides, if we did somehow manage to make contact, where else would a spaceship land? The tunnels were the perfect hiding places for small ships, and there was lots of flat, barren rock to take the weight of larger ships.

On Halloween night, the three of us headed for the quarries on our bikes long before sunset, and long before official trick-or-treat time began. We wore Army surplus gear, and had cameras, snacks, and those nifty Army surplus folding shovels in our backpacks. Other kids in military costumes (camouflage was a very popular costume that year) laughed at us because we didn't have camouflage greasepaint on our faces like them. Tell me, what good would greasepaint do us if we *did* contact aliens?

We set up the IGT, made sure it would keep broadcasting even when Kurt stepped out of range, and headed into the tunnels to do some serious exploring. Just in case anything or anyone came out of hiding, in response to our signal. We had night vision goggles Kurt had made last year for the science fair. He had beat out Reggie Grandstone with his lame volcano that burped red gelatin.

"What's that?" Felicity said.

Kurt took another new gizmo from his backpack. He plugged a car battery into it, making it flash, temporarily blinding our goggles, and give off a rattling buzz.

"Geiger counter." He flashed a grin at us. "Radiation always brings out mutant powers, right? Maybe there was a lot of radiation when we landed."

The quiet of the growing twilight didn't bother us. Not the compressed feeling deep inside the tunnels. Nor the damp and the moan of the wind across blowholes leading into the tunnels.

We explored the easier tunnels, first. The ones that went through sections of rock above ground, and had visible beginnings and endings. Then we explored the ones that took us down, almost entirely below the surface of the ground, that we had to descend into down slopes worn by running water, or steps carved by time, wind, or explorers who had gone before us. We still kept to the ones that were relatively straight, so we could see moonlight through the opening at the other end.

After about an hour, we had explored all the tunnels with their niches and dead-end branches that we were already familiar with. When we came back above ground, full night had fallen, with only a few streaks of sunset gleaming dull crimson on the far horizon. The air felt even cooler than the damp air underground, heavy with the smell of stone. I glided across the open space to check on the IGT, to make sure it was still broadcasting and that no one had come to the quarries while we were underground and interfered with it. We ate our snacks and discussed our strategy. With the damp and chill settling in, we decided our camouflage clothes weren't quite as warm as we imagined. Plus trick-or-treating had started, and we wanted to get some candy. While the Halloween party at the community center would be fun, and we would get some candy there, it wasn't enough to satisfy any of us. Should we take the chance of someone sneaking around the quarries while we were away and messing with the IGT? After all, if we were willing to come here after dark, against all the posted, official rules, what was to stop other people from coming, too?

We agreed to go into one more tunnel, one we had never explored before because it went down far enough that it had several inches of water on the bottom at all times. Then, after we came up the other side, we would decide if we would leave or keep going. Kurt almost left his Geiger counter behind, because it was getting awfully heavy. The wind picked up a little as we took the first of ten stair steps carved in the rock, down into the tunnel.

On the fifth step down, I was positive I heard a soft humming coming from the Geiger counter. The rising moan of the wind made it hard to tell, though, so I said nothing. Felicity said nothing, and she was walking between Kurt and me, with him in the lead. If she couldn't hear anything, then it was probably just my imagination.

At the bottom of the steps, as we started down the tunnel that curved just enough we only caught a bit of reflected moonlight from the other end, the hum got loud enough to be a slight rattle-buzz. Now I knew it was real. It sounded even louder when the wind quieted and all I could hear were our wet footsteps, our too-loud breathing, and the hum of the Geiger counter in Kurt's hand.

"Is it supposed to do that?" Felicity asked, when we stopped at the lowest downward curve of the tunnel, where the walls looked wet even in the green-tinted vision of our goggles.

"Nope." Kurt glared at the green-white readout screen. "I never designed it to…"

"To what?" I demanded. Then I felt the same thing that stole his voice.

The stone under our boots buzzed, almost the same buzz from his Geiger counter. Not good.

My goggles changed to one solid green-tinted mist in front of my eyes. More not-good.

"Uh, Lanie—" Kurt said, as Felicity latched onto my arm with both hands.

"Go!" I leaped forward so we were all jammed together, our arms brushing the walls of the tunnel and wicking up the moisture from the stone. We linked arms and ran.

For a second, a sense of utter doom smothered me, like during dreams where the ground turned to glue and I couldn't run no matter how fast my legs churned. That buzzing in the rock grew stronger. It followed us. The Geiger counter buzzed louder.

My goggles adjusted back to normal, shades of green, showing us the opening of the tunnel, and starlight beyond.

The buzzing in my feet turned audible.

"Fly," I gasped, as we burst out of the tunnel. Felicity lifted both feet, Kurt leaped, and I pushed hard with my mind.

I lifted us hard enough, I got that spike-through-both-temples strain headache, but I was scared enough I didn't care. We flew lopsided, since Felicity didn't push. That moment proved beyond a shadow of a doubt that I couldn't actually fly, just keep going forward, prolonging the momentum and direction from the moment my—our—feet left the ground. I could glide to beat the band, though. I gasped out just enough disjointed words, Kurt understood what my stammering brain couldn't quite get down to my tongue. He latched onto my talent and boosted it.

With him helping, we swooped out over the deepest part of the quarries, where the river had filled it and rangers regularly patrolled to keep kids from swimming. Right then, I was ready to believe monsters patrolled the cold, dark depths. I pulled my legs up, making us wobble, in case something decided we were fishing bait. Anything big enough to see our legs as tasty worms wouldn't have any trouble leaping up twenty, thirty feet in the air and taking us all in with one gulp. No thanks. Not tonight.

When we landed on a plateau above our campsite where we had left the IGT running, it was taking short jumps like it wanted to launch. Kurt didn't build it to move on its own. We heard the same buzzing sound that had come after us in the tunnels, now trying to come up through the rock under the IGT. I looked at Kurt, he looked at me, and I knew we had the same thought. But exactly how did we get down there and turn it off without getting caught? Glide? Yes. Hover? Yes. Fly down there and stop precisely over the IGT, holding Kurt, so he could turn it off? No.

Then I almost laughed, when I saw Felicity down on her knees, gripping an outcropping of rock in front of her. Tiny sparks of anxiety-based electricity caught on the ends of her hair, where it had escaped her cap. When I took off my goggles, to see better in the moonlight, those sparks were pink and blue. I reached across her and tugged on Kurt's arm, pointing at her. He froze, then he tore off his goggles and looked at her. Then he shook his head.

"Why not?" I whispered. That was all the volume I could manage.

"Not strong enough."

He was right. Several other times when Felicity had been so scared sparks came out of her hair, that was all she did, like a slow leak. What we needed was an explosion.

An angry explosion.

Kurt grinned, and I knew he not only got the same idea I did, but he got another idea, too.

"Hey, Felicity. Is that Sylvia Grandstone?" Kurt tugged on her arm to make her look at the shadows beyond our campsite and the bouncing IGT. "Is she trying to take your bike?"

"She better not!" Felicity snarled and clenched her fists and jumped up to her feet. Those sparks got darker, shifting to white and red with increased intensity. Before I could do more than hold my breath and take one step back, an EM burst rose up from her feet in a visible ring—that had never happened before—to shoot out from her chest in a spray of light.

Kurt managed to focus all that angry-frightened energy. The light narrowed into a beam that covered the distance between us and the campsite. It hit the IGT and fried it, just like Felicity's uncontrolled EM bursts had fried so many others of Kurt's inventions. But this time, as glowing pieces flew in all directions, he let out a whoop of triumph.

Felicity's EM bursts were usually unpredictable because they linked with her emotions. We had experimented, but irritating her into a burst was very different from frightening and infuriating her. This was our first moment of real control. Who knew?

We knew better than to sit around and discuss what had just happened. Analysis could wait for later. We had to get out of there. Someone was bound to have seen that burst of light that rose up at least one hundred feet in the air. Who knew what kind of energy readings official, government-type watchers might have caught? With more coordination this time, we linked arms and took a running leap off the plateau, glided over the wreckage of the IGT, and landed just past our bikes.

No buzzing remained in the ground. We were so relieved, we were shaking and giddy. That made it kind of hard to ride our bikes for a few minutes. Fortunately, the road from the quarries that came up into the backside of town was downhill most of the way.

We figured by the time we got there, we would still have half an hour of trick-or-treating. We decided to skip going to houses for candy and go straight to the Halloween party at the still-unnamed community center. There were all those donuts and cider and other goodies waiting to be devoured. We were scared and shaky and had expended a lot of energy, so we needed to refuel.

Just as we came up the park road from behind City Hall, a car pulled out of the municipal lot into the street to block us, and flashed its brights. None of us would have been surprised if scientists in those silver-white radiation suits got out and came toward us.

"Go," Kurt rasped, but Felicity and I put on our brakes and he didn't abandon us.

A lone man got out of the car, a silhouette in a military cap. He stepped in front of the headlights and I recognized Col. Hayward. He crossed his arms and settled on the front of his car and gave me a weary kind of smile, then looked past me. I turned around, and I half-expected to see the glow from the IGT explosion still hanging in the air.

"Those are good costumes, and I dare anyone to prove for sure you three weren't going door-to-door tonight. Army surplus was a popular theme this year." He sighed. "Might be smart to go a few towns away and buy some candy to fill your bags, though. Just as more evidence."

"Evidence of what?" Kurt stepped up in front of me and Felicity. He sounded kind of angry and his shoulders were pulled back like he was trying to look bigger.

"It's okay," I said. "This is Col. Hayward. He's a friend of my folks."

"More important," Hayward said, "I'm a Neighborlee kid from way back. Your folks decided it might be smart to call me, just in case something … more strange than usual decided to happen this year. They thought I needed to know what you were trying."

"Why?" Felicity's voice squeaked and cracked. The headlights dimmed and flared a couple times, and I had an awful vision of her killing the colonel's car.

"There are people who aren't friendly, when it comes to Neighborlee and the things Angela is charged with protecting." He smiled, kind of grimly, when all three of us inhaled and sort of drew back and closer together. "To protect her, I stay away as much as I can, so those unfriendly people don't connect me with her. And now with you." His shoulders slumped a little. "Kids, be careful, will you? Just promise me you'll be careful. They were here tonight, but they went down another road toward that …" He flicked his fingers in the direction of the quarries. "They didn't see you. I'm good at deflection and subterfuge, but you're safer the farther away I am, understand?"

"Yeah," Kurt said. "Thanks."

"We all guard in our own ways. I'm sure if you get over to the town party, Angela will be waiting. She can take over from there." He got up from his seat and looked toward the quarries again. "Now, I need to do my job. It's a good thing I just happened to be here, visiting your folks for some research they were doing for me. Funny how things work out like that, here in Neighborlee."

"Yeah. Funny." He got back onto his bike seat and nodded for me and Felicity to go ahead of him. When he saluted, the Colonel nodded and saluted back.

Later, Mum and Pop told me something very interesting. Col. Hayward was a Lost Kid, too.

While the party was great, that didn't exactly make up for not contacting aliens or finding spaceships. The ruckus when the military showed up by morning made up for it. We were kind of proud of ourselves, to be honest.

There was some arguing between different groups of authorities over who would have custody of the melted, burned, exploded equipment found in the quarries. Chief Tanner came over after everything calmed down, and told my folks what was going on. He apologized when some reporters showed up at our farmhouse. They wanted to know if my folks were there to investigate the rumors of aliens trying to land. Mum laughed and said she and Pop were researching a new cookbook of healing recipes. Then she told them about a bunch of local kids who made a ruckus a week ago, after a showing of *E.T.* Maybe the reporters should go talk to them, and find out who tried to contact aliens? I was watching from upstairs. The reporters looked very disappointed when she told them that. They went away soon after.

After that mess we made, the three of us decided to wait until we were much older before we tried that again. Like, when we had graduated from college. Like when we had hopefully found other Lost Kids with superhero powers. And most important, when Kurt had built a much better version of the IGT, so we could cut the connection if something weird picked up on the other end. Maybe, we agreed, it would be safer to be mutants or escaped experiments.

Because it occurred to us there was no guarantee that all aliens would be friendly explorers like E.T. After all, there were two basic explanations for why we were here without parents or instructions. Either we had been kidnapped, or we had been separated from our homes and families by some catastrophe. If true, then finding who we belonged to might turn out to be a good thing.

On the other hand, what if we were thrown away, sent into exile because there was something wrong with us, or even to punish our families or homeworld? There was an old joke that speculated that Earth was the dumping ground for the universe's lunatics and other rejects. If we made contact, wouldn't that kind of tick off the powerful people who wanted to get rid of us?

Waiting until we were stronger, smarter, with more superhero powers at our disposal, was the smart option.

Chapter Eighteen

With our gazes taken off the stars, we were let with our Earth-bound options. Besides, Kurt was in high school, heading toward fifteen, and that meant a little over three years until he had some big changes in his life. With his savings account and a growing reputation as the guy to come to for stubborn mechanical problems, he didn't have that much to worry about once he graduated from NCH. His options were to take college classes year-round and live in the dorm, get an apartment, or share a house with some other graduates. After sharing a cottage with eleven other boys, Kurt looked forward to having his own place. Choosing his own food, his own clothes, even his own furniture, getting up when he wanted, going to bed when he wanted.

I totally agreed with Kurt's plans to get out on his own. Funny thing, with all the discussions we had about his options, and looking forward to getting out of his cottage and away from his "brothers," I didn't feel any envy. I looked forward to living in the dorms at Willis-Brooks, and maybe going home every weekend. The big part of that was the joy of knowing I had a place to go. I wasn't stuck, like other NCH graduates.

Felicity didn't care. She was eight. She had ten years to look ahead, and it went without saying that if she was in a tough spot, Kurt or I would take her in. She didn't need to think about her future for a few more years. Besides, who knew what the world would be like by the time she hit eighteen?

We did think about what we, as semi-pseudo-superheroes, should do with our powers. Even though there hadn't been any hints of the return of the threat of interdimensional invaders from underneath Neighborlee, we always had the thought in the far recesses of our minds that we were its guardians. Even if we were never needed to do anything spectacular, like Stephanie had done that Halloween, strengthening the weak spots in the walls that kept the monsters out. Guardians didn't have to be limited in their duties to just the weird and wonderful, did we? What about the jerks and bullies who came over the borders into our town from Darbyville or Cutterville, or farther away, like Medina or Akron or Cleveland? People came to the quarries and Metroparks to explore, relax, and to find a private place to make trouble. The rangers and the Neighborlee police were constantly finding abandoned tents, or signs of people camping or having drinking parties in places where they didn't belong, and broken glass and wrappers and labels and chemical bottles. We didn't have to let creeps like that invade our town and make things dangerous for the people around us.

After all, what was the use of having superpowers, even as quirky as ours were, if we didn't use them for good? Angela said we were guardians. So shouldn't we do some guarding?

We were limited to the short time between school and NCH's curfew to learn to be guardians. Still, that left us several hours every school day, and every weekend, when we could be on unofficial patrol duty. After all, everyone around us said, at one time or another, Neighborlee took care of its own. Ever since that run-in with Col. Hayward, we had become much more serious about our superpowers and the responsibilities that came with them. It was about time, as young as we were, that we stepped up and become some of those who helped take care of *our own.*

By the time the Christmas shopping season started, we had worked out a little bit of a routine. Lots of people came into Neighborlee for Christmas shopping and to enjoy the decorations. Our town went all out. Lights and little animated figures in public locations. Music playing in the business district and the Mall. Lighting competitions in some neighborhoods.

Neighborlee had a reputation for being a fun spot just to walk around outdoors and enjoy the sights and sounds of Christmas. We could almost guarantee that snow would be falling at dusk, for that perfect Christmas card look. Most of the stores in town were independently owned, or else parts of very small chains, locally based, so we didn't have big chain stores and big box stores, and the nasty customer problems that came with them. When people knew chances were good the person they talked to about the problem was likely to be the owner, rather than just an employee a dozen steps away from any real authority, they tended to be a little more reasonable.

Yes, we had bullies and arrogant twits in Neighborlee, shoplifters and cheats and vandals, but somehow the everyday nastiness and stupidity didn't rear its ugly head quite as much during the Christmas shopping season. I speculated over the years that Divine's Emporium pumped some kind of magic, or at least a really good, strong aromatherapy that affected moods, into the air, and that protected us. It always smelled good at Christmas in downtown Neighborlee, of hot chocolate and cranberry candles, peppermint and Christmas cookies, and pine trees.

In fact, Christmas trees were a big part of the first real, definable act of "guarding" the three of us performed. Keep this in mind as I tell the story: Every year, civic groups decorated trees in the center of town, a Neighborlee tradition going back to the founding. Another tradition, at any time of the year: Grandstones having a snit if they were not consulted about civic events or given some authority that would make for good press.

Kurt, Felicity, and I went on the second Saturday morning in December to check out the newly decorated Christmas trees. The tree decorating had taken place on Friday during the day, with the various sponsoring groups and organizations taking turns working on their trees. They had a specific schedule so no one would be bumping into each other, and there would be no fighting over the city equipment, like the hook-and-ladder, for getting ornaments and lights up to the tops of the trees. In Neighborlee, we insisted on tall trees, nothing shorter than ten feet. None of the lights had been turned on other than testing the strings, and the official lighting ceremony was set for Sunday night. The trees for Neighborlee Children's Home and Neighborlee Gospel Church were supposed to be right next to each other.

Technically, they still were, but NCH's tree lay pointing into the open grassy area that the decorated trees surrounded, while NGC's tree pointed to the street. The two downed trees were in the center of the line, across the street from City Hall, with the Grandstone tree at the far right end. Remember what I said about the yearly snit.

There had been some snow during the night, but it had started around ten, after the last decorating teams had left, and only lasted about two hours. Enough time to cover the tracks of those who were supposed to be there, meaning all the boot prints walking around the downed trees belonged to people who *didn't* belong there. The little boot prints with spike heels were a dead giveaway.

Sylvia Grandstone boasted about her tiny foot size and wore boots that needed a stepladder to put them on.

We got close enough to see the boot prints and stare in dismay at the fallen decorations. Including decorations we had helped make. We stayed on the curb and didn't disturb the crime scene. At least, we hoped it had been declared a crime scene. We saw no other footprints in the snow, other than the ones going around and around the downed trees. It was just after nine in the morning. Maybe no one had time to react and investigate the scene?

"Chain saw." Kurt gestured at the spray of sawdust in the snow, all around the two-foot-high stumps and the piles of dirt heaped up around where the trees had been set into holes in the ground. Whoever had cut down the trees had pulled up the thick metal stakes that braced them. Those stakes were completely missing. No doubt they would appear somewhere else, used in a nasty trick in the new year.

We speculated for a while how the vandals had managed to cut down two trees in the middle of the night, with a chain saw, without the police noticing. This was the center of town, across the street from the municipal complex, with City Hall, the Fire Department and the Police Department, plus the maintenance garage entrance just around the corner. There were lights on all night. How could someone not have seen?

We decided the Grandstones had had help of some kind. Maybe their minions, the troublemakers at school, had been keeping the police busy somewhere else in town, while Sylvia and her two jerk cousins did the dirty deed. They were the kind of snobs who would disdain to do manual work unless they thought the task that got their hands dirty was fun. Why leave it to their underlings to hurt people, when they could experience it firsthand?

Unfortunately, all that thinking and reasoning led us to one important and disappointing conclusion: while everyone was very sure the Grandstone cousins had cut down our trees, there would be no proof. They would have a dozen people verifying their alibis, and without proof, there was no way to make them pay to replace the trees. Forget about forcing them to apologize publicly. Grandstones went into anaphylactic shock at just the thought of admitting they were wrong and apologizing.

"We gotta do something," Felicity said.

Kurt looked at me, nodded at the fallen trees, and lifted one eyebrow, ala Spock, before tipping his head back and looking upward. Translation: *Can you lift it into place?*

"Keeping it there is the problem," I said, and stepped back, my hands in my pockets. I liked the idea of Sylvia's gloat shifting to frustration.

"Leave that to me." He whipped out the notepad from his back pocket and crossed the street to sit on a bench and scribble ideas.

"I meant get back at Sylvia," Felicity said.

"Can you turn her hair green?"

"Nope." She shrugged. "Just my own. Sounds kind of cool. Maybe braid in red ribbons?"

"Hmm, maybe. Can you zap her braces with an EM burst?"

"Dunno. But I'll try."

We threw ideas back and forth for greater and stranger and more visible punishments, until Kurt finished sketching. Then we got on our bikes and headed back to NCH. Need I say that Kurt had upgraded his light, strong netting that covered bicycle tires, giving the effect of chains to let us drive in snow and on ice? We were the envy of many of our peers. Those who envied us the most called us freaks and weirdos, because only insane people rode their bikes in the winter. A year later, Kurt shut them up by creating blades that snapped onto bicycles, allowing riders to ski and ride their mountain bikes.

We waited until dusk, and not just because our comic books had taught us to hide what we could do. Kurt had to put his tree-mending gizmo together.

Problem: The Service Department hauled the trees away, as we discovered when we returned after dark, at seven that evening. The ground was frozen, so they couldn't dig up the stumps. That left a hole like a missing tooth in the line.

"Now what?" Felicity said.

Kurt shrugged, turned his bike, and headed for the garages behind City Hall. Both trees were there, still decorated. I mind-lifted the top tree, and Kurt and Felicity held up our bikes so the tree lay across the handlebars. Hey, I could not carry it all the way back with the power of my mind—I was only eleven. Talk about killer headache.

When we got there, most of the lights around the area hadn't come on yet. Lots of decoration lights had been hung and were already lit at dusk, but the timer hadn't been activated. Only the trees were waiting for the official tree-lighting ceremony the next evening. We had time to work half-hidden in the thickening darkness, but how much?

The Neighborlee weirdness effect meant nobody saw us at work. Granted, the shopping district was a block away, with city park and office buildings between us and all that traffic, and the tallest office building was only four stories high, with lots of room between them. But seriously? Sometimes I wondered if we generated an invisibility field we didn't know about.

I got the tree upright, but the weight was beyond my strength limits, so the top kept wobbling. That made it hard for Kurt to wrap his metal corset around the cut trunk. Time was running out, so I jumped up and hovered near the top, holding on to keep it steady.

Right then, all the lights everywhere else in the municipal center came on.

"Ten seconds," Kurt snapped, and ducked under the branches.

Felicity ran to the library gazebo with her bike when headlights swept the trees, coming from the City Hall driveway.

I was stuck fifteen feet up in the air, holding onto the tree.

"Kurt!"

Ever try to shout and whisper at the same time? It hurts the throat.

"Almost…there."

Truck headlights swept past me.

Came back.

Passed me again.

Came back and *stayed* on me.

"Kurt!"

"Got it. Let's book!" He rolled out from under the tree, grabbed his bike and mine, and raced across the street. The trees partially shielded him.

I was caught in headlights like tractor beams.

"Lanie!" Felicity looked out from the gazebo. "Run!"

Yeah, right.

"Hey! What the— Bud, you see what I see?" A guy leaned out of the truck and gestured at me.

"Lanie!" Blue sparks shot out of Felicity.

Every light on every plywood figure and decorative house, every bush lining the garden paths through the park area, every streetlight, and all the decorations on City Hall died for about fifteen seconds, with a pop-flash that felt like a percussion cap went off. Forget Sylvia's braces. Felicity zapped downtown Neighborlee. I got out of there before the lights returned.

Then we finally did the smart thing. We told my parents what we were up to.

I learned once again that I had the greatest parents in the whole world. Mum and Pop laughed first. Then instead of calling Pastor Rocky and the deacons of our church, who had started the process of finding a replacement tree to put up and redecorate in time for the lighting ceremony, they helped us repeat the job for our church's tree. That involved getting permission from Mrs. Silvestri for Kurt and Felicity to stay overnight at our house. Then we snuck out at two in the morning. Pop knew the schedule for patrols through town, because he had helped Chief Tanner create a new schedule, to deal with the increased traffic during the holidays. We got the second tree up twice as fast, with Pop helping Kurt and me, and Mum and Felicity got the strings of lights untangled and re-attached to the power. That really freaked out the people who went to the center of town the next day to make final repairs, and discovered they didn't have anything to do.

The story went around town past New Year's, more convoluted with every re-telling: An angel had fixed the NCH and NGC trees.

Seriously? Nobody saw the metal corset Kurt had designed for both trees? Nobody automatically thought of either him or Mr. Longfellow, our resident inventors, and asked either of them if they knew what had happened? Of course, maybe they only thought of Mr. Longfellow, and he told them the truth: he had no idea what had happened.

But still? An angel? I was wearing a dark green parka and a silver scarf. Everybody knows angels wear all white.

That was a typical Neighborlee Christmas.

~~~~~

Because of all the contact I had with the people at the *Neighborlee Tattler*, thanks to delivering the paper, I had the proverbial inside scoop on developing events in town. Some were
~~~~~

just rumors, and some were fragments of the strange and weird and wonderful tales that served as town history. I got the news even before our teachers or the principal, when Sylvia Grandstone ran away from home to join a traveling theater troupe, and her family packed her off to a boarding school in England. The sad part was that I didn't get all the details—or maybe the people at the *Tattler* didn't get all of them—because when my family went to England, I had the misfortune to run into her. Some advance warning would have been helpful.

More important, I heard before everyone else at the middle school that the *Tattler* was going to have a writing contest. The prize was to let the winners become junior reporters over the summer and assist the staff, learn the ins and outs of the newspaper business. I picked the sports reporting category and interviewed my track coach and did a retrospective on our last season, if a grand total of five track meets counted as a season. That junior reporter internship turned into a stringer job at the *Tattler* all through high school, and college. That link with the newspaper became my safety net when I ran into some trouble during Senior Prank Night many years later. In Neighborlee, a good rule to follow is to expect the unexpected, and never make plans that are set in stone. Stone crumbles too easily, and sometimes turns into cement galoshes.

Just as crumbly were the superhero rules we had developed. We got the pattern wrong for predicting when another semi-pseudo-superhero would show up. Worse, the year we were getting ready to turn seventeen, fourteen and eleven, we had proof that enemies moved among us, and we missed the warning signs until it was almost too late.

Chapter Nineteen

Kurt came back from an afternoon visiting junkyards and odds-and-ends stores with Mr. Longfellow, and reported that his mentor was in a bad mood. He had seen something when he was bringing Kurt back to NCH and stopped in the middle of a sentence. Mr. Longfellow just sat and stared out of the side window of his truck, watching something. When Kurt leaned forward to see, he caught just a glimpse of movement. Something dark, a vehicle of some kind. Mr. Longfellow shifted into top gear and was all in a hurry to get Kurt home and out of the truck. He nearly drove away before Kurt could get his crate of parts out of the back. Kurt was no dummy. He threw the crate into his workshop and hauled out his bike and followed Mr. Longfellow. That part was pretty easy, because Kurt had been refining the motors he added to his bike over the years, and could do about twenty-five or thirty miles per hour for a short distance.

Fortunately, most of the streets were residential or business district, so he didn't have any trouble keeping up. Unfortunately, it was a sloppy wet spring day. In Northeast Ohio, a spring day could go from warm rain to snowflakes in the space of an hour, with accompanying winds from the rapid drop in temperature. That afternoon convinced Kurt to stick a crowbar in his bank account and get a car. Still, before he had to give up and head home, he saw enough to satisfy him, and mystify all of us.

Mr. Longfellow pulled up in front of the Neighborlee Arms, the old brick mansion that had a long and checkered past in the center of town, and now served as our hotel. He sat in his truck for maybe ten minutes, giving Kurt time to get into a good position under a store overhang to see where he was looking. The object of his angry attention was a windowless, dark blue van with out-of-state plates. Kurt couldn't get close enough to read the plates, he just knew the colors weren't right for Ohio. Whoever drove the van just sat there, never got out during the short time it sat there, half a block down the street from the Arms.

When the van pulled away and continued down the street, Mr.

Longfellow followed, so Kurt jumped back on his bike and followed, too. The drizzle changed to a downpour, and got colder with every block that passed in that weird chase. Kurt was soaked and had ice forming in the cuffs and collar of his jacket and his hair by the time he came to my house to report. He gave up the chase when the van reached our part of town, where farms took over from the residential area. Once they got out of the residential and business district, the speed limit jumped to thirty-five, and then forty. Kurt's bike kept up as best it could.

Then came the really weird, exciting, and mystifying part, and the reason why Kurt came to my house. The dark van pulled over to the side of the road, in the gravel lot where local gardeners held a farmer's market every Saturday morning from June through September. Mr. Longfellow pulled his truck over, sort of blocking the first driveway into the lot. That didn't do much good, because there were three driveways.

Kurt got close enough to see two people sitting in the van, but between the thickening rain and the overcast sky and the distance, he couldn't make out much more than that. Mr. Longfellow got out of his truck and left the engine running, which showed just how ticked off he was, because normally he wouldn't do something like that. He took two steps away from his truck and jammed his fists into his hips. Kurt felt sure he was going to start yelling. When something riled up Mr. Longfellow enough to yell, it was wise to duck for cover, because whatever it was deserved to be verbally reamed and scorched.

Kurt had ducked for cover into some overhanging trees that didn't have any green of new growth yet, but were interwoven from all the vines and kudzu and other parasite plants that had filled the roadside trees on that side of town. It was enough to put him in shadows, so he was pretty sure he couldn't be seen, and it also gave him a break from the icy rain.

Then it happened. The humming—yeah, *that* humming—rose up, vibrating in the air, and then making Kurt's bike buzz as it picked up the resonance. By this time, we had done enough experimenting, Kurt could judge from the humming just how far away someone was when they used their talent, and he could also tell if Felicity or I were generating the energy. The bubble of power lasted just long enough for him to estimate two people, using their talents, in the van. A loud *bang*. A second *bang*. Mr. Longfellow's truck sort of leaned over to the right. Kurt recognized the sound of tires bursting, and looked just in time to see the back right tire visibly grow—and then *bang*, it went too.

Mr. Longfellow shook his fist at the van as it seemed to leap forward with a visible backwash of mud and gravel, and beat it out of the lot. Kurt left his bike in the shelter of the trees and vines and ran over to help. For a few seconds, he thought Mr. Longfellow was going to yell at him. He just stood there, eyes narrowing, mouth flat with fury. Then he shook his head and closed his eyes and sort of sagged against the side of his truck.

"Well, just be grateful those tires were due for replacing about a hundred miles ago," he said, and lifted up the door for the back cap, and reached in for the jack. Then he shook his head again, let out a soft chuckle, and slammed it shut again. "One spare tire isn't gonna do me much good, now is it?"

"Want me to—" Kurt gestured down the road, where the van had vanished.

"Good boy. Be careful. Those aren't the usual two old..." He shook his head again. "For all I know, there are more than just them, spying on our town, looking for a weakness. It's not just creepy-crawlies from other realities trying to get through, it's people trying to tear down the defenses and reach out. That's something new." He gestured at the blown tires.

Kurt got going, pushing his bike as fast as he could, giving himself a headache to get extra speed from the motor. He got close enough to determine the vehicle ahead of him was the dark van, but then when the road crossed the border into Cutterville, the speed limit went up to fifty and that was it for him.

He got back to Mr. Longfellow's truck just after the third truck pulled into the lot and someone got out to see if they could help. Mr. Longfellow told Kurt to get home and get dried off, and promised he would tell him what was going on later. So Kurt came to my house, since it was only ten minutes away from the farmer's market lot. Felicity was sleeping over for the weekend, and the three of us talked and speculated for a long time.

From that evening's talk, and the little bit of information Mr. Longfellow gave Kurt a few days later, we decided it was time to live up to the label Angela had given us—guardians. All we knew, all Mr. Longfellow knew or guessed, was that the people in the van were not the usual two old men in dark suits who showed up every few years to spy on the orphanage. Maybe they were taking over from the original two old men, or maybe they were someone new, someone else who knew or suspected about guardians and Lost Kids. What did it matter? People in a dark van, watching the orphanage, meant trouble. They might even have been the same people Col. Hayward saw on Halloween night.

Those people, giving off the same hum we did when we used our semi-pseudo-superhero powers, were looking for Lost Kids who weren't careful about hiding their *tricks*. Was it a good thing or a problem that Kurt didn't feel any humming inside the orphanage grounds? Maybe someone was using their talents when he wasn't there to sense it, or their power was so weak and so far away that Kurt couldn't feel it at work.

"Maybe they just practice when they're asleep," Felicity offered.

We both just stared at her for a minute or two, feeling really stupid, and then really proud of her.

That started our nighttime patrols. Yes, we broke a number of rules, like the curfew at NCH and Neighborlee's graduated curfews for children under the ages of twelve, fifteen and eighteen. I'm not going to say that the ends justify the means, but just how could we *get* permission without wasting a lot of time and raising a big fuss, maybe getting all three of us thrown into a hospital? The claims we were making could only come from feverish, hallucinating minds, or maybe someone had put LSD in the water supply for the schools. Right? My folks, Angela, Stephanie, Mr. Longfellow and Col. Hayward would believe us, but we would get them all in trouble if they had to get us out of trouble. We couldn't ask permission. We just had to hope we never got caught and needed to apologize later.

We did one thing right, though. We flew. Nobody, especially at night, looked up. Not without noise or some bright light or movement to attract their attention. With Kurt providing auxiliary controls and sharing energy, the three of us could link arms and fly, and stay up for nearly half an hour before Kurt and I got the headaches that meant we had pushed too far. We also rigged a harness to keep us fastened together, in case our grips slipped.

To be extra safe, we didn't go out and up every night. Every third night, patrolling the night sky over the orphanage grounds, and the roads leading to it. If there were more Lost Kids like us, experimenting and exploring and learning their powers, we had to find them and teach them the rules of survival and staying unnoticed. Fast.

Years later, we learned we were too late. By several months. The only good part in it was discovering that the men in the van that rainy afternoon hadn't got her. Someone else did, months before. It was a little embarrassing, though, during a low population period at NCH, we didn't notice when a girl our age just vanished. In several different ways, actually. In our defense, she didn't live in Felicity's cottage, she was quiet, she was little, she was pale, and she was so caught up in figuring out what she could do—and a little freaked out by it—she avoided notice. Correction: she avoided our notice, but not the two old men's notice.

But that's a story for later.

To be honest, despite the cold, the weather, and a few near misses when someone with powerful flashlights caught us in their beams, and the exhaustion from late night hours, it was kind of fun. We felt like we were doing something good, something worthwhile, and living up to the definition of guardians. Sometimes I wondered if we would have done it any differently if we had gone to Angela for advice, or at least her approval. For some reason, we needed to do it our way, figure it out for ourselves. The rules. The official flying gear: dark, warm, waterproof clothes, hoods, gloves, and Kurt's night-vision goggles.

Maybe we just expected her to know, without being told. Maybe we expected her to tell us if we were making mistakes or doing unnecessary work. How were we supposed to know what Mr. Longfellow and Stephanie, and maybe even Col. Hayward were doing, in their role as guardians? Well, duh, we could have asked. We didn't.

In our defense, we just expected Angela to know, and at the right time, offer advice to suit the situation. Most of the time it was cryptic. We had to think hard to apply it to the events or problems. Maybe that was our punishment for not just going up to her and saying, "Here's what we're doing. What do you think?"

Kurt got his car. Meaning he got pieces and parts from the junkyard and made his own modifications and improvements. There was no law, was there, that said a car on the road had to be a recognized brand? He took the chassis of one car, and then installed parts from probably every brand of car then available on the road — or in his case, in the junkyard. Mr. Pucket let Kurt do all his building and modification at the high school garage, as his self-designed practicum. That meant he earned points toward graduation and a grade with it. Part of the official reason was so Mr. Pucket could keep an eye on Kurt so he didn't do anything dangerous. Plus, he could make sure other boys didn't sabotage Kurt's project, or get in trouble trying to follow his example.

Unofficially, Mr. Pucket confessed he wanted a front row seat for whatever amazing thing Kurt did next.

Kurt made the car work, earned his driver's license, then underwent an inquisition to get his car registration before he could sign up for insurance. We were finally able to take short jaunts just before school let out for the summer, his junior year.

He took his car out of the high school garage and parked it at our house for the summer, to protect it. Rumors said some graduating seniors wanted to "borrow" his car for Senior Prank Night. While some troublemakers just wanted to use a car that didn't belong to their parents, others were jealous and wanted to inconvenience Kurt or embarrass him. Better to get his baby out of harm's way.

When the car wasn't parked in our barn, it was at the Longfellows' house, where Kurt and Mr. Longfellow and Jinx spent long hours tinkering with it. Funny, but Kurt usually chose to walk around town, between NCH and his job at Eckleman's Garage or doing maintenance for two lawn care companies.

Kurt's car really did, legitimately and verifiably, work. Anyone with the keys could drive it. At the same time, his ability to make broken things work when they shouldn't was as strong as ever. For all anybody knew, that Frankenstein's monster of a car was starting to become sentient. What mattered was that despite all the laws of physics, when we needed that car to work, it did.

Several important parts of our growth and training as guardians of Neighborlee had to do with Senior Prank Night, so I need to explain the roots of the tradition.

The Willis twins were the sons of Arabella Willis, the founder of Neighborlee. They graduated from an East Coast college with engineering degrees. The engine that provided power for hauling the blocks of stone out of the quarries and several cutting tools had been malfunctioning for a couple years by that time. There was no manufacturer's name on the engine, so when it started to break down, there was no one to turn to for schematics or an early version of an owner's manual. Various mechanics worked on it through the years and coaxed it to keep going, but time was running out.

The Willis twins came back to Neighborlee, eager to prove themselves. What better way to do that than take apart the engine and put it back together so it worked properly? However, while they managed that, they also moved it to the other side of the quarries, and down two levels. Granted, the new location was more efficient for the expanded boundaries of the quarries, but according to the town records, the quarry manager and foreman were in a state of panic when they showed up for work the next morning and the engine was gone. The twins hadn't *told* anyone their plans.

On a side note, the engine worked almost like new for another twenty years, until a Grandstone who wanted to sell the quarries a newfangled, smaller engine managed to roll a boulder from a high cliff in the quarries and smash the engine, so it couldn't be repaired. He didn't make the sale, despite the forged order form.

Thus began the tradition of harmless, clever pranks performed by graduating seniors. It started out with town natives who returned to Neighborlee, showing off what they had learned. Then when the population had grown enough to warrant our own school district, it shifted to our own high school seniors showing off and giving hints of what they planned to do when they got out into the big, wide world.

Over the years, the "harmless" element got tossed aside, and "clever" turned into sometimes outright stupid. Or bizarre. Such as the year Jinx Longfellow and some of his goofball friends attempted a chemistry experiment in the Metroparks. From what I overheard at the time, it was supposed to be a light display that would keep growing and changing colors, and only last for a few days. Things were hushed up pretty quickly, which was a good indication that something had gone very wrong.

From then on, that little corner of the Metroparks, close to the quarries, was kept cordoned off. People said there was a new pond where there had been solid, rocky soil that didn't let much of anything grow. Rumors circulated for years about the stereotyped military personnel in black government cars who regularly showed up, unlocked the chains across the barricades that stood eight feet tall, with barbed wire on top, and went in to examine the contents of the pond.

Senior Prank Night was always the first Wednesday in June. Nobody could ever give me a definite answer why. It was simply tradition. The rest of the tradition, by the time we showed up, was that it was the senior's last chance to ensure they didn't walk through their graduation ceremony the following Friday.

Kurt's junior year, we went out to the quarries the day after graduation for a picnic, to celebrate the end of the school year, and discuss all the crazy stories going around. Naturally, we talked about the pranks from four teams of seniors, along with the lame solo tricks played by people who either weren't cool enough or crazy enough to be included in the teams. The tricks ranged from simply toilet papering the homes of teachers to an elaborate chain reaction, triggered by the first person to unlock the back door at the high school the next morning. In a series of falling balls, swinging pendulums, water filling pots that raised levers, striking matches, and more, the chain reaction ran around the entire outside of the school, setting off whistles and bells and blowing horns, until finally a confetti cannon went off on the front steps and released a huge tarp holding down three dozen balloons filled with helium, to lift a banner into the air over the school, saluting the graduating class.

That was clever, even if it was messy. The perpetrators of the prank were right there to record it all on video tape, and then helped clean it up. Unfortunately, the idiots who filled the school swimming pool with over two hundred family-size boxes of gelatin didn't show up to help clean up the mess. Remember what I said about the "harmless" quotient being tossed aside over the years.

The hunt was underway for the idiots. They were sloppy enough to put all the empty gelatin boxes in the school dumpster. Chief Tanner and outgoing Principal Hawthorne made lots of noise about getting the boxes dusted for fingerprints, to identify the perpetrators. Not only would they have to pay for emptying and cleaning and refilling the pool in time for summer swimming classes to start in two weeks, but they would have to pay for the fingerprint technicians. Amnesty was offered for those who turned themselves in before that happened. Not that they were actually going to dust for fingerprints. Chief Tanner came over for dinner the day after Senior Prank Night and laughed with us, because the dummies hadn't left just the gelatin boxes, they had left their store receipts. The next idiotic mistake was that they had bought in huge quantities. How hard would it be for store clerks to remember high school kids who bought out the entire stock of gelatin at one time?

We laughed about that, and groaned about the dummies who tried to put a cow on the roof of the elementary school building, the only one with indoor stairs up to the roof. The cow had gotten irritated about halfway up the stairs and sat down on two of the unfortunate pranksters pushing her. They had required a trip to the hospital, but fortunately only came away with bruises, filthy clothes, and much embarrassment.

That day at the picnic in the quarries, I shared with my two co-conspirators and erstwhile guardians of the town what Chief Tanner had said at dinner on Thursday night. Because of the growing population in the schools, meaning an increasing number of seniors pulling pranks every year, the time had come for some of the adults in town to help the police department on Senior Prank Night. Nothing very active. Just patrol the town, ride around the business district, through the Metroparks, watch for unusual activity, and hopefully deter stupidity by being visible. Those on patrol would need to be ready to deal with accidents resulting from bad planning or malfunctions or deliberate sabotage. Some people who couldn't get on a team, or get helpers for their plans, spent Prank Night trying to ruin someone else's prank.

"Yeah, maybe we should have been out on patrol Wednesday night," Felicity said.

"Who would we have stopped?" Kurt said, shaking his head. He winked at me and stretched out on his back.

We had left his car in the remains of the main parking lot of the quarries and climbed up to the highest plateau, where we had an incredible view. All the pits and steep paths, the tunnels and mazes dug in the quest for sandstone, as well as worn by wind and water through the years. Years of experience had taught us to bring a plastic tarp and at least two blankets, if we wanted to be comfortable in our picnic spot. With protection against the damp of the stone, as well as the uneven ground, we had a great location for sunbathing and lazing around, and lots of privacy. No one came to the quarries, so it was like our private playground. Or so we thought. We were so naive when we were in high school.

"Nobody got hurt, and how could we have stopped those jerks who bombed the swimming pool without getting caught?" I said, understanding what Kurt was thinking.

Sometimes I wished we did have telepathic communication, as it would have made our increasing guardian duties just a little easier. Sometimes, like that afternoon, or in other tense or crazy situations, we didn't need it. We knew what each other was thinking, what we needed to do.

Chapter Twenty

"Should we plan on helping next year?" Felicity said.

"Heck no!" Kurt sat up halfway. "Next year is my senior year. I am not spending Prank Night on duty." He grinned at me, then at her, and all three of us laughed. The next moment, we got to work planning Kurt's glorious, record-breaking prank. We had a whole year to put it together, so it was going to be the best ever.

We had so much fun, plotting and laughing, we didn't hear the crunch of gravel under tires, or the rumble of engines when a bunch of what could only be described as junior grade hoodlums and gangster wannabes came into the quarries. We found out later that the acoustics were such that everything we said at normal speaking volume on that high plateau could be heard throughout the quarries.

I managed to see and remember some of their license plate numbers on our way out of the quarries, and gave them to Chief Tanner. When he did a little research, he found out all the drivers were involved in low-level organized crime and drug running. Chances were good they were scouting the quarries that day for a base of operations, assuming, as we mistakenly did, that "nobody comes to the quarries."

Either way, we didn't know we had company, but they heard us loud and clear and came looking, to scare us away. When we realized they were there, they were heading up the steep path to our plateau. We would have been trapped, unable to get off the plateau without jumping. No problem for us, with all our practice in flying as a trio. Yet at the same time a big problem, because rule number one was to never, ever, use our superhero powers in daylight, in public, except for really big, dangerous, life-or-death emergencies.

We were warned when some of our would-be attackers fell or tripped over stones and holes in the landscape as they climbed to the plateau where we were still having a silly, loud good time, plotting Kurt's prank. We heard the stones falling and rolling, and the ones who cursed and the ones who laughed at them. Definitely wannabes, because if they had any experience or common sense, they would have been quieter. Even more evidence they were idiots? They came from nearby towns, but ignored the rumors of what happened to people who tried to make trouble in Neighborlee. They should have known better.

Felicity mind-called some of the wild dogs roaming the quarries and sent them running to investigate. She couldn't exactly see through their eyes, but by age eleven-going-on-twelve, she got impressions from her dogs. Enough to know there were a lot of people approaching us, and the dogs didn't like how they smelled. That was good enough warning for us. We jammed our leftovers into our backpacks and hurried down that one accessible path from the plateau.

The gangsters, bullies, whatever or whoever they were, confronted us on the next level down. Fortunately, the landscape opened up there, and we had lots of avenues for escape.

There were nine of them. Observers might have considered us outnumbered three to one. Our biggest handicap? We were kind of cocky, after dissecting what this year's crop of pranksters had done wrong. We were also feeling pretty good about our superpowers. When the leader of the group started into his evil mastermind monolog, meant to intimidate us, I ignored him in favor of checking our exit routes. That ticked him off, so he devolved into cussing, and not doing a very good job. I had heard better cussing in Australia, from the aborigines and the Aussies.

"Yeah? You and whose army?" Kurt blurted, which just got the others riled up.

Looking back, that was kind of stupid, but like I said, we were cocky. The nine of them must have spent more time on their costumes and posturing than actually learning how to be gangsters. Maybe scouting out the quarries for whatever they were going to do was a test from the big bosses.

"Let's make like Rocky," Kurt said.

"The squirrel or the boxer?" I said.

"Theme song from *Rocky* and the squirrel."

Translation: Time to fly.

Felicity laughed, which meant she wasn't anywhere close to being upset enough to set off an EM burst. With all the chains and piercings in the wannabes, it would have been quite a light show.

The dogs' first howl startled a couple of the gangsters. We ran in those seconds of hesitation.

More howls. Curses thrown at us. Claws scratching on the rocks of the quarries. Barking. Shouts and demands for us to stop. Then screams as the first of the dogs raced up some of the thinner access slopes and trails and collided with the gangsters. We just kept running and didn't look back.

As soon as we were out of sight, around a bend in the road going down to the parking area, Kurt linked arms with both of us. I gave a hard mental shove and he took over, aiming us straight for the rusty, dented remains of the guard rail that was supposed to keep people from going over the edge, straight down to the main pit of the quarries. We went up and over, and for a few seconds yeah, we went straight down. In ten seconds, we were down in the parking area and racing for Kurt's car. Walking, that switchback path would have taken us maybe fifteen minutes.

We landed a little harder than usual in the gravel of the parking lot, which showed that Kurt was just as rattled as me. Felicity was the only one still grinning. That showed how much she trusted us, sure that we would get out of this mess without a scratch.

About three steps later, we realized something. Kurt's car was blocked on three sides by the gangsters' cars. Kurt never parked against the sheer rock wall that towered up over the parking area, so he wasn't completely blocked in.

"You ain't going nowhere!" someone shouted from behind and above us.

I looked back as we reached the car, and saw the gangsters trotting down the trail. That made no sense. They weren't making much of an effort to get down to us before we could escape. Maybe ten, fifteen seconds tops to get in the car, crank up the engine, make a sharp turn, and pull out of there. Did Kurt really need to be careful not to hit their cars?

Kurt pulled out his keys. "No problem. We'll be gone by the time they get down here."

"What if they chase us?" Felicity said.

"We'll take the road that leads up behind City Hall, take them right to the police station before they know where they are."

We all laughed, until Kurt put the key in the lock and something kept the mechanism from turning. By this time, I was on the other side, ready to open the passenger door as soon as Kurt got in and reached over to unlock it. He tossed me his keys and I tried the lock on my side. The same problem.

"Something's jammed in there," he said, pressing his face against the window, and prying his fingertips in to peel back the rubber gasket seal between the window and the slot it slid down in the door. "Opposite of a slimjim."

"Huh?" Felicity was standing next to me, waiting to slide into the back seat, her assigned spot.

"Should have built a convertible," I said.

He screwed up his face at me.

The cursing coming from the gangsters mixed with laughter now. No wonder they weren't hurrying to catch us. They had sabotaged the car before they came up looking for us.

"Duh, duh, duh," I said, and pried back the gasket on my side, to get a glimpse of what had to be blocking the lock. I still needed to see what I was manipulating before I could put my personal whammy on it.

Kurt laughed, that low, nasty sound he could make sometimes when he was really ticked off. A chunk of metal, maybe a quarter-inch thick and maybe an inch wide and five or six inches long, leaped up out of the slot, scratching the window.

I didn't want to take the chance on wasting time by getting in the car and trying to open his door from the inside, so I did a modified vault over the car, only partially helped by my superpower, and looked into the narrow gap in his door. Another, longer bar came out. Kurt snatched it before I could let it drop.

"Get in," he growled, as he unlocked his door. He lunged across the front seat by the time I got around the front of the car and had the door open.

By the time Felicity was in the back seat, Kurt had the key in the ignition and cranked the engine hard. I stopped short when there was no response from his car, whatsoever.

The gangsters were now in the parking lot and sauntering toward us, laughing and saying things I only halfway understood. Kurt growled and turned the key again. He pressed his other hand against the dashboard.

"Come on, baby," he whispered.

"Looking for this?" one of the gangsters shouted, and held up his arm, with something big and mechanical-looking in his hand. He waved it for good measure.

I slammed the door and reached for the seatbelt as I said, "Break all the rules?"

Kurt grimaced, shook his head, and closed his eyes. A strong thrumming went through the entire car, threatening to become discord, and for a second there I expected to see blood come out his ears and nose from the effort.

An answering thrum came from the ground below us. That vibration was familiar enough. It was the same frequency we had felt that terrifying, exhilarating Halloween night when we had tried to "phone home."

Felicity let out a squeak and reached over the seat to grab Kurt's shoulder. A big blue spark erupted where she touched him, and I nearly shrieked myself, positive she had finished killing his car.

Kurt yelped and the car roared into life, almost deafening loud. He jammed it into gear and turned the steering wheel hard, and then grinned at me with teeth bared as we scraped the car to the left and behind us, making a hard right turn, and got out of there in a shower of gravel.

"Zap 'em," he growled as the gangsters shrieked and howled.

Felicity leaned out the window and shook her fists at the ones who tried to chase us. Faint blue and green streaks of light swirled out from her fists and hit the three cars with loud *pops*. Faintly behind us, nearly drowned out by the sound of the racing engine, I heard the screams of car horns. Headlights flashed and died.

We zipped around the first bend in the ramp that led us upward and out of the quarries. Kurt was visibly shaking, his face flushed, his teeth still bared in a fierce grin. His car sounded louder, the engine's song higher pitched than I had ever heard it. Did that come from Felicity's borrowed energy, or from him, boosted by his anger? I shuddered a little bit, knowing just how furious Kurt had to be. It was near-sacrilege for someone to mess with one of his precious gizmos. Especially his car.

"You are one mean drunk, Superman," I muttered.

Felicity squeaked and collapsed in the back seat. She giggled all the way out of the quarries and down the park road straight to the parking lot of the police station. Kurt glanced once at me, let out a gasping kind of chuckle, and his shoulders and hands visibly relaxed. His grimace melted into a shaky kind of grin. He did let go of the steering wheel when we reached the station. I had seriously expected to find dents from his fingers in the plastic.

We sat there for a few seconds, looking at the back door of the police station. Kurt didn't turn off the engine. Considering what I had seen in the gangster's hand, that was probably smart.

"I don't get it," Felicity said.

"Get what?" he said.

"Superman."

"It's an old joke Mr. Kimberly told. Back when we were little. Remember?" I said, and finally gave in to the need to squeeze Kurt's hand. Both our hands were still shaking a little. Whether from the expenditure of energy to rescue ourselves, or the tension finally releasing, who really knew?

"Pretty much," Kurt said. "Basically, these two guys are in a bar and they're both drunk, and one tells the other that the wind in the city is so strong, it'll blow you to the top of the tallest skyscraper. The other guy doesn't believe him, so the first guy takes him to the top of the building to prove it. He jumps off three times, and each time, just before he hits the ground, he zooms back up to the top. So the second guy tries it, only he goes splat. The first guy jumps again, and he lands hard, cracking the sidewalk, and one of the onlookers turns to him and says, 'You're one mean drunk, Superman.'"

"That's…" Felicity sighed and seemed to deflate. "That's kind of stupid. But yeah, I kind of get how that applies." She shuddered a little. "Did we really do what we did?"

"Teamwork." He nodded to me, tugged his hand free, and nodded at the back door. "We're probably gonna get in trouble, but those jerk-alerts aren't smart enough to be scared away. If we don't report them and get the cops to do something, they'll keep coming back and looking for us."

"Sucks, being superheroes," I muttered, and reached for the door latch to get out. Then I had an idea. "The Chief is my folks' friend. He's in the band with Pop. Let me handle it, and you go to Mr. Longfellow and figure out what they did to your car. If we can prove part of their story wrong, even without the evidence they took from your car, maybe things will go easier on us."

In the end, we did get in a little bit of trouble, but that old Neighborlee magic worked in our favor. Plus, we did the right thing by reporting the invaders and admitting our guilt right away. Chief Tanner didn't make me finish telling my story before he got on the radio and called the park service, then sent two patrol cars. The gangsters were still there, cursing and fighting and blaming each other when the authorities arrived. Another mark against them was that they had coolers full of hard liquor and bags of pills and worse, with all the indications they had planned to camp out and get stoned.

A search of their vehicles was justified after a check of their license plates revealed all of them had outstanding warrants for a laundry list of activities. The officers found several guns, lots of ammo, and written instructions for finding an ideal spot to set up a meth lab.

Being heroes helped tone down the trouble we were in for trespassing in the off-limits part of the quarries.

Kurt and Mr. Longfellow found a handful of wires and cables had been ripped out of his car's engine, along with the cap for the radiator, and the carburetor had been removed. His car shouldn't have started, plain and simple.

By the time Chief Tanner drove me over to the Longfellows' to get Kurt and Felicity's part of the story, Kurt and Mr. Longfellow had found enough replacements to fix his car, neatly turning some of the gangsters' counter-claims into a lie.

That was Neighborlee. What was freaky for outsiders was essentially, "So what else is new?" for those of us who lived there.

~~~~~

Kurt's senior year was relatively peaceful. Granted, what was peaceful for ordinary people in other towns did not mean the same thing as it did in Neighborlee.

The Grandstones were remarkably restrained, passing over opportunities to try to take over pieces of the town for the third year in a row. Something was up. Could it possibly be they were learning some sense of reality?

Portia Longfellow had big plans to change the world through the Peace Corps and other altruistic activities, but never found the right guy to chase those dreams with her. She wanted kids, so she had gone to a sperm bank. Just about a year after giving birth to
~~~~~

Athena, she came home, announced that she was a lousy mother and she loved her baby too much to make her suffer, stuck with the wrong mother. She left Athena for Ford and Charlotte to raise and headed for the other side of the world to pursue her goal of making that world a better place. By this time, Stephanie and Ben Miller had a daughter, Bethany, who was the same age. The little girls were best friends from the moment they met in the church nursery. I loved babysitting them both, and often did.

Lenore Longfellow went off to college in England. She became a researcher and wrote huge, scholarly, socially conscious books that exposed injustices throughout all levels of society and cultures. She married a man named Halliday, doing the same kind of work. The Longfellows adored him. On their visit home to prepare for the wedding, he passed the all-important test of Divine's Emporium. Neighborlee not only accepted him, but welcomed him.

The Halliday family, however, were not just rich but pretty much cut from the same cloth as the Grandstones. How Lenore's husband turned out so nice, no one could figure out. I later learned that he was considered the black sheep of the family.

Why am I telling you all this? Portia and Lenore were daughters of a guardian, and even if they didn't follow in their father's footsteps… Let's just say that Neighborlee has claims on its own, as well as takes care of its own. Guardians need to look out for each other, because their stories will all be important in time.

Chapter Twenty-One

My freshman year of high school, Mum and Pop and I headed to Cancun between Thanksgiving and New Year's. I thought it was a little odd, because they were in the final phases of their newest book coming out. Granted, this one was a cookbook, using food as medicine, so there wasn't the usual frantic back-and-forth with galleys and last-minute trips to check details. Those kinds of trips usually entailed Mum or Pop going off by themselves, so I didn't go on three-day trips to Australia or Peru, for example.

I couldn't figure out why my folks were starting to research a new book when the current one was still in production. This was the time they spent in what they called "mental vegetation and recuperation," and all their energy was reserved for doing renovations to our farmhouse, setting up book tours, and just enjoying life.

Col. Hayward showed up at our cottage at the resort nine days after we arrived. The curly-haired, seven-year-old boy who trotted along beside him was our reason for being there.

His name was Jeraldo, but by the time we left the resort to come home, we were calling him Harry. He was one smart little guy — and stubborn — but pretty polite, and cute, so he wasn't really irritating when he insisted that if he was going to live in *Norte America*, he was going to have a *Norte Americano* name. He also insisted on speaking only English. Every time I tried to get him to teach me Spanish, so I could navigate the market and some of the less-touristy parts of town, he turned it into an English lesson. He always laughed, and I guess it was funny. And yes, I kind of liked being a big sister.

That was why we went to Cancun. To adopt Harry. I never got all the details from Pop, but Harry's parents were researchers like him and Mum, and they knew each other from years before. Harry's parents were into much more serious research, and I had the very strong impression that while my folks did occasional work for the military and the U.S. government, Harry's parents were full-time investigators. Maybe even spies. Whatever it was, they had gotten in so much trouble that Harry needed a new family.

If Harry's parents were just facing a hard time and had to get him out of danger, or if they had been killed, or maybe being held prisoner somewhere in South America, no one said. At least, nowhere that Harry and I heard. I knew better than to ask my folks after the first time, when they looked so sad and a little frightened. I decided I didn't want to know.

Col. Hayward knew all the right strings to pull, so that a process that could take years and thousands of dollars only required a couple visits with the right people in Cancun, about six inches of paperwork all stacked together, and a few changes in our plane tickets, so we all could fly home together the day after New Year's.

We got home late in the evening, exhausted from the flight. So the first thing the next morning, we went to Divine's Emporium. We needed furniture for Harry's bedroom, and guy stuff to decorate and make it all his own. Angela "just happened" to have Harry's favorite Latino treats. The hot pepper candy wasn't to my taste, but I kind of liked the *bocadillos* and *plantanitos*, basically, candy made of guava paste, and fried plantain chips. The used furniture room at Divine's "just happened" to have a full set of boy's bedroom furniture; a captain's bed with drawers built into the frame, a desk, and a long chest of drawers. Harry loved it.

He liked building things. Models, blocks, Lincoln Logs, Erector Set, it was all fun for him. We found lots of building toys at Divine's, and all at maybe one-fourth the new price, so we hauled it home for him. Yeah, maybe I was a little jealous, but I remembered how Mum and Pop worked so hard to make me feel comfortable, and like I had come home, from the very first day. Harry Zephyr had a right to make a place for himself, from the moment he came into our lives.

Then something weird happened that I totally hadn't expected. Mum sat me down to explain to me that it wasn't like they didn't like Kurt or Felicity, and I wasn't supposed to feel hurt or anything that they adopted Harry but not my best friends. They did kind of love Kurt and Felicity, it just never occurred to them to adopt anyone else.

Adopt Kurt and Felicity? I never thought about it before, either. They were like my brother and sister, but we didn't call each other brother and sister. I couldn't really think of any time when either of them had tried to hint that maybe my folks should adopt them. I kind of dreaded going to school the next day, when school started up again, and facing my friends. Would they immediately think that my folks should have adopted them instead of Harry? Would they get angry and blame me? Would they put pressure on my folks and on me, to adopt them?

I understood. Mum and Pop adopted Harry because Col. Hayward had asked them. They hadn't sought him out specifically. Adopting him didn't mean they didn't like Kurt or Felicity. To be honest, I couldn't get my head around the idea of Kurt and Felicity becoming my brother and sister.

To my folks' relief—and mine—neither Kurt nor Felicity really said anything about it, except they thought the whole story of adopting Harry was kind of cool. Our cover story was pretty close to the truth. Harry was the son of people my folks knew a long time ago, and when he was orphaned, his guardians asked my folks to adopt him. End of story. No need to explain that if Harry's parents ever got out of their dangerous situation, they would come get him.

Harry thought my newspaper catapult was cool, and he wanted Kurt to teach him how to make things like that. Naturally, that endeared my new brother to Kurt from day one. Harry tried to help me deliver newspapers, but getting up so early, combined with Ohio winters, kind of chilled his enthusiasm. No pun intended. When spring returned, and he had developed a new routine and was more used to his new environment, Harry helped me. Most of his help consisted of just riding with me as I drove the streets of my route, until he got used to riding a bike. Then when he built up some muscle, we attached the wagon with the un-rolled newspapers to the back of his bike, and the catapult was all I had to tow on my bike. That made for a little faster ride, without all that weight. Harry got to be very handy, helping me roll the newspapers and reload the catapult "magazine," so my route went even faster. That meant I expanded my paper route with another neighborhood when it came available. Harry and I split the money. Three years later when I graduated from Neighborlee High and went to college at Willis-Brooks, he took over the route completely.

Our freshman year of high school was the year that Sylvia Grandstone frustrated and frightened her family enough that they shipped her off to boarding school in England. That frightened her cousins into a temporary increase in their intelligence and common sense, so Reggie and Freddie stayed out of trouble of the Grandstone variety. Think the kind of adventures Pinky and the Brain would have gotten into if they were five feet tall instead of being three-inch-tall mice, and aiming at taking over just Neighborlee, instead of the whole world.

Harry made friends quickly enough, especially since his second grade teacher decided during Christmas break that the class would learn Spanish. Everybody wanted to be his friend and get some help learning words that weren't part of the workbook. They got extra points, which they could trade in for treats, like whistles and gum and neon-colored water pistols and stickers, if they learned extra words and then used them during conversation time at the end of the week. Harry picked up his own clique of friends. It helped that a lot of the kids in his class went to our church, so he got to spend time with them outside of school.

Still, Harry spent a lot of time with Kurt and Felicity and me. Despite our "rules of survival," it never occurred to us to hide what we could do and what we were, when my new brother tagged along with us. They thought he was cool and smart, and Harry looked up to them. It helped that he didn't freak out the first time Felicity had an EM burst and fried a radio that some jerk kept turning up to chop-and-liquefy volume during open gym time at the community center.

Harry thought we were just like the superheroes in the comic books. He earned a lot of respect from Kurt when he was able to sit for hours and explain the superheroes in the Spanish-speaking comic books that he had read, and related the storylines to Kurt with only a few pauses to think and translate.

He came in handy when we got to work on gathering up the materials Kurt needed for his Senior Prank Night extravaganza. He was a builder, after all, and offered new ideas and variations. Then he sketched out what he meant, and Kurt liked it. He came in very handy when we went to the junkyard and the scrap heap behind the town service center, looking for pieces and parts. Harry could keep the plans in his head. He had a knack for looking at a piece of wood or metal, or spare parts like wheels and cables, and knowing if they would fit or wouldn't work.

What was Kurt's prank? It was such a huge project, he recruited a dozen other seniors to help the four of us build a track that went around the three schools. When it came to driveways, the track went over them, raised up on bridges. It was all-electric, powered by truck batteries, and the movement of the little one-seat cars along the track generated more power and replenished the batteries. It was like a self-replenishing perpetual motion machine. Only it wasn't continuous motion, because at the front door of each school, Kurt built a mechanism to let people ask for a ride. The cars would stop if there was an empty seat available. They could go from one school to the other, or take a round trip. School started about an hour late the next morning because everybody wanted to ride it, even the teachers. Everybody who was involved in helping to set it up was so tired, most of us were even later getting to school. We worked from about ten at night until four in the morning. Mr. Longfellow and Jinx helped us, Mr. Pucket from the shop class, all the houseparents at NCH, and Principal Wellington.

Kurt's electric train made the *Neighborlee Tattler* and the Cleveland *Plain Dealer* and the *Akron Beacon Journal*. Some millionaire from Texas called that evening, once the train showed up on the national news, when Channel 5 and Channel 8 both covered it. He wanted to buy it. Kurt could have been in a jam if it had been one of those never-should-have-worked inventions of his that died as soon as it got out of his field of influence. Fortunately, the track and the train worked when Kurt stepped away from the main control panel. In point of fact, it worked even after Reggie and Freddie and some of their brainless cronies tried to sabotage it. They failed. Miserably and publicly, and got in a fight over their failures, which was also public. The millionaire paid for Kurt to fly back to Texas with the pieces and assemble it all for him. They made an agreement that if there was a malfunction, he would fly Kurt out to fix it.

Kurt went to Cuyahoga Community College and took business administration classes, to help him set up his own business as a repairman and designer of personalized security systems. That Senior Prank Night established Kurt's reputation in the county, and most of Northeast Ohio. It also solidified the growing sense of competition in the upcoming classes. Jinx Longfellow had started something with his prank, so there was always someone each year who tried to top the previous year's best prank. If not for weirdness or cleverness, then with sheer guts and recklessness.

Bottom line: college didn't have much to teach Kurt about engineering or physics where it applied to machines and such. He read constantly, determined to learn everything possible, all the newest discoveries and theories where they applied to inventing and engineering.

The following year, my sophomore year, was Reggie and Freddie Grandstone's senior year. Reggie had failed so many classes in middle school, he had been held back a year, so he went through high school with his younger brother. The Grandstones held true to form, first fighting the decision of the school board with lawyers. Then they insisted they had *asked* for Reggie to be held back, to support his brother, and also to give him more time to "mature without the usual, debilitating pressure of other high-spirited young men his age."

Common sense said with those two combining their demented creativity and nastiness, we needed to change our night patrols from twice a week to every other night as Senior Prank Night approached.

Two weeks before Senior Prank Night, Gordon Priebe came to me. He was a friend from church, one of the instigators of a Star Trek club at the community center, and in that year's graduating class. I make the distinction here between *class* and *graduating class*, because despite their money and expensive clothes and cars and vacations, Reggie and Freddie had none. Gordon, despite being huge and the head defensive bruiser on the football team ever since elementary school, was a teddy bear. A true gentleman. He planned to take law enforcement classes at Willis-Brooks, and work his way up to detective in the Neighborlee PD.

This was a guy with class oozing out of him. So naturally, Reggie despised him. Guys like Gordon were expected to be the single-digit I.Q. brawn, and guys like Reggie with their manicures and fancy clothes were usually the brains behind illegal activities. However, in a battle of wits, the only way Reggie could win was if he stayed away from Gordon and hired people to fight for him. Of course, Reggie had avoided Gordon since elementary school and didn't make fun of him, so maybe despite the handicap of being a Grandstone, he at least had enough intelligence to be a survivor.

Gordon put to use the things he had learned from years of reading detective novels and true crime books, and working Safety Patrol in elementary and middle school. He asked questions and listened hard everywhere he went. It was amazing how a guy as big as Gordon Priebe—think Godzilla with a shave—could make himself invisible when he wanted to be. He could step into a room, and just by sitting still and appearing to ignore what was going on around him, get people to forget he was there. Then they would relax and talk, and eventually say things they shouldn't.

Gordon overheard enough snickering and things like, "Make them forget Jinx Longfellow," and "Hanson's wimpy Disneyland ride," and "make our mark in history," he got suspicious. He mentioned what he had overheard when he picked up Felicity, Harry and me for our Star Trek club meeting, after a week of listening and putting pieces together. Gordon felt like he should try to do something, but he didn't know what. His summer job with the police department was mostly helping with office work. It didn't give him any authority to arrest Reggie and his gang of idiots, especially when there was nothing definite to use against him.

"So we got to do something," Gordon finished. "What do you guys think?"

I was watching Harry and Felicity, sitting in the back seat. He looked at her and grinned, then leaned forward to rest his arms on the back of my seat.

"Don't make me angry," he said very quietly, his breath tickling the back of my neck. "You wouldn't like me when I get angry."

Felicity laughed, instantly muffling it behind her hand. Harry had found the entire collection of the Bill Bixby/Lou Ferrigno *Incredible Hulk* TV series on video tape at Divine's, and we had been binge watching, sometimes ten episodes every weekend.

We both got his reference, though. If Felicity got angry, or just startled enough, we could blow up whatever Reggie and Freddie and their gang of idiots tried to do. That was if—a big if— there was something electrical involved in the whole thing. Of course, we could use our old standby of flying overhead and dropping water balloons on them. Only in the case of the Grandstone jerks and their friends, water balloons in the past had been filled with ammonia, glue, paint, turpentine, and other noxious substances.

It was amazing and most gratifying, to see what sort of damage could be done with a half-dozen water balloons dropped from fifty or one hundred feet in the air, coating car windshields so bullies heading for mischief couldn't drive. Or we gummed up the works in a bucketful of sand or sugar they were going to pour into the gas tanks of their enemies at school events. Or we settled for just marking them with paint or other smelly substances, to prove they had been in the area after we had been unable to stop them from sabotaging something and fleeing. We had taken to keeping a stockpile of water balloons filled with an assortment of substances in Kurt's car, when we went out on patrol, just in case we needed to "tag" someone.

At our Star Trek meeting, Gordon brought up the problem again. There were only ten of us, in those early days, and we treated the mystery like a landing party mission. We were all in high school, other than Harry, and we all had been the recipients of Grandstone nastiness. So it wasn't hard to agree to spy on them and their co-conspirators and figure out what they were going to do for Senior Prank Night.

Sunday afternoon, Ryan Perkins called to report that Leo McRory, a notorious jerk and bully at NCH, had been snooping around Perkins Hardware, asking all sorts of questions about the pallets of fertilizer. Things like how long people stayed at the store once they closed up for the night, what kind of alarm system they had, and if they had security cameras in the alley behind the store.

Holly Sullivan was in Felicity's class and her cottage at NCH. She was a bookworm to the nth degree, and managed to get a job at the Neighborlee Public Library despite being in middle school. She only worked an hour every afternoon after school, and four hours on the weekends, but she had first crack at all the books that went into the Friends of the Library sale, and the librarians all loved her. She noticed that Freddie Grandstone and his two current favorite henchmen had been spending a lot of time at the library. That was a rare enough occurrence to attract attention. A lot of us were sure Freddie didn't even know what a library was. So Holly went through all the records to find out what books the trio of jerks were investigating.

That was easy enough to do, since the slobs didn't put the books away when they were done, and they didn't know how to clean their hands after they had lunch. Their greasy-grimy fingerprints revealed what pages and chapters had held their attention. They were investigating the history of the quarries, which pits had been turned into fishing holes, which were used as reservoirs, and where dams had been built along the course of the river through the Metroparks area that had been made from the old quarries. Plus, they had looked through more than a dozen books on creating explosives. They even left a book on the copy machine, open to the page on creating a bomb from—that's right—fertilizer.

Gordon and I went to Chief Tanner, to tell him what we had found out. While he believed us, the new generation of Grandstones had a reputation for being more swagger and threat than action. The Chief couldn't arrest them for doing suspicious research, because their history proved they were weak on follow-through.

There was no law against being self-centered, loudmouth, double-standard, whiny jerks. Otherwise most of Congress would have been thrown in jail so many times, there would be a revolving door on every facility surrounding the capital beltway. What the Chief could do, though, was warn the Perkins family about the planned theft, and put the park rangers on alert at the various dams and spillways through the Metroparks, just in case someone managed to get their hands on fertilizer anyway.

We couldn't figure out why the Grandstones wanted to blow up the dams in the Metroparks. It wasn't like there was enough water at that time of the year to cause any flooding. Neighborlee essentially sat on a hilltop, looking down into the park system and the quarries. There wasn't enough water in some of the streams for decent wading, much less swimming. In fact, once the spring rains gave way to early summer heat, the favorite sport of disgusting middle school boys was to find fish that had gotten stranded in the shallows and died for lack of water, to toss the stinking carcasses at any girls who happened to be nearby.

By then, most of the others in our team got busy and had to drop out of the investigation effort. Well, they had final exams to worry about, and homework. Gordon had begun the investigation as a matter of pride, and to prove his instincts were correct. Holly had been tormented a little too often by all the Grandstones and their single-digit I.Q. followers. As the town's preeminent bookworm, she had been threatened and blackmailed, to force her to do their homework. Her glasses had been stolen and broken, along with other nasty tricks. Besides, they had broken library rules multiple times, and if she didn't do something to protect the sanctum of knowledge and learning, who would?

Kurt, Felicity and I talked with Angela about our suspicions. She agreed with us that it would be wise to keep an eye on Reggie and Freddie, because what damage they couldn't do through nastiness and cleverness, they could do through pure dumb luck and stupid clumsiness. We couldn't disappoint Angela, or let down our town.

We met up with Gordon and Holly at the library to keep gnawing on the problem. Kurt got a brainstorm. He grinned at us for a few seconds, then grabbed a piece of paper and started scribbling notes on it.

"The water," he said, without raising his head. "The water level is the key." He sighed, scribbled a few more notes. For an engineer, Kurt had such awful handwriting that I could barely decipher it. Forget about trying to read it upside down. "What can you do if you raise the water level through the whole length of the waterway through the park?"

Chapter Twenty-Two

Holly tipped her head to one side, eyes narrowed, as she studied him for about ten seconds. Then she raised a finger, signaling us to wait, and jumped up from our table in the corner. She ran back behind the shelves of history books and dashed to the other side of the library. Kurt snatched another piece of scratch paper and got to work sketching. By the time Holly got back, he had a rough map of the river through the park.

She laughed and put a big book down on the table next to Kurt. It was open to an official map of the waterways through the quarries and the park system, only two years old.

Kurt compared it to his map. His grin died.

"What?" Gordon said.

Kurt pointed to a square, about a quarter inch away from the big retention basin that had been made from one of the deepest and widest of the quarry pits. According to local legend, that pit had been dug to get massive slabs of sandstone for some ambitious building project in Canada. The architect and owner wanted solid walls of sandstone, not blocks. Slabs ten feet wide, twenty feet tall.

"Oh," Holly leaned closer and even took her glasses off to read the fine print of the map. She stepped back and waited as Kurt shoved the book over in front of Gordon, with his finger just below that spot on the map.

Gordon shook his head, muttering a few words that sounded like Klingon.

"Okay, I get it," Felicity said. "They want to raise the water level so they can ride inner tubes or rafts or something from one end of the river to the other. Sounds kind of dumb. Why couldn't they just ask for help lowering the gates? Okay, sorry, this is the Grandstones we're talking about here. First, they bully someone into helping them with their plan. Then when that doesn't work, they find people to go behind other people's backs and pay them to get what they want."

"Not all the dams are adjustable, for one thing," I said, as a light of understanding finally glimmered, even before Gordon passed the book to me. "They're just high, sloping walls to hold back the water and keep it backed up until it gets to a certain level, then let it spill over. Some of them aren't even official dams, meaning they were built more than a hundred years ago."

I looked at the map, and there it was, laid out and making concrete what had been struggling to come up from the back of my mind. In this case, information I had picked up last summer, when I did an internship at the *Tattler* and helped cover a series of public information meetings on the park system.

"Even if they get away with raising the water level and riding the river from one end to another, there are two big problems in the way," I said slowly, as ideas tangled and fought for dominance.

"Drunkard Falls." Kurt slid the map book over to Felicity to let her look. "If they go over that drop, they'll get pulled under and churned around long enough to drown."

"And if they don't drown…" Gordon slouched back in his chair and rubbed his face. He looked so tired, I had a good idea of what he would look like after ten, twenty years as a police officer, dealing with the resident weirdness of Neighborlee. "There's the water treatment plant and the power station that both take advantage of the force of that water shooting through there. They'll either get sucked into the turbines, or they'll get pulled down and sucked into the treatment tanks."

"Water polluted with Grandstone?" Felicity made a face. I admired her attempt at humor. "No, thanks."

"So what do we do to stop them?" I said, sensing what the others were thinking. "We can't depend on guards at the store to stop them from getting hold of the ingredients for their bomb, and we can't depend on the park rangers to guard all the places where they can blow a wall and let the water out."

"Would it take that long to fix the turbines or the treatment plant?" Gordon said with a sigh.

"Again," Felicity said. "Water tainted with Grandstone? Ick."

"Double ick," I said. We three semi-pseudo-superheroes exchanged looks. Once the law enforcement people did what they could, the rest was up to us.

We were the guardians, after all.

First step: go to Angela and Mr. Longfellow and Stephanie. They supported our theories, and they promised to go to Chief

Tanner and others with the authority to stop disaster striking. They agreed with our tactics, which mostly consisted of watching.

We recruited some people to keep an eye on Reggie, Freddie, and their cohorts. Then Donnie Slocumb got caught trying to steal an inflatable raft from Maynard's, a sort of second-hand store that specialized in sports-related equipment and outdoor gear. Donnie was a Grandstone descendant. Most of the time, the Grandstones had only sons. The majority of them managed to wipe themselves out before they could reproduce. Every few generations, a daughter or two were born. They showed they inherited most of the brains for that generation by convincing their husbands to leave Neighborlee, and most of the time cut off all contact with their brother's family. Well, Donnie's great-great-grandmother broke the tradition. She ignored the "go away, you're not welcome here" ambiance. That meant she and her descendants went kind of stupid nasty crazy.

Which explained why Donnie got along so well with the Grandstone boys, and also explained why and how they got him to do all their dirty work. And why he got caught so often, yet never learned anything. I'm not talking about just nasty stuff, like stealing things and going over to the elementary school playground to beat up little kids to get their milk money. I'm talking dirty work: hauling things, destroying things, sweaty work, dirt-dirty work.

After Donnie got in trouble trying to steal the raft, and was dumb enough to claim that he had paid for it but Mr. Maynard forgot to give him the receipt, Gordon went to Chief Tanner with our theory. Mr. Longfellow had done his prep work. The Chief was ready to act. He sent out requests to local stores, asking for reports on stolen fertilizer and stolen canoes, rafts, kayaks, anything that would go down the river, once the water level rose.

Not a lot of thefts, but a lot of attempts. The Grandstones and their henchmen just didn't learn. It was amazing that they actually got grades good enough to graduate.

All too soon, the first Wednesday in June came. Senior Prank Night. The moron brigade looked a little too excited and smug and satisfied for anyone's taste, but at least they were so busy whispering and plotting and smirking, they didn't cause trouble during the last week of school.

The teachers were all busy following up on rumors and things they had overheard the other jokesters in the senior class planning and plotting. They wouldn't be able to deal with the possible explosion that might still go off in the Metroparks. Chief Tanner and the chief park ranger were getting a little irritated with Gordon by the fifth time he had gone to them with more ideas and rumors he had picked up. They insisted that no one would get into the Metroparks on Senior Prank Night with boats, rafts and trunks full of fertilizer and all the other ingredients for a bomb. Now could he please let the professionals do their job in peace?

"He's right," Kurt said, when we met at Miller's for shakes and plotting. No Holly, this time, since she had to work right after school. "What are we worried about? We've done everything we could, and those guacamole-brains couldn't make a bomb go off even if they did manage to get past the guard posts at the roads into the park. This is your Senior Prank Night, too, Gordon. Are you going to have any fun?"

For the next twenty minutes or so, Gordon just lit up and told us about the elaborate scheme to dress up all the statues in town — bronze and sandstone and marble, indoors and outdoors — in crazy costumes and fake beards and wigs. The statue of Captain Willis was going to get a "bang" flag sticking out of the barrel of his gun. One of the girls on Gordon's team had figured out a way to attach poles to the three statues with horses, to turn them into carousel horses. Despite our laughter, I could sense Kurt's tension and then his sharp relief when Gordon had to leave, to join his team and make final preparations. By then I realized that Kurt had thought of something, and whatever it was would require our semi-pseudo-superhero talents. Which meant we couldn't have Gordon as a witness. He was our friend. We didn't want to fry his brains. Besides, yes, he had the right to enjoy Senior Prank Night.

"What did you think of that we missed?" I asked, as soon as Gordon's wide back vanished around the corner outside.

"All the roads leading into the park," Kurt enunciated with special care. "Just because those roads are being watched, that doesn't mean the roads into the quarries are being watched."

"Because they're chained and blocked," Felicity said. Then she got that "oh, right, duh," look and slumped a little. "Since when do **Keep Out** signs work on Grandstones and their pals?"

"They'll go through the quarries and take those back roads, the really steep ones, to get into the park," I said with a sigh. "What are our chances they'll go over the side and mess themselves over and save us the trouble?"

"Well, someone getting hurt being stupid is also a Prank Night tradition," Kurt said with a shrug. "Any chance they'll find something to blow up in the quarries, and ride that flood of water into the river, oh guardian of all watery knowledge?"

I kicked him under the table, but not very hard.

Our next stop was the archives at the *Tattler*, to get the notes for that very informative series of stories on the park system. It was nice to have an in with the boss, so he didn't even ask me what we were looking for. He just waved in the direction of the archives when I asked, and got back to a phone call that he had certainly looked glad to interrupt, when we walked through the door.

I didn't pull out the map created for the general public. We needed the one compiled from historic records, with notes from geologists and engineers, predicting what would happen or could happen to various rock formations and geologic features in the quarries if there was some cataclysmic change or shock or damage. Say if there was a massive flood, or an earthquake.

Or some idiot detonated some fertilizer bombs in just the right or wrong places.

Just like we feared, there were a couple "delicate" spots in the quarries, in the section where people weren't supposed to go. We were proof that lots of people went into the quarries who weren't supposed to. There were always a few people who genuinely got lost. They could be excused. The ones the park service and police had to worry about were the ones who ignored, stepped over, drove around, or cut through the chains across roads, the barricades, and the warning signs. People with that kind of "you can't tell us what we can't do" attitude turned out to be talented at evading the regular patrols of the park service and the police. The three of us led the list, but in our defense, we never did any damage, and we only went up there to have some privacy and clear skies for practicing our flying or trying to tame Felicity's EM bursts.

The most dangerous, and ironically the most accessible of all those delicate spots, was a place named in local legend as Pickle Falls. It was attached to another legendary spot in Neighborlee's weird history, Black Water Pool. Essentially, Black Water was formed when there was a problem with blasting in the quarries, and a huge section of quarry wall at a high level didn't disintegrate like it should have. Instead, a deep pool formed, filling within a day with strangely black water. Hence the name. The falls were named for a member of the explosives crew who died, or might not have died, in a second attempt to empty Black Water. Legend claimed that Black Water had no bottom. It wasn't too big of a stretch of the imagination to believe that water wasn't exactly water, but came from a not-quite-Earthly source.

Chapter Twenty-Three

In light of the geological studies made while transforming part of the quarries into the Metroparks, Pickle Falls was the best place for the Grandstone band of morons to find something to blow apart and release lots of water. Modern measuring and sensing equipment had determined that a strong enough blast or blow would start an avalanche that could, at least in theory, topple Pickle Falls, and finally, after more than eighty years, empty Black Water Pool. Forget the fact that wiser minds had chosen not to empty Black Water because of the devastating, uncontrolled consequences that might result.

That was something a Grandstone would give up his life for: a chance to change the physical face of Neighborlee, prove he had power, and make a mark on the history books.

Maybe it wasn't very nice or mature of us, but our greatest concern was keeping Reggie and Freddie and the idiots and bullies who supported them from reaching the water treatment plant. Like Felicity said, *Grandstone-flavored water. Ick.* A close second was keeping them from destroying Pickle Falls. While we and maybe half the town were curious about what lay at the bottom of Black Water Pool, and seeing if there really was a bottom, we weren't willing to lose a piece of Neighborlee history and lore. Neighborlee protected its own, and part of that was the weirdness quotient.

Gordon let us know that the police had received a few more reports of canoes and rowboats being stolen. The police weren't too concerned because, first, they were on patrol three times more on Senior Prank Night than any other night of the year. Second, they were on the watch for the Grandstone crew. And third, most of the stolen rowboats and canoes and other smaller watercraft had been recovered within a couple hours of the thefts. Such things weren't that easy to cart across town at high speed, without people noticing them. It was the *most* that worried us. There were maybe eight guys in the Grandstone crew. How many could they fit into a stolen canoe or rowboat or inflatable of some kind? The more idiots who got out on the water, if we somehow couldn't manage to halt their plans, the more bodies we had to try to rescue. And, yes, to be thoroughly mercenary and selfish, the greater the chances of someone realizing who had saved them and how, and our secrets being blown.

It wasn't like we had secret identities or even costumes or even superhero nicknames. Granted, Kurt was generally known as the Handyman, but not for his superpower. When we were either in a silly mood or wanted to rile her, we called Felicity "Zap." The bottom line was that we were safer, more secure, and freer to go about our duties as guardians if hardly anybody knew what we could do or what we had done. That was part of the reason why, other than creating our flying gear with night-vision goggles and hoods, we didn't really pursue the question of costumes. Ninja-style clothes were much easier to cover up than figure-hugging outfits and capes in bright colors with mystical symbols on our chests. We had already decided that masks did more harm than good. After all, who would people look at twice? Someone wearing a mask, or someone who didn't?

Bottom line: protect the secret identity, even if it didn't have an official name or costume or logo.

So that meant trying to be as un-flashy as possible. Which meant avoiding notice. Which meant preventing idiots from doing things that required rescuing.

It was exhausting being a superhero, even just a semi-pseudo-superhero, because of all the prevention and preparation work.

On Senior Prank Night, we joined the patrol of city officials and municipal leaders and teachers who supported the police. Just the knowledge there were adults driving around after dark, or stationed at strategic locations, had an odd effect on the pranksters. Some toned down their pranks, some didn't even try, while others felt freer to take stupid risks, because they knew someone would be there to rescue them. Then there were the ones who took it as a challenge, both good and bad. Good challenges were to be as stealthy, as humorous, and as silly and harmless as possible. Preferably to get so much applause and admiration that when the pranksters revealed their identities and took credit, they wouldn't be required to fork over some cash to pay for the clean-up bill. Bad challenges were the ones who wanted to be as flashy, as loud, as messy as possible, without getting caught. That year, there were just under two hundred in the graduating class, and a lot of parkland, open fields, forests, and municipal property to patrol. The odds of catching everyone and stopping damage or stupidity were fairly low.

Our team didn't care about the people who would soap moronic messages on all the windows of a strip of stores on one street, or hang Christmas lights across the front of City Hall, making it impossible to get through the maze to reach the front door, or set up chain reactions of all sorts of falling objects, or the equivalent of buckets of water — or more noxious substances — over doors. We focused on the Grandstone crew.

That evening we settled in on the highest point in the quarries, where we had a good view of Black Water Pool and Pickle Falls. I made sure to say a prayer of thanks that our generation only had three Grandstones to start with, and Sylvia was out of the picture. Granted, she might return to town in time to graduate with our class, but Sylvia wasn't the type to make much physical effort, other than with her makeup and clothes and hair. Chances were good she wouldn't get involved in Senior Prank Night unless she could talk a bunch of hormone-stupefied guys into doing the dirty work while she claimed all the credit. So we really only had to deal with Reggie and Freddie. Thank You, Lord!

After about an hour of waiting, we developed some doubts about our sleuthing skills and our theory. Twilight thickened, and neither Grandstone showed his arrogant, surgically enhanced face. Nor did any of their minions show up to prepare the way. Kurt had brought the newest upgrade of his police scanner, to follow all the police chatter. It was one-third the size of the previous model, which meant it was lighter, and also needed fewer batteries. He pulled it out of his backpack and plugged in one earbud, to listen. Our confidence in our theory and our preparations fluctuated like a roller coaster when Kurt confirmed that no one had spotted the Grandstone crew anywhere else in the park or the more accessible portion of the quarries. Maybe they hadn't been able to get enough fertilizer and other necessary parts for the bomb? Maybe they had car trouble?

Felicity groaned when Kurt said that. In hindsight, we realized we should have thought of that tactic, and just gone around and sabotaged all their cars during the day. We could have saved ourselves a chilly early June night's watch in the quarries. We had to leave Kurt's truck a good distance away and fly in with what gear we could carry, just to avoid suspicion.

The problem was that, knowing the Grandstone brothers, we were pretty sure they wanted to pull off their stunt in enough light that they would have witnesses, as they rode the flood surge down the river through the park. What was the fun of blowing Pickle Falls if no one saw them riding the higher water? One part of the calculation we didn't take into consideration was that they would be dumb enough to try their stunt in the dark. No one could be that reckless and stupid, could they?

The obvious answer was yes, when it came to the Grandstones and the morons who looked to them for leadership.

The half-moon had just broken free of the horizon. The dark gray of twilight softened back to silver when the poison green convertible Reggie got for his graduation present careened down the last curve and into the gravel field to the left of the pool below Pickle Falls. He and Freddie were the only ones in the car. Before we could revise our theory, Dougie Winslow's filthy pickup truck chugged up the steep drive to the top of Pickle Falls and the small area of flat land around Black Water Pool.

Dougie was another Lost Kid, but didn't have any semi-pseudo-superhero powers, unless being a selfish jerk with a perpetually runny nose was his Clark Kent persona to throw people off the trail. If there was anyone we would have wished on the mysterious two old men in the dark van, or the other men in the dark cars, he was the one. (Of course, knowing what we learned years later, maybe it was a good thing they didn't take him. We totally left out the evil minion portion of the calculations.) The only good thing about Dougie was that he basically left people alone and focused on earning as much money as he could, to buy that truck. He would have been tolerable if he had learned to carry tissues with him and hadn't let the Grandstones draft him as brainless muscle for their schemes.

The pickup truck was visibly heavy with bags of fertilizer and wires and bottles of chemicals and batteries. Dougie and three other guys climbed out of the truck and got to work unloading everything. They consulted several sheets of paper that looked like diagrams and lots of written instructions, when I turned the binocular portion of the night vision goggles on them. The placement of the bags of fertilizer in three strategic spots confirmed our research and theory. Sometimes, being proven right was no comfort.

Down below at the foot of Pickle Falls, another truck showed up, with three canoes lashed in tight to the truck bed. The rest of the gang got to work unloading the canoes, then truck and convertible drove away.

"Darn, no chance of burying that sleaze-mobile under a pile of rocks," Felicity muttered.

"Even if we dared to wait until they put the bomb together," Kurt said, "those meatheads are just oblivious and stupid and stubborn enough to try to drag everything back into place if we move it. And that's if Lanie and I even have the strength between us to mind-lift all the parts into the right place to make the landslide go a different direction. Who says we'd even have the time to calculate the positioning and all that?"

"You don't need time," I said.

The three of us got those stupid grins on our faces. I knew my partners-in-crime-fighting well enough to be sure they had pretty much the same utterly satisfying image in their heads that I did. Bags of fertilizer with the bottles of other chemicals on top, and one or two members of the Grandstone crew hanging off each one while they floated around about fifty feet in the air, as the counters ticked down to zero.

"You can eyeball something within an inch of where it needs to be, and I've seen you calculate the placement of cuts and connections spot-on," I continued. "The problem is that helping these scuzzbuckets give themselves paybacks for the dirt they've done to the entire school ever since Kindergarten would mean letting them wipe out the falls. There'd still be a flood heading down into the park. Let's face it, we're here to save Pickle Falls and Black Water Pool, not Reggie and his moron brother and the lobotomized jerks who follow them."

We laughed, and immediately ducked down, muffling the sound to snickers and snorts, just in case the acoustics worked against us. Everybody was now at the top of the falls, working to set up the bomb piles. The Grandstone crew were making enough noise, setting up the fertilizer bags and other equipment, they probably wouldn't have heard us. Still, people who were arrogant enough to trust entirely to luck and "but it worked that way the last time," usually got some nasty surprises. Tonight was not the night to take the risk of surprises working against us.

We waited, and didn't have long to wait. For a bunch of guys who slouched through high school and only did the bare minimum to get by, all of a sudden they were quick, irritatingly cooperative, knew what they were doing, and didn't pass a task off on someone else. Guys who whined when they were asked to pass out papers in class now heaved fifty-pound bags of fertilizer into place without a whimper, and didn't complain when Freddie, who had pretensions of being an engineer or architect or something highly technical someday, kept consulting the diagram he brought with him, and adjusting the placement of those bags.

The moon had risen about halfway up the horizon. Everybody piled back in their cars and trucks and rode down the curving, steep ramp from the top of the falls to the bottom. Then to add insult to injury, when Reggie climbed out of his car, he had a video camera and tripod. The worst, most aggravating and insulting part wasn't that the jerk-face crew had the foresight to record their prank for posterity. Or at least bragging rights. It was the fact that Reggie had a camera. More specifically, that camera.

Three weeks ago, he had nearly been suspended because of his video camera. Someone noticed grit on the floor of the girls' locker room at school, and then found a hole in the wall tiles near the ceiling. The investigation found a pretty high-tech lens feed in the hole, going back to a video camera in the school furnace room, which was right behind the locker rooms in the gym. The video camera was fancy and expensive, and it wasn't too hard for Gordon to make the right connections and track down the store it came from. Not many stores within an hour's drive that carried something so high-tech and expensive. *Expensive* being the operative word.

While the police and school officials were waiting for the store owners to cooperate and identify who had purchased the camera, the three big brothers of one of the girls who had been in the locker room at the time the setup was discovered followed up on their own suspicions. They found the receipt for all the equipment in Reggie Grandstone's gym locker, and verified that the four numbers on the receipt matched the last four numbers of his credit card.

Reggie talked himself out of suspension by pointing out that while, yes, he had bought the camera and all that other equipment, he hadn't set up the equipment. In fact, he had brought the equipment to school for a project for video arts class, and he was positive that everything was locked up, or should still be locked up, in the storage closet of the classroom. Reggie was planning on being a lawyer someday to solve a constant Grandstone problem of having to replace their lawyers. Constantly. Their clan had a habit of running through lawyers like other people ran through gym socks. In the end, no one could prove that Reggie had set up that equipment, or that it hadn't been stolen from him as he claimed, or even that he had loaned the equipment to the slimebag peeping Toms who had actually done the dirty work.

"That sleazeoid," Felicity muttered, as we watched Reggie and Freddie set up the camera.

Unfortunately, it was well back from the projected line of descent of all those rocks when the falls blew. Proof, maybe that Freddie might just know what he was doing if he ever sought legitimate employment as an engineer?

"He shouldn't have that. How did he get it back? I thought Gordon said the police had confiscated that camera until they could get the prints and compare them and..." A growl of frustration escaped her, rising until it sounded like a steam whistle before she could muffle it.

"Well, money," I said. "Either his father bribed someone or harassed someone until he got it out of the evidence locker. Or he just bought a new one."

"Not fair," she said, crawling forward a few more inches, as if that would give her a better look at the camera. "Three of the girls in my cottage were in the locker room. They take showers every day before and after school, just thinking that sleazeoid might have seen them..."

"Good job," Kurt whispered, and traded grins with me as the first blue and green and silver sparks of energy swirled off the ends of Felicity's hair. More sparks formed little bubbles on the ends of her fingers. He nodded to me, and twirled his hand, gesturing for me to keep things going.

Great. Why me?

"What're their names?" I asked. "The girls in your cottage."

"Amy, Shania, and Liberty."

"Okay, I know Liberty. Dang, she's planning on being a model. I wouldn't put it past those jerk-face Grandstones to sell nude pictures of her to those smut magazines." I blanked for a minute. "Isn't that like…like…violating her copyright? I bet they all feel pretty violated. Like Reggie and the other jerks actually touched them."

That was the right mental image. Felicity flinched and her scowl deepened and the sparks left her hair and fingers and swirled up into the air. Any minute now…

"Time to lift and dump." Kurt gestured at the dark lumps of fertilizer bombs sitting along the top of the falls. Little flashes of red light showed where the timers were ticking down. We couldn't see the numbers from where we were, but Reggie and the others hurried away from the camera, some of them giggling like filthy little third-graders. That was a good sign the bombs were about to go off.

"Gotta stop them now," he whispered, leaning closer to Felicity. "Before they hurt someone else. They're probably laughing about Amy and Liberty and the other girls. Maybe they still have the video tape in that camera. For all we know, they're going to celebrate by looking at film of the girls getting their showers and all that after they watch—"

A shriek built up fast, as the ball of sparks stopped spinning and corkscrewed down through the air, from our watching point to the camera at the side of the falls. At the same time, stray streaks of light arched out and up and blasted the timers on each fertilizer bomb, one after another, *ping-fizz* and *ping-fizz* and *ping-fizz*. Kurt and I clamped our hands over our mouths and just stared at each other, smothering whoops and laughter, while that expensive video camera blew apart in an eruption of sparks worthy of the Death Star turning to dust. For a final salute, the tripod somersaulted up high in the air, pinwheeling three times before coming back down.

We didn't need to be quiet. The screams and curses coming from the Grandstone crew were loud enough to drown out a bomb going off. None of which did. For good measure, Kurt and I held hands and focused on the fertilizer bombs, one after another. I lifted and he attached the steering mechanism to my telekinesis. Two of the three bombs slid backward into Black Water Pool. An odd bubbling went up, and then some fizzing, making me think that the destruction of the timer mechanisms had torn open the bags and maybe punched holes in the liquid chemicals. The third bomb went forward off the falls, spinning slowly through the air as it fell. A few flashes in odd colors and streaks lit the darkness, proving there were leaks, as the tumbling descent mixed the spilled ingredients. Then it hit the pool at the base of the falls with a loud splash and a gusher of water. Maybe that was a delayed explosion, maybe it wasn't, but the entire crew of idiots were stunned silent for a count of ten. Then they started in on each other, cursing and laying blame.

"Time to fly," Kurt said, when Freddie said those magical words:

"Somebody sabotaged us. Somebody's here."

"I still say you should have learned to go invisible," Felicity muttered, as we pulled our lightweight black ski masks down over our heads and faces, and shrugged into our navy windbreakers.

"Yeah, like I have any more control over my superpowers than you do," I retorted, as the three of us linked arms and hurried away to the far side of the plateau where we had been either sitting or lying for the last two hours. I pushed with mind and legs. Kurt took over, and we leaped high and zoomed away, entirely out of the quarries, to where he had left his truck on a park access road. The shrieks and curses of the Grandstone crew followed us, mixed with our laughter. Come to think of it, their yelling was probably just in my imagination after about ten minutes, but it was still beautiful to hear.

To celebrate, we went to Miller's Diner. Stephanie was there, with Bethany toddling around. Her giggles and her outstretched arms when she saw me just added to the euphoria of the successful evening. Is there anything better than being loved by an adorable toddler? We stayed at Miller's, eating onion rings and fried mushrooms and malts and listening to reports of the various Senior Prank Night escapades as they came in.

Wednesday nights were always slow at Miller's Diner, and tonight it was nearly dead. Lots of people were out that night, either trying to see what pranks were going on, participating in the pranks, trying to stop the pranks, or just staying off the streets so they didn't get caught, or pranked, or accused of being part of a prank. Ben Miller had a police scanner, and he brought it out into the dining room since there were only ten of us, total, and we listened and laughed. It took a long time to get a report of the Grandstone crew. We learned that Felicity's EM burst had not only killed the video camera and the fertilizer bombs, but it had killed all their cars and cell phones. That was a pretty big fury-bomb. They were stranded, on foot, in the far reaches of the quarries, which were chained off at sunset. Aww, poor Reggie and Freddie, they had to walk to ask for help.

Thus began our tradition of helping with the patrolling during Senior Prank Night. Of course, while people might have guessed that we were involved in ensuing years, we noticed a tendency for people not to ask what we had seen, who we had stopped or fished out of trouble, or in the case of the really clever pranks that didn't hurt anyone, who we had helped. When we were older and out of school, people just assumed we were involved in patrolling. We were adults, and we already had a little bit of a growing reputation for stepping in and helping and watching out for people. Of course, that grew over time.

That weekend, we went into Divine's to look for any pieces and parts in the junk room, just to see what brainstorm Kurt could come up with for a new invention. And to report on what we had done. When we stepped into the main room, Angela was just putting four rainbow-striped shakes down on the little soda fountain table on the far side of the main counter. She turned around and smiled at us and gestured at the table. That raised left eyebrow, and the twitch in one corner of her mouth made it somewhere between an invitation and an order. We came in and sat down. Rainbow-striped shakes were created in tall glasses with vertical stripes of flavored syrups, and of course, the combinations suited each of us. Kurt had three different intensities of chocolate and vanilla and peanut butter. I had mint and chocolate and vanilla. Felicity had essentially a banana split—strawberry, chocolate, butterscotch, caramel, banana. How Angela knew we were coming and when wasn't as hard to believe as her ability to have all those flavors of shakes ready and waiting to pour into the glasses, and how she kept the flavors and stripes from mixing as she put them in. Still, we just accepted even the little bursts of magic and weirdness, because this was Neighborlee, and this was Divine's Emporium, and she was Angela.

"Hail the conquering heroes," she said, as she sat down with her shake—blue and green and pink stripes, which I assumed were fruit flavors. "Tell me everything."

"Don't you already know everything?" I said, which probably wasn't smart. Even if Angela did know everything, the fact that she *wanted* us to tell her meant there was a good reason why she *needed* us to spill.

"There are facts, and then there is the fun of hearing the story. Besides, my sources only give the basics, a newspaper article versus a two-hour documentary, so to speak." She winked at me and inserted her straw in the center of her shake, which had a dark red spot that I suspected was cherry.

So we told her. What else could we do? The telling didn't take two hours. Just under an hour, actually, with all the details and backing up to give more information.

Angela nodded, pleased, when we speculated on how Reggie had gotten hold of that video camera, and how Felicity had utterly blown it to dust. She didn't say much, but she promised she would make sure all the girls who had been frightened by the idea of Reggie Grandstone having video tape of them taking showers would know the tape had been destroyed.

My general impression was that she was more satisfied with our saving Pickle Falls than with stopping the Grandstone crew, and more satisfied that Black Water Pool hadn't been disturbed, than by the saving of the falls.

"Do you think..." I immediately wished I hadn't started to voice the thought. Angela gave me that raised-eyebrow look that made me think she knew what I was about to say, even though it wasn't quite clear in my head yet. "Well, was there anything hurt, or changed or something, by the fertilizer bombs going into Black Water? There was all that bubbling, and no matter how deep that sinkhole goes, and how much water, all those chemicals and everything... Did they... I don't know...change anything?"

"There are some places I can't see, some things I am not permitted to know, and some things I do not want to know. Some things are better left unknown, left to sit quietly in the corner, so to speak. As long as we don't think about them, as long as we pretend they aren't there, they don't wake up, I supposed you could say." A sighing little laugh escaped her and she put her glass down on the table. "I found that article you wrote in the school newspaper very clever, and insightful. The one about rules of magic, and people who try to circumvent prophecies just bring them to pass. You started out by complaining about people who put curses on someone as a punishment."

"Right. I couldn't see the logic in putting some horrific curse on someone that would just make things even worse for the innocent townspeople a hundred years in the future, when the curse was broken. Why not just kill the guy, instead of making it possible for him to come back from hell and take vengeance on everyone?"

"Exactly. And you were very right to point out the flaw in what is essentially a Hollywood construct. So many things we take as fact in folklore were actually created by Hollywood. The rules of vampires and werewolves and other fantastical creatures aren't the actual rules. If there are any such creatures," Angela added with her trademark smirk and sparkles of mischief in her eyes. "The point I'm working up to is that on the surface, some things might not make sense, and you can think of a dozen different options that seem more logical and efficient to you. But that's it, just on the surface.

"There are some things that you need to go down through many layers, and years of history and mystery, to find the answers. It could take your lifetime to just start to unravel the reasons and justifications, and the stopgap measures. What does that have to do with the mysteries and legends of Black Water Pool?" She gave us a delicate little shrug.

"Sometimes what seems a tragedy, a mess, might turn out to be a plug filling a very nasty hole, with even nastier things kept firmly on the other side. If the fertilizer and other things dumped into Blackwater will have any effect, for good or bad, we may not live long enough to know. What matters is that the three of you have proven yourselves worthy and honorable and I am so dearly proud of you. I know that you would love to tell the world of your triumph, but you will just have to be satisfied with Rainbow and Charlie, Ford and Stephanie, and me knowing. And perhaps other allies who join our guardianship in years to come. We serve the cause of right, the cause of life. I know I speak for the ultimate authority who we will all answer to someday, at the end of time, when I say, 'well done.'"

END

Neighborlee, Ohio

(Title, Original Title, Release Date)

Confessions of a Lost Kid (Growing Up Neighborlee) 05/20
Semi-Pseudo-Superheroes (Dorm Rats) 07/20
Virtually London (London Holiday) 09/20
Living Proof (that no good deed goes unpunished) (Living Proof) 11/20
Night of the Living Proof, 01/21
Quitting the Hero Biz (Hero Blues) 03/21
Bride of the Living Proof, 05/21
Shrunk: The Exile of Maurice (Divine's Emporium) 07/21
Return of the Living Proof, 09/21
Allergic to Mistletoe (Have Yourself a Faerie Little Christmas) 11/21
Dawn of the Living Proof, 01/22
Angela's Knight (Divine Knight) 03/22
The Living Proof Gets the Blues, 05/22

ABOUT THE AUTHOR

On the road to publication, Michelle fell into fandom in college and has 40+ stories in various SF and fantasy universes. She has a bunch of useless degrees in theater, English, film/communication, and writing. Even worse, she has over 100 books and novellas with multiple small presses, in science fiction and fantasy, YA, suspense, women's fiction, and sub-genres of romance.

Her official launch into publishing came with winning first place in the Writers of the Future contest in 1990. She was a finalist in the EPIC Awards competition multiple times, winning with *Lorien* in 2006 and *The Meruk Episodes, I-V,* in 2010, and was a finalist in the Realm Award competition, in conjunction with the Realm Makers convention.

Her training includes the Institute for Children's Literature; proofreading at an advertising agency; and working at a community newspaper. She is a tea snob and freelance edits for a living (MichelleLevigne@gmail.com for info/rates), but only enough to give her time to write. Her newest crime against the literary world is to be co-managing editor at Mt. Zion Ridge Press and launching the publishing co-op, Ye Olde Dragon Books. Be afraid … be very afraid.

www.Mlevigne.com
www.MichelleLevigne.blogspot.com
@MichelleLevigne

Also by Michelle L. Levigne

Guardians of the Time Stream: 4-book Steampunk series
The Match Girls: Humorous inspirational romance series starting
    with **A Match (Not) Made in Heaven**
Sarai's Journey: A 2-book biblical fiction series
Tabor Heights: 20-book inspirational small town romance series.

Quarry Hall: 11-book women's fiction/suspense series
For Sale: Wedding Dress. Never Used: inspirational romance
Crooked Creek: Fun Fables About Critters and Kids: Children's
    short stories.
Do Yourself a Favor: Tips and Quips on the Writing Life. A book
    of writing advice.
Killing His Alter-Ego: contemporary romance/suspense, taking
    place in fandom.
The Commonwealth Universe: SF series, 25 books and growing
The Hunt: 5-book YA fantasy series
Faxinor: Fantasy series, 4 books and growing
Wildvine: Fantasy series, 14 books when all released
Neighborlee: Humorous fantasy series
Zygradon: 5-book Arthurian fantasy series